The Family Business 5:

A Family Business Novel

The Family Business 5:

A Family Business Novel

Carl Weber

with

La Jill Hunt

www.urbanbooks.net

Urban Books, LLC
300 Farmingdale Road, NY-Route 109
Farmingdale, NY 11735

The Family Business 5: A Family Business Novel

ISBN 13: 978-1-60162-093-4
ISBN 10: 1-60162-093-4

First Hardcover Printing February 2020
Printed in the United States of America

10 9 8 7 6 5 4 3 2 1

This is a work of fiction. Any references or similarities to actual events, real people, living or dead, or to real locales are intended to give the novel a sense of reality. Any similarity in other names, characters, places, and incidents is entirely coincidental.

Distributed by Kensington Publishing Corp.
Submit orders to:
Customer Service
400 Hahn Road
Westminster, MD 21157-4627
Phone: 1-800-733-3000
Fax: 1-800-659-2436

The Family Business 5:

A Family Business Novel

Carl Weber

with

La Jill Hunt

This book is dedicated to the fans of
The Family Business.

Also, to the Cast and Crew of The Family Business TV Show.

—Carl Weber and La Jill Hunt

Prologue

After circling the Brooklyn Heights block for a fourth time unnoticed, the Ford Escape stopped, and Denny Torrez emerged. The handsome, athletic-looking young man had a natural street swagger that was more cute than threatening. He lit a cigarette, stepped onto the sidewalk, and leaned against a telephone pole as the car continued its loop around the block. From the way he kept looking from one end of the street to the other, it was obvious that he was scoping out something . . . or someone.

A baby blue Bentley GT convertible pulled up and parked. Normally, he'd just stand there admiring the car, but that was impossible when two of the finest women he'd ever seen stepped out of the luxury vehicle. Paris Duncan, a mocha sister with curly hair that fell past her shoulders and looks that rivaled any supermodel, was the passenger. The driver of the luxury car was her equally beautiful cousin, Sasha Duncan. Both women were dressed in designer jumpsuits and carried expensive handbags that matched their outfits.

"Twelve o'clock," Paris mumbled, boldly studying Denny with seductive eyes. She glanced at her cousin, who hit the lock button for the Bentley as she gave Denny the once over.

"I'd do him," Sasha replied, walking around to the front of the car. "But he's more your type than mine."

Realizing the women were checking him out, Denny squared his shoulders slightly and semi-posed. If they were window shopping, he was damn sure going to let them see the merchandise.

Paris smiled, lifting her sunglasses before taking a second look. "Yeah, he's definitely my type, isn't he?"

Paris was expecting her cousin to quickly cosign, but instead, she growled, "Dammit, I hate Brooklyn!" loud enough for half the block to hear.

"What the hell, Sasha?" Paris yelled.

"This has got to be the most ass-backward borough in the entire city. In Manhattan these things take cards." She glared at the parking meter with frustration. "You got any change?"

Paris made a face, shaking her head. "Please. You know I don't carry change. You just gonna have to eat the ticket. We're five minutes late for our appointment."

"Uh, hell no. Not after the way Uncle LC cursed your ass out about tickets when your car got towed last month."

"That wasn't my fault, Sasha. That was Daddy's fault for not paying the tickets on time."

"They were your tickets, Par—" Sasha stopped midsentence when she realized Denny had sauntered over.

He smiled at them, but his attention was mostly on Paris as he put four quarters into the meter. "Here you go, ma. That should hold you for an hour."

Paris grinned seductively. "Thanks. Nice kicks. Those the new Jordans?"

"Yeah, they just came out." Taking advantage of the moment, he reached into his hoodie and handed her a postcard flyer. "I'm a DJ at this new spot that just opened uptown. Y'all should come through for ladies' night. Let me buy you a drink."

Paris casually took the postcard and said, "Maybe," before she and her cousin walked away, giggling.

Denny watched the ladies for a moment, then went back to his spot on the corner. He'd been so distracted by the girls that he almost forgot why he was there and what he was supposed to be doing.

The Ford Escape circled back again, and Denny gave the driver a nod as he passed by slowly. The driver pulled into an empty spot, and Roman Johnson, an almond-colored man with a mustache and goatee, jumped out, wearing a brown UPS uniform and sunglasses. He headed up the block, carrying a box, and stopped in front of Louis Franks Diamonds, a boutique jewelry store that catered mostly to entertainers and sports stars.

Roman rang the bell and looked up at the security camera, lifting the box until a buzzer went off, unlocking the door. He pulled it open and used his foot as a wedge to keep it unlocked. Within seconds, Denny was at Roman's side, wearing a black ski mask. He pulled a large semiautomatic handgun from his waistband. Roman quickly removed his sunglasses and pulled down his brown skull cap, which turned out to be a ski mask as well. He opened the box, removing a sawed-off shotgun along with a large black satchel. Locked and loaded, they stepped into the jewelry store, which only had two customers—Sasha and Paris—and four employees, including the security guard.

"Okay, everyone. Hands up! This is a robbery!" Roman announced, taking charge. He slid a shell into the shotgun chamber and pointed it at a female employee's head when she reached for a security button. "You don't want to die, do you, lady?"

"No." The woman shook her head, pulling back her hand.

Roman glanced over at Denny, who had already disarmed the security guard and zip-tied his hands. He tossed him the satchel. "Time to go to work, cuz!"

Suddenly, the store was rocked by a startling crash.

Denny was smashing the showcases with his gun and dumping trays of jewelry into the black satchel as Roman covered everyone with his shotgun. They were moving fast. Clearly this was not their first robbery.

As Denny smashed and grabbed, he was making his way toward the Duncan cousins. Sasha casually slipped her hand into her oversized purse and wrapped her fingers around the 9 mm handgun she carried at all times. Unbeknownst to the boys, she and Paris had been trained at Chi's Finishing School in Paris, one of the world's most renowned mercenary and tactical training schools. Taking these amateurs down was going to be a piece of cake.

Sasha was about to spring into action when Paris, whose trained eyes had been studying both boys since the minute they walked in the door, calmly grabbed her cousin's wrist and shook her head. Reluctantly, Sasha backed down and watched Denny smash the showcase in front of them and clean it out.

"Time to go, cuz!" Roman shouted, looking out the window. "Our ride's here."

"I'm done," Denny replied, looking over at Paris. Their eyes met for a brief moment.

"Then let's get the fuck outta here," Roman said, backing up toward the exit. Denny headed for the door, and just like that, they had cleaned the place out and were gone.

As the store employees scrambled to call the police and untie the security guard, a confused Sasha turned to Paris, and said, "What the fuck was that? I could have stopped them!"

"For what? They didn't rob us. Last time I checked, your ass wasn't Supergirl, and I damn sure ain't Wonder Woman." Paris glared at her defiantly.

Sasha shot back, "Paris, they just cleaned this place out. We shouldn't have just let them get away like that."

"Why not? Nobody got hurt other than the security guard's ego." Paris shrugged. "If you had taken them down, we'd be dealing with the police for the next five hours and probably have our faces all over the six o'clock news." She gave her cousin a pointed look. "And who the hell was going to explain that to my mother and father? 'Cause it damn sure wasn't gonna be me."

Paris's words hit Sasha hard as she glanced around the room. "Now that you put it like that . . . I'm sure this place is heavily insured."

"Exactly. Besides, I got a feeling we're going to see those two again real soon." Paris flicked the postcard Denny had given her earlier and smiled knowingly.

Nevada

1

"Oh my God, that was so much fun. Paris and Sasha are going to be so jealous when they see these pictures on Instagram," Uncle Rio shouted, showing off the selfie he'd taken as we walked toward the parking lot. I had spent the entire day at Splish Splash with Rio, Kia, Danielle, my dad, and his girlfriend, Marie. "Aren't you glad you came now, Nevada?"

"Yeah, it was a blast," I replied, checking out Danielle and Kia's backsides, which were barely covered by their bikinis, as I walked a few feet behind them. I tried to be subtle about my gaze, but when I glanced over at my dad, he gave me *the look*, letting me know I was busted. I swear between him, my mom, and my grandmother, there were always eyes on me. I was just thankful that Marie didn't notice, because Danielle and Kia worked for her, and I didn't want her to think I was some disrespectful pervert.

Thanks to Uncle Rio's horrible sense of direction, it took us almost half an hour to find the Mercedes Sprinter van we were traveling in, but everyone was still in high spirits. My dad climbed behind the wheel, and Marie sat up front with him. The rest of us slipped in the back. Although there was plenty of room, Danielle, an exceptionally pretty white girl with long blonde hair and a body like a swimsuit model, sat right next to me, pinning me to the van's wall with her body and spreading out across the seat. Danielle was the more aggressive of the two girls, and it was clear all day that she enjoyed being the center of attention, especially mine. I made sure to play it off like it was no big deal, but my dad seemed to always be looking.

"Look how sunburned I got." She pulled back the top of her bikini that barely held her full breasts to start with, so that I could see the lighter pigmentation of her skin compared to her bright red sunburn. I tried not to let my eyes linger on her breasts too long, but it was a challenge.

"You wouldn't be sunburned if you'd put that sunscreen on like I told you," Marie scolded her, more like her mother than her boss. "I don't understand why you don't listen. Your skin is way too fair to be exposing it to the sun like that."

"Okay, okay, Marie. Damn, you act like I'm as red as a lobster or something." Danielle pouted, sliding her bikini top back in place and then resting her head right in my lap. She began playing with her phone, and all I could do was look down at her beautiful body laid out across the seat. To make matters worse, I had no idea what to do with my hands.

"You a'ight over there, nephew?" Uncle Rio could barely contain his laughter as he took a picture with his phone, which meant he and Aunt Paris were going to be joking and teasing me for the next two weeks.

"Yeah, I'm *cool*." I placed my hands behind my head and sat back like it was no big deal. I noticed my dad looking at us in the rearview mirror, and once again, he had that smile on his face.

"Y'all hungry?" Dad asked as we pulled out of the park. "You wanna stop and get something to eat?"

"Yes!" Danielle quickly answered.

"Definitely," Uncle Rio yelled.

"Yes." Kia, the other girl Marie had brought, raised her hand and smiled. Unlike Danielle, she was quiet and reserved. I'd overheard her tell Uncle Rio that her father was black and her mother was Korean, which was probably why she looked so exotic.

"What about you, Nevada?" Kia asked. The way she stared at me was kind of creepy and sexy at the same time, and it gave me butterflies for some reason. "You hungry?"

"Yeah, I could eat, but I'd rather go home and have a barbecue than eat fast food," I replied. Kia grinned as if I'd come up with the right answer.

"A barbecue does sound good," Uncle Rio added. "What do you say, Vegas? You're the grill master."

Dad nodded. "I've got some steaks and burgers from last weekend, and Ma's always got a fridge full. Why not?"

"Let me find out you can cook . . ." Marie said playfully.

"Cook, no. But grill? Baby, I can grill my ass off," my dad bragged.

"All righty then, I guess we're having a BBQ!" Uncle Rio cheered, solidifying our plans.

"I love barbecues. Are we invited?" Danielle lifted her head from my lap and turned from her phone. Marie looked back, cutting her eyes disapprovingly, but Danielle pressed. "Please, Marie, I want to taste Vegas's cooking."

"Grilling," Dad laughed, reiterating his previous point. "And yes, y'all can all come."

Marie glanced over at him with uncertain eyes. "You sure about this? I don't want to upset your mother by bringing the girls to her house, Vegas. She's just starting to like me."

"Trust me, my mom loves a full house," Dad said, squeezing her hand. "I'll text her and let her know."

"Tell her she won't have to lift a finger. I'll pick up everything we need," Marie told him. "And the girls will clean up."

"And I'll make drinks," Uncle Rio added.

"Yes for the drinks!" Danielle clapped.

"No for the drinks. You're only nineteen, Dani," Marie reminded her. "And you too, Kia."

I was surprised to hear that. I knew Danielle and Kia were the youngest girls that worked for Marie, but I thought they were in their early twenties, not their late teens.

"What? That's some bull, Marie. We're not at work," Danielle snapped.

"Rules don't change just 'cause we're not at work. Until you're twenty-one, you don't drink around me or any of my friends. You got a problem with that, then we don't have to have a BBQ. We can go back to the house." Once again, Marie sounded more like a mother than a boss.

"No, I wanna stay," Danielle replied humbly.

"Okay. Now, give Nevada some space and cover yourself up. We're not at the water park anymore."

Danielle sat up, shifting a little farther away from me and covering herself up with a beach towel. It was nice being able to stretch, but I can't say I didn't like her lying on me.

Marie turned back to the front, and a few minutes later, Danielle and Uncle Rio were asleep. I looked across the van at Kia, who turned from looking out the window and smiled at me timidly.

"What grade are you in?" she asked out of nowhere.

"I start my junior year next week, but I have enough credits to graduate. Right now, I'm taking all AP classes—except for gym."

"Are you some kind of genius or something?" She laughed. She must have thought I was a brainiac freak.

"No, not really. I'm just—"

She cut me off, giggling. "It's okay. Smart is sexy. Don't let anyone tell you different." She winked at me, and I could feel the heat from my face turning red. "So, you think you can help me study for my GED test sometime? I'm having a lot of trouble with the algebra. Math's not my strongest subject."

"Sure. I tutor kids in math and science at my school all the time. It's not really that hard once you learn the formulas. Most of the kids get A's and B's once they work with me."

"I bet they do," she replied, giving me that stare that caused butterflies in my stomach again. "So, here's a question for you. If you're so smart and can graduate, why stay in high school? Why not go off to some fancy college?"

"It's kind of a long story, but I just came to live with my father and his side of the family about three years ago. Before that, I spent most of my life in boarding schools in California because my mom was trying to keep me a secret from her husband."

"That's deep," she said. "But boarding school sounds fun. Did you have to wear the uniforms like they do on TV?"

"Yeah, and I hated it. I hated the whole experience. I just wanted to be with my mom and have a real family," I said sadly. "I thought I was all alone in the world until I came to live with my dad's side of the family. I never thought anyone could show me as much love as the Duncans have. And now all I want is to hold onto it as long as I can."

"That's sweet. I'm glad it worked out for you, but from my experience, family is way overrated," she replied morosely. I could hear in her voice that there was way more to that story.

"Vegas, can you turn some music on? These two are trying to bore me to death," Danielle yelled out of nowhere, interrupting our conversation. A few seconds later, the sound of hip-hop music came through the speakers.

Kia and I stared at each other, but neither of us said a word. Fifteen minutes later, we were both asleep.

LC

2

"Sign here and there," I said, marking an X next to the two places I wanted Davis Taft's signature. He scribbled his name by both, smiling like he'd just won the damn lottery. And why shouldn't he? He'd just signed the paperwork to purchase a $600,000 Lamborghini Hurricane.

"Congratulations." I extended my hand, and Davis took it with a firm grip. "Young man, you just bought yourself one of the finest cars a man can own, and in the process, scratched off one of the bucket list items of half the men in America. How does it feel?"

"Amazing," he replied. The man looked like he was going to soil himself from excitement.

"Good. Let's get you into that car." I spotted Phil, our sales manager, and waved him over. "Phil, this is Davis Taft. He's here to pick up the yellow Hurricane we've got down in service."

"Nice. That's a beautiful car. Congratulations." Phil shook Davis's hand.

Davis couldn't get rid of the shit-eating grin on his face. "Thanks."

"Why don't you take Davis down to service and get him acquainted with his new car?" I tossed Davis a set of keys and shook his hand again before the two of them exited. When they were both out of sight, I leaned back into my plush leather chair and pumped my fist in the air. Other than my family, there was nothing that I loved more than selling an expensive car. It was like a drug. God, it felt good to be back at work.

"Mr. Duncan?" I was startled out of my personal moment by a light tap on my office door and a female voice. I looked up, and there was Sherry, one of our administrative assistants.

"Yes?" I answered.

"There's a Mr. Brooks here to see you. He was here earlier to see Vegas, but he wasn't in, and now he's back asking for you," she said.

"Brooks? Is that a first or a last name?" I took off my glasses and rubbed my eyes.

"I assumed it was his last name, but I can go—"

I shook my head. "No, send him in. If he's looking for Vegas, I probably know him."

A few minutes later, Johnny Brooks was standing in my office doorway. I recognized him right away.

"Hey there, Mr. Duncan," Johnny said humbly, his smile revealing a shiny gold tooth.

Johnny was a long and lanky two-bit hustler with an unkempt beard. He used to drive trucks for us a few years back, and he wasn't a bad guy when he was sober. Johnny had a drinking problem, and the only person who could keep him on the straight and narrow was Vegas. When Vegas went to jail five years ago, Johnny damn near fell in the bottle, and regrettably, I had to let him go. This was the first time I'd seen him since.

"Johnny Brooks! It's been a long time, son." I stood and offered my hand, wondering what he could possibly want with me or Vegas after all these years. I knew one thing was for sure—he wasn't there to buy a car. "What brings you down to Duncan Motors?"

"Well, I'd heard Vegas was home, and I needed to see him. It's kinda important." He had an uneasiness to him, and I couldn't tell if he was intimidated by me, was drunk, or both. Whatever it was, he was nervous as hell.

"It must be for you to stop by twice. But Vegas isn't here on the weekends. Is there something I can help you with?" I asked.

He scratched his head, looking around like someone might walk in the room and kill him right then and there. "Nah, I probably should just speak to him about it. No disrespect."

"None taken." I had a pretty good feeling why he was looking for my son. "Johnny, you looking for a loan? You need a few bucks?"

"I ain't gonna lie. I could always use a few bucks, but I'm not here to borrow money. I've got a job . . . or at least I think I do. What I need is to get in touch with your son. You think I could leave you a number? It's real important."

He'd piqued my curiosity. "Why don't I do one better? Why don't I give him a call?"

Johnny looked hopeful for the first time since he'd walked in my office. "Could you, sir? This is really important." There was that "important" word again, the third time he'd said it since he walked into my office.

"Sure." I pulled out my phone and made the call. When it began ringing, I handed Johnny the phone and waited. I would ear hustle to satisfy my curiosity.

"Hey, Vegas," Johnny said, covering the phone. "It's Johnny Brooks, man. Listen, I need to talk to you real bad, brother. Can you give me a call?" He left his number, and then finished up with, "It's important!" There was that word again.

He hung up the phone and handed it back, frowning. "Voicemail."

"Yeah, he's out with his son today. I'm sure he'll call you when he finishes." I tried to play it off, but as hopeless as Johnny was, he was starting to make my Spidey senses tingle. "So, Johnny, how about a drink?"

"Sure, that sounds good. I haven't had anything to eat or drink all day," he said.

I stepped over to the bar located on the far side of my office. "What can I get you?"

I was already reaching for the decanter of cognac when he said, "Coke is fine."

"Coke? I was gonna offer you my good cognac. You sure you want Coke?" I knew Johnny liked my cognac because he and Vegas used to sneak into my office for a taste.

"Coke's fine, Mr. Duncan. I don't drink no more," Johnny replied seriously. "It's been about two and a half years since I took a drink."

Now, that surprised the hell outta me.

"Two years, huh? That's good, Johnny." I handed him a can of Coke from the mini fridge. "Glad to hear you've cleaned yourself up."

"Yeah, me too." I heard the words come out of his mouth, but I could see him eyeing the decanter as I poured myself a drink. "You sure you won't have one?"

"Yeah, I'm sure." I could hear the hesitation as he sat down in a chair across from my desk and took a sip of his soda.

I sat down and stared in his eyes. "I hope you don't mind me saying this, Johnny, but you look troubled."

"That's 'cause I am in trouble, Mr. Duncan." Johnny took a long sip then glanced up at me. He had tears in his eyes. "More trouble than I've ever been in, and I don't know what to do."

"What kind of trouble, son?" I asked.

"The kinda trouble where you end up in a body bag," he said matter-of-factly.

I leaned forward in my chair, more concerned about my son than anything else. "And how exactly is Vegas involved with this trouble?"

"He's not, but he's the only one I could think of to help me out of it."

I tried to mask my relief. "You do know I'm probably the first person Vegas is going to come to with your problem, Johnny, so why don't you tell me what's going on? Maybe you and me can figure this situation out without getting Vegas involved."

"Yeah, maybe you're right." Johnny sat up for a second. I was sure he was about to tell me what was going on, but we were interrupted by Sherry.

"Excuse me, Mr. Duncan. A gentleman who says he's your business partner insists on seeing you."

She handed me his business card, and I almost pissed myself when I saw the company name. "Where the fuck is he?"

"He's in the conference room," Sherry replied.

"Johnny, hold tight for a second. I gotta take care of something. I'll be right back." I didn't wait for a response. I was on my feet and out the door so fast. Sherry was on my heels, but I quickly dismissed her. "This is a private meeting, but if you want to do something, take Johnny down to the breakroom and get him a sandwich and another Coke. This shouldn't take too long."

She stopped in the corridor and said, "Yes, sir," as I trudged away, prepared to whip somebody's ass.

I stormed into our conference room. Sitting at the head of the table was KD Shrugs, a short, fat, middle-aged redneck who was as mean and ruthless as they come. He was dressed in a blazer, jeans, and cowboy boots. To his right, standing in the corner, was a refrigerator-sized redneck bodyguard wearing a Make America Great Again T-shirt. I thought about slapping KD's fat ass for having the audacity to show up at my place, but at my age, going up against the bodyguard without shooting him could prove to be painful. It was times like these I wished one of my sons were around—or maybe even Paris.

"Nice place you have here, LC," KD said in his long Southern drawl. "And that secretary of yours makes a real fine cup of coffee." He lifted up a black Duncan Motors coffee mug as if he were an invited guest. "Oh, and she's got a nice ass, too, if you're in the mood for a little brown sugar." He and his bodyguard began to laugh hysterically, until I raised my voice.

"What the fuck are you doing here?"

"God damn, who the hell pissed in your corn flakes this morning?" KD slid a black duffle bag across the table. "Here. Maybe this'll make you feel a little better."

"What's this?" I unzipped the bag. Inside were stacks of money. Without even counting it, I knew there had to be at least a hundred thousand dollars.

"That's your cut for the month. Business is good. I'm thinking about buying a few more trucks."

"Not good enough for you to be showing up at my fucking place of business," I growled, zipping the bag up. "We have a deal. You don't come to my office, my home, or anywhere else I do business. Obviously, you don't understand that."

"What I understand is that *we* have a problem." He pointed back and forth between me and him. "So, I don't give a shit if your black ass is having dinner with the fucking queen of England. We need to talk."

"Well, we're not talking here, and I don't give a shit if your redneck, white-sheet-wearing, cross-burning, fat ass likes it or not!" I stated in no uncertain terms. "I don't think you want me to take this little incident to our mutual friends, do you?"

We stared at each other for a moment, and he finally relented. "Fine. Tonight, the usual place, the usual time. Don't be late."

I nodded, and without saying another word, he struggled to get his fat ass up out of the chair until the bodyguard helped him up. He picked up his cup of coffee, finished it, then walked out unceremoniously.

Damn. This was not good.

I took a few minutes to get myself together and figure out my next move before I returned to my office to deal with Johnny. However, when I walked through my office door, I found Sherry alone.

"Where's Johnny?"

She shrugged skittishly. "He left."

"What do you mean, he left? I asked you to keep an eye on him. Where'd he go?"

"I took him to the break room to get him something to eat like you asked, and on our way back to your office, he just dropped his sandwich and ran. Disappeared out the back door."

I was confused. "And this all happened out of nowhere? He just took off unprovoked?"

"Well, I don't know if I'd call it unprovoked." She looked out of sorts, and I could see why. Between that asshole in the conference room and Johnny disappearing under her watch, I was fuming, and I was sure she could see the agitation on my face. "It all happened so fast, but as we were leaving the breakroom, we saw that man you were talking to in the conference room leaving the building. I'll admit he's a pretty scary-looking man, but Mr. Brooks looked more than scared—he looked petrified when he saw him."

"So petrified that he took off out the back way?" I asked.

"Yes, sir," Sherry replied. "I don't think I've ever seen anyone look that scared before in my entire life."

Nevada

3

"Rise and shine, everybody!"

Dad's yelling woke me. I looked out of the window and saw that we were pulling through the gates at our house. The last thing I remembered was Danielle asleep on my shoulder and seeing him and Marie exiting the van to go into the grocery store. I must have fallen back to sleep after that. But it was good to be home, because I was hungry, and I couldn't wait for my dad to start grilling.

"Damn, this is where you live?" Danielle sat up, excited.

"Yep," I said pridefully.

"Y'all rich!" She leaned forward to look past me, not caring that her breasts were all over my face.

I glanced over at Kia, who just kind of shrugged.

"Can you give me a tour?" Danielle asked.

"Ah, sure," I replied, and she grabbed hold of my arm as we exited the van.

"Nevada!"

We were halfway to the front door when my dad shouted my name. We stopped and waited for him to catch up.

He said, "Danielle, can you give me and Nevada a minute? Rio will take you inside."

Danielle let go of my arm and grabbed Rio's, and they continued toward the house. I could see Kia hesitate, but she followed Rio when he waved her on.

"What's going on?" Marie eased over when she realized we'd stopped.

"Nothing. Everything's cool, babe. We're just having a little father and son talk. We'll be right inside."

Marie looked skeptical but didn't protest. She gave him a kiss and then left us alone.

Dad turned to me. "You all right?"

"Yeah, I'm fine. Why? What's up?"

He gave me a knowing look. "Danielle's what's up. I saw how she's pressing up on you. She's definitely trying to offer you an opportunity. I just wanna make sure you're good, in case you plan on taking it."

"Would *you* take it?" I asked. "I mean, if you were me? Would you take that opportunity?"

Dad looked away for a second, taking a deep breath. I could tell this was not the direction that he'd planned our conversation to go in. "You and me are not the same person, son. But back in the day, if a pretty woman like Danielle offered me some . . ." He hesitated briefly, then just said it: "Yeah, I'd probably have taken her up on it. But that was me. I was a little more out there than you."

"I've had girlfriends before, Dad." I wanted to make sure he didn't think I was scared, although there was some scariness to what we were talking about.

"This ain't no high school cheerleader we're talking about, son. This is a grown-ass, experienced woman. I've seen grown-ass men lose their minds over women like her."

"I can believe that," I replied.

"Good, because time spent with her could be invaluable—or detrimental as hell." He placed his hand on my shoulder. "Unfortunately, this is something you have to decide for yourself. Just know this: whatever you decide, I got your back."

Since the day we'd met three years earlier, my dad had not only proven to be a great father, but also my best friend. However, in that moment, I could tell he was finally beginning to see me as a man and not his little boy.

"I appreciate that, Dad, but the truth is, Danielle isn't exactly my type. She's a little too loud and aggressive for my taste." I took a deep breath. "Don't get me wrong. She's beautiful and nice, but not my type."

"That's kind of what I thought. Good luck getting that message across. But that being said, it's still my job to make sure you're prepared for anything." He chuckled, taking out his wallet from his back pocket. He opened it and handed me a gold foil–wrapped condom. "Why don't you hold onto this just in case? Not necessarily for Danielle, but you never know when these kinds of things are going to happen. Always better to be prepared than not. I keep a box in my top left-hand drawer."

I stared at it, not knowing whether to laugh from the hilarity of the moment or die from the embarrassment. After all, this was my dad handing me a condom.

I didn't have time to choose a reaction or even respond because suddenly, an SUV pulled up, and of all people, my mother stepped out. I shoved the condom into my bathing suit pocket.

"What's she doing here?" my father mumbled.

I shrugged, putting on a fake smile and heading toward the car. I loved my mother and knew she was flying in from the West Coast to spend the week with me before school started, but she wasn't supposed to arrive until the next day, and her being there was not a good look at all—especially since she had that angry look that usually made me find somewhere to hide because there was about to be a whole lot of cursing in Spanish.

"Vegas Duncan, what the fuck have you gotten my son into?" she snapped, stomping toward us.

I wasn't sure what she was talking about because I was positive she hadn't seen the condom . . . *or had she?*

"I trusted you to take care of my son, not corrupt him!"

"What are you talking about? We just got back from the water park," Dad replied, shaking his head. "I told you I was taking him. Why are you tripping?"

"You told me you were taking him—not him and a bunch of half-naked whores," she hissed at my dad angrily. "Those women were all over my child."

"Stop right there, Consuela," Dad shouted back in warning. "First, he's not a child. He's a young man. Second, no one was half naked or all over Nevada. You're out of line."

"No, Vegas, you're the one out of line and out of touch. I told you to keep that whore and her tramps away from my child! And your brother had the nerve to put it on his Instagram page?"

Damn. Uncle Rio must have put that picture of Danielle lying on my lap on his Insta.

"They're wearing bathing suits, Consuela. We were at a water park. You're being ridiculous." I could see Dad trying to hold his ground, but he didn't have much ammunition. Best thing he could do was shut up and let her shout until she was burned out, and not take it personally. I knew this from experience.

"No, ridiculous was me even bringing *my son* around you. This is what I get for thinking you would be a good father to him." Mom shook her head in frustration, but it wasn't her I was worried about. I could see my dad was hurt by her comment.

"I am a good father, Consuela." Dad's voice remained calm.

Mom stood with her hands on her hips, her face full of doubt.

"I love my son more than anything in this world. I would never do anything to hurt him."

"Is that why you bring him around whores and prostitutes?"

Okay, it was time for me to intervene. This was getting a little too emotional. I touched my mother's arm to defuse the situation. "Mom, you're overreacting. He's a good father, and you know it. He's everything you told me he was, and he's teaching me to be the man you want me to be." I stared at her, putting on my "cute and loving son" face that always won her over. But of course, that's when the condom fell out of my pocket.

Oh, crap. I looked up at my mother then down at the condom. The three of us stared at it for what seemed like an eternity before I reluctantly reached down and picked it up.

"What's that?" my mother asked rhetorically, snatching it from my grasp.

It took me a while to answer, but I finally did, trying to sound grown. "A condom."

"I can see that," she said between gritted teeth. "Now can you tell me why you have a condom in your bathing suit? Is that required equipment along with goggles and swim shoes at the water park?"

Once again, there was silence for a while, but this time Dad threw himself under the bus and came to my rescue. "He has it because I gave it to him, Consuela. He's a young man—"

Dad couldn't finish his sentence before my mom started cursing him out in Spanish. She was using profanity and slang in ways I'd never even heard before, and I spoke Spanish fluently. At one point, I tuned her out until she switched back to English and said, "Nevada, get in the car. We're leaving. I'm taking you back to California."

"What? No!" I yelled a little louder than I expected, surprising all three of us. I rarely, if ever, spoke back to mother, and I never raised my voice—until then. "You're not taking me from my family and throwing me in some boarding school! I have a family now, a family that loves me, and I love them. Why can't you understand that?"

"Lower your voice, young man. Now, you heard what I said. Get in the car!" She turned to my dad, fuming. "This is all your fault. You have no one to blame but yourself."

"Consuela, don't do this," Dad pleaded.

"You think I'm going to leave my son here with you and that whore and her mini thots? Nevada, come. Get in the car."

"Mom, don't do this, please." I tried to reason with her. I couldn't believe this was happening. "What about the rest of the family? Can I at least say goodbye?"

"*Súbete al carro inmediatamente. No juegues conmigo,*" she yelled in Spanish, letting me know she was not to be played with. "Your father will say goodbye for you."

I gave my father a hug and slowly walked toward the black SUV. This wasn't a bad dream; it was a nightmare.

"I love you, son."

"Love you too," I replied, feeling totally dejected.

"Don't worry. We'll work this all out," Dad said.

"I can't believe you're doing this," I murmured under my breath to Mom, heading to the car.

"You will understand when you're older," she said. "It's for your own good."

Roman

4

It was a well-known fact in the South Bronx that Lex Diamond had the ability to find anything you wanted, no matter what it was—appliances, electronics, steaks, cell phones, guns, you name it. Hell, he was even known to get green cards and Social Security cards if you had enough money. Yep, ol' Lex was the guy you went to when you needed something, and he was also the person you went to when you needed to unload shit; hence the reason he was the first person Denny and I sought out when we needed to fence our stolen goods.

"Whatcha got going on, fellas?" Lex, an Israeli immigrant in his forties, asked when we showed up at the counter of his Boston Road hardware store.

"We got some primo goods for you, Lex, my man," Denny bragged.

Lex's lips twisted into a sarcastic smirk, and his brow furrowed. "Is that so?"

"You damn right. Best shit you've seen in a long time," I replied, making Lex raise an eyebrow.

"All right, then let's see what you got." He gestured for us to follow him into a back room, which had a metal desk with a large computer monitor and a calculator on it. There were also two large safes and various padlocked strong boxes scattered around the room.

Lex sat down at the desk, and Denny placed the large black duffle bag in front of him. Lex unzipped the bag, and his surprised eyes went from Denny to me, and back again.

"Holy shit!" I was sure he was expecting us to have some stolen iPhones or some cocaine or heroin like usual, but he'd never anticipated us having what was in front of him then. "Y—you knocked off Louie the jeweler, didn't you?"

"Well, we didn't rob the tooth fairy," I joked.

Lex reached into the bag and took out a diamond-studded bracelet. "The balls on you two. You do know Louie's connected?"

"No risk, no reward," I responded.

Lex smiled at me. "Kid, you don't have *balls*. You have fucking coconuts between your legs. I'm impressed."

"Enough of this petty chit chat," Denny snapped. "You gonna take this merchandise off our hands or what?"

Lex continued going through the bag, taking out a jeweler's loop and studying several of the pieces. "*Hmmmmm*. It's a possibility."

"Possibility? Man, you full o' shit. This is good shit and you know it," I argued.

Lex looked up and sat back in his chair. "You're right. It is good shit, but where the hell am I going to unload it? You think the cops don't have a description of this shit?"

Denny glanced over at me with raised eyebrows as if to say, *He's right, Roman.*

"Look, Lex, you gonna make an offer or what?" I was quickly growing impatient, mostly because I knew what he was about to do.

"Tell you what. I'll give you fifty grand for it," he said nonchalantly, as if he were sitting at the final table of the World Series of Poker.

"Fifty grand? What the fuck? Are you crazy?" I gave him the finger. "This shit is worth at least five hundred K. Fuck that and fuck you." I reached for the bag and zipped it. "Come on, Denny."

"Hold up, Rome." Denny put his hand up to stop me. "Let's not be hasty. We're all businessmen here. We can negotiate a fair price. Right, Lex?"

"Hey, I told you what I was willing to pay." Lex shrugged as if it were no big deal. His nonchalance irritated me even more, especially since I knew he had to want the merchandise.

"Fifty grand seems a little low for product of this quality. How about seventy-five?" Denny sounded like he was pleading, and I wanted to reach out and smack him.

Unlike my friend, I wasn't willing, nor in the mood, to haggle with Lex. I looked over at Denny and said, "Man, let's go. We can find another buyer. One who ain't tryna lowball us."

"You can try," Lex replied confidently.

"Lex, I'm trying to work with you," Denny explained. "You know us. We been bringing you stuff for years."

"That's the reason that I'm willing to give you fifty grand for this shit." Lex finally sat up and looked alert, leaning against the desk as he spoke. "This shit is hot as hell."

"Are you kidding me? Everything you get is hot!" I was amused by his statement. "You buy hot shit, you sell hot shit. That's what keeps you in business, because it damn sure ain't hardware."

"You fellas don't understand the severity of the situation. Everybody and their mother is talking about this fucking robbery. It's been all over the local and national news. I'm gonna have to sit on this shit for six months before I start to unload it. Now, you either take the fifty grand and walk out of here with some money in your pocket, or you can leave and be stuck with it. Because I can promise you this: nobody's gonna offer you that amount. Hell, real talk, ain't nobody gonna wanna touch it until that shit cools down."

The reality of what Lex was saying changed any leverage I thought we had. There had been some talk about the robbery, but we'd been so proud of the fact that we'd pulled it off that the possibility of not being able to get rid of it hadn't even crossed my mind.

"I guess we'll see," I said sternly, unwilling to admit he had a point. I took a few steps toward the door with the bag in my hand. "Come on, Denny."

"Wait! I'll tell you what. I'll give you sixty, and you can each take any piece you like as a parting gift. But this is a one-time offer. You leave outta here with this shit, the price will be thirty when you come back," Lex said firmly.

"Just give us a sec to talk," Denny pleaded, pulling me aside.

We stepped into the corner, and he whispered, "Look, I need you to take this deal. I need the money, bro. My ass is broke, and I can't be waiting to find another fence." I could see in his face he wasn't lying.

"He's robbing us. You know that, right?" I stared at my friend hard.

"Yeah, I know, but sixty grand's the biggest payday we've ever seen."

"A'ight, man." I nodded. "But I get the jewelry."

"Bet. I already took out a bracelet." Denny turned to Lex. "We'll take the sixty."

Lex gave him a satisfied smile then walked over to one of the large safes and pulled out a duffle bag similar to the one holding the jewelry. He pulled out six banded stacks.

Denny and I stared at the money.

"It's all there. You wanna count it?" Lex encouraged.

"Nah, we good," I said, picking up three stacks and shoving them into my hoodie pocket. Denny did the same. I took two pieces of jewelry out of the original bag, then we shook Lex's hand before exiting the same way we had entered.

"So, what'd you think?" Denny asked, getting into his sister's car. We'd had Li'l Al, our driver, ditch the stolen Ford Escape right after the robbery.

"Thirty grand a piece, minus the two grand we gotta give Li'l Al for driving." I gave him a thumbs up. "I ain't complaining."

"It's more money than I ever had, and I've been stealing shit since I was thirteen." He drove out of the parking lot.

"So, what you gonna do with your cut?" I asked him.

"Man, I gotta get me a new whip first and foremost. Probably give my baby mama a couple dollars to shut her the fuck up." Denny laughed. "What about you?"

"Pay my momma's rent up for the rest of the year," I said proudly. "Then I think I'm gonna take ol' girl Kandace down to Miami and wax that ass for a couple of days."

"Man, you still fucking with that chick?" Denny looked across at me like I'd lost my mind. "It's a million other bitches out there, and you gotta mess with her? Shit, you crazy as hell."

"Bro, there's just something about her that I can't get enough of," I admitted.

"It's that good-ass pussy and that phat ass of hers you can't get enough of." He laughed.

"True, she does have a phat ass," I replied, laughing along with him.

"Just don't let that phat ass get you put in a pine box," Denny said, suddenly getting serious. "'Cause ain't no pussy worth dying over."

LC

5

"We're almost there, Pop," I heard Junior say.

I nodded, staring out the window as we exited I-95 not far from the tunnel in Baltimore. With my son Orlando, the Duncan Motors CEO, somewhere in the Caribbean trying to work out his relationship with his son's mother, I had decided to take Junior to my meeting instead of Vegas, who usually handled this type of thing. Truth was, Junior was the least inquisitive of my sons, and right now I didn't need a lot of questions. I needed someone to watch my back, and that was Junior's specialty.

Ten minutes later, we drove down a dark road and past several abandoned warehouses. At the end of the road, we parked by the water next to a black Ford pickup truck. I could already see the irritated look on Junior's face when he spotted the Make America Great Again license plate as he exited the car. He stayed on task, though, surveying the area for unexpected guests.

A minute or so later, Junior gave me the signal, and I stepped out of the car, walking up to the truck with him at my side. We were greeted by KD Shrugs, the fat redneck from the conference room, and his refrigerator-sized bodyguard. To look at the two of them, I could see why Sherry and Johnny were intimidated. KD had all the markings of a gun-toting redneck, complete with Confederate flag and KKK identification. But that shit didn't scare me.

"Just like old times. Right, LC? Except now they got casinos on the other side of the water." He gazed across the bay at the casino lights, gesturing for me to walk with him. Junior and his bodyguard followed, but far enough away that they couldn't hear our conversation.

"Where does the time go? Remember when me, you, Sal and Tony Dash, plus your brothers Lou and Larry used to meet here?" He chuckled. "Those was the good old days."

"For you maybe. But then again, you and your good ol' boys were calling the shots back then, weren't you?"

"Somebody had to keep you and your goombah buddies in line. We couldn't have you running around unchecked, spreading that crap in the wrong neighborhoods. That shit was getting out of hand. Besides, with me no longer a civil servant and you with all your high-falutin' connections, you're the one on top now." He glared at me with disdain, and I glared right back, wishing his fat country ass would have a heart attack and die. The only problem was that we'd had a codependent relationship for so many years. We both needed each other—or at least we used to. But I'd made a few calls before I arrived, so that might not be the case anymore.

"But just remember, what goes up must come crashing fucking down eventually," he warned.

I grinned. "So I've heard, but you would know that better than me. You're the one who spent all those years in prison."

Frustration took over his face. "For your information, I only spent two years in prison, and if I remember correctly, you, Sal, and the rest of your criminal buddies were waiting for me at this very spot with bags of cash when I got out. Do you remember that?"

"Like it was yesterday, Sheriff," I replied, taking a step closer. I'd called him Sherriff to aggravate him, because KD used to be not only the president of the National Sheriffs Association, but also sheriff of El Paso, Texas, a job he'd held for almost twenty years. Shakedowns, bribery, and the largest protection racket this country had ever seen had made him one of the wealthiest law enforcement officers in the country, if not the world. "I also remember that we were the only ones here when you got out. Where the fuck were your good ol' boys?"

He just stood there in silence because we both knew they'd abandoned him, and from that day forward, he was one of us. A fucking criminal.

"Kiss my ass, LC."

"I don't have time for this, KD. Why the hell am I here?" I asked.

"We had a problem, but I've already taken care of it. No thanks to you," he replied. I think my little history lesson had snapped him back to reality.

"Good. Now, in the future, if you want to talk, there are protocols for that. I suggest you use them."

I was about to walk back to the car when he said, "Fuck you! And fuck your protocols, you uppity black son of a bitch! I should be able to talk to you any damn time I please."

"KD, these protocols were put in place to protect my anonymity."

"That's kind of interesting considering we've been business partners for twenty years." He huffed his response. "I came to tell you in person that we had a problem. That's what business partners do."

"You keep talking about a problem. What kind of a problem was it?" Now I was curious.

He turned and looked across the water. "We lost a truck."

"You broke a fifteen-year arrangement and showed up at my office because you lost a fucking truck?" I almost hit him.

"It was a truckload of your merchandise. Over three hundred pounds of marijuana from across the border. I was trying to show some good will and let you know from me personally, considering we ain't never lost a shipment," he said proudly.

"That's awfully nice of you, but let's stick to the protocols."

"Again with fucking protocols. We're partners," he said adamantly. "Why the disrespect?"

"No disrespect. As long as you follow the protocols, you can talk to me any time you want. Now, is there anything else you wanna talk about before I leave?"

He was not pleased, but I didn't give a fuck.

"Well, yeah, actually there is. I hear you're thinking about getting out of the business."

His words surprised me, and suddenly he had my full attention again, because somebody was talking that shouldn't be.

"Yes, me and my family are discussing getting out of the marijuana business. With legalization sweeping the country, the business is starting to show a diminishing return with very little upside."

"So, basically, it's true?"

I nodded my head. This news did not make him happy.

"Well, if you get out, what's that going to do to me? You're my biggest client. . . . Or am I just fucked?"

"Don't worry. You'll be compensated. Most likely there'll be a buyout. We'll use the trucks and facilities for some of our other operations." I actually expected him to find some comfort in my words. Like me, KD was getting up there in age, and a buyout would set him up pretty well. But his eyes told a different story.

"Buy me out! What the fuck do you mean, buy me out? I don't wanna be bought out," he said angrily.

"I don't think you have much choice in the matter."

"It's my fucking company. Of course I have a damn choice!" he shouted.

I gave him a skeptical look. "KD, we are all going to need to distance ourselves from the company. Liquidation is the safest bet, legally and financially."

"Are you trying to steal from me? Are you trying to take my company, you black bastard?" Even in the dark, I could see his entire face was bright red.

I glanced back and could see Junior and the bodyguard were both at the ready.

I raised my hands defensively. "There ain't shit you got that I want, KD. The only reason we ever got into business was because I was assured my product would make it unmolested to its destination. So, no, I'm not trying to steal a damn thing from you, but there are people who want you to be kept in check."

"Like who?" he asked between gritted teeth.

I placed my arm around his shoulder like we were old friends. "Let me give you a little advice. Those good old boys you used to be friends with . . . you know the ones who sent you up the river to teach you a lesson? Well, they're placing another man in your old job, and he looks more like me than you. He does what he's told, and they like that because all they give a shit about is money and power, which, these days, you have very little of by their standards. So, I wouldn't be making any demands or threats right now, and when the time comes, I'd take the buyout and retire. Better to live your old age in a rocking chair than rotting away dead in the hot sun of the desert."

He shook my arm from around his neck. "You always did think you were better than me."

I gave him a smug smile. "Only because I am better than you, KD, in every way imaginable. But this isn't about me. Ask around. You'll see."

Vegas

6

"Dad!"

Before I could step into the hotel suite, my son pulled me into a hug that nearly knocked me down. Though it had only been a few days since we'd seen each other, it felt like an eternity, so I could understand why he was so happy to see me.

"What's up, son? You good?" I asked when he let go of me and we went inside.

"Yeah, I'm good. I just want you and Mom to stop fighting so I can go home."

"I know. That's what I want too."

"I think we all want to stop fighting," Consuela said as she walked into the living room. She surprisingly greeted me with a smile and gave our son an encouraging look.

Maybe this wasn't going to be as hard as I thought.

"However, there are some ground rules we have to discuss if we are going to co-parent. Rules that are not up for discussion."

Then again, maybe she was going to be her usual hard-ass self.

"Consuela, before you even go there, I just want to say I'm sorry. I should have never given Nevada a condom. I was wrong." I didn't think I could get any more sincere.

She shook her head, and I could tell from her disappointed look that my apology wasn't good enough. "This is not about a condom, Vegas." She turned to Nevada. "Go to your room. I need to talk to your father privately."

He turned to me, looking ready to protest.

I gave him a sympathetic look but told him, "Let me talk to your mother for a second, son."

Nevada hesitated, but ultimately, he gave me another hug, whispering, "Don't blow this. I wanna come home."

"I won't," I promised.

He looked at me, then his mother, then finally left the room. I remained in the same spot. The tension was thick, and Consuela and I stood staring at each other in silence for a full minute before I decided I might as well be the one to speak first.

"What is this really about, Consuela?"

"Nevada's not here because you gave him a condom." She walked over to the bar and poured herself a glass of wine. She lifted another glass, offering me some, but I declined. "You're his father. You're supposed to give him condoms. That's why I sent him to you, so you could teach him how to be a man."

"Then what the hell is the problem?" I couldn't help raising my voice. I was confused as hell and getting pissed.

"The problem? The problem is . . ." She sat on the sofa, staring up at me, and sipped her wine. "The problem is your whore."

Oh, Lord. Here we go!

"Are you serious? What does Marie have to do with this?"

"She has everything to do with this. Do you think I want my son at a house where a whore and her working girls are welcome? What kind of mother would I be?"

I could see this leading to an argument, which was the last thing I wanted, but I couldn't let Consuela distort the truth. "She's not a—"

"No? Then what is she? What do she and those girls do for a living? 'Cause they sure as hell aren't candy stripers."

There was nothing I could say that would be right. I wanted to call Marie a madam, but I realized that wouldn't have been any better, so I just stared at Consuela in silence.

"I don't want my son influenced by a prostitute, Vegas, and neither should you," she said. "The life we lead is hard enough."

"What do you want from me, Consuela?" I asked in frustration.

"Same thing I've always wanted since the day I found out about that whore," she snapped back.

"You want me to keep Nevada away from Marie?" I asked, and she nodded. "You are so wrong for this."

"Call it what you will, but that's what I want."

"Fine," I hastily agreed. At this point, I was willing to say whatever I had to so I could take my son home.

"That's not all," Consuela announced. "I want you to stay away from her as well."

"What?" My voice was an octave higher than usual. I knew Consuela could be unreasonable, but this was over the top. "I'm not doing that! She's my fiancée."

"And you deserve someone better."

"Someone better like who?"

"I can think of somebody in this room that would be perfect."

The conversation was becoming more confusing by the minute. I didn't know what kind of scheme Consuela was planning, but I had too much going on in my life and with my family to deal with it.

"You?" I shook my head emphatically. "No way."

"Why not me? Don't stand there and pretend that at one time you didn't have feelings for me; that we didn't have feelings for one another. And who can forget our chemistry?" She started winding her hips.

"Do you know how long ago that was, Consuela?"

"And?" she shot back.

"Where the hell is all of this coming from?"

"I've been thinking about it for a while, and even more since I found out about the whore," Consuela replied. "Listen to me, Vegas. You are smart and successful. You need a woman by your side who can match the kind of man that you are. One who can help you plan and execute. You can't be a power couple with a woman with no power. They'll laugh at you."

"Whatever we had between us died when you chose to go back to your husband—and then hide my child."

"*Our* child. I hid our son to protect him. Alejandro would have killed all of us, including Nevada. I didn't want anything to happen to you or to him, so I did what I had to. I saved us. And now, Alejandro is dead, and we are alive. Don't you want us to be a family?" She sounded like she fully expected me to understand and agree with her. I suppose there was some logic to the argument in her mind, but if there had ever been a chance of us becoming a family, this was a conversation we should have had a long time ago.

"He has a family. We don't have to be together to be his parents," I replied. "He not a baby anymore. I just want my son home, Consuela."

Our eyes locked, neither one of us willing to bend to the other.

"Okay. Have it your way. But understand this: if Nevada comes back to your home, he won't be coming alone. I'll be coming with him, or else he'll be on a flight back to California. Either way, our son will be living with me. Now, it's up to you where he'll be staying."

"We'll see about that." I was two seconds away from putting my hands around her neck, so I turned and walked out before I hurt her. She might have thought she had me backed into a corner, but I would never let her keep me there. Consuela would soon find out she couldn't win this fight.

KD

7

The temperature when I got back home to El Paso was damn near 110 degrees, and I was sweating my balls off. Even with the air conditioner in the truck on full blast, sweat dripped down the sides of my face. It was almost five o'clock in the evening, but the heat and humidity were still suffocating as hell. Patrick, my gorilla-sized nephew and driver, pulled off the main road and onto the long dirt roadway that led to the seventy-five acres of land bordering Mexico that we called the ranch. For ten miles or so, the only thing you could see was produce being farmed by migrants, and cows and horses, but eventually a large farmhouse and barn would appear, along with six out-of-place steel warehouse buildings a little farther in the distance. Alongside the buildings were about twenty cars, some farm equipment, and six or seven tractor trailers.

"Boss," Patrick said, gesturing to the front of the barn, where three Texas Highway Patrol cars were parked randomly.

I nodded my head, and Patrick parked in front of the house, quickly getting out of the truck to help me out. Retrieving my Stetson, I walked around to the back, past the barn, to the entrance of one of the buildings.

"Welcome back, KD." Wilbur, one of the ranch foremen, who was unloading boxes of fresh fruit and vegetables from the back of a pickup truck, tipped his hat at me. "How was the big city?"

"As good as one can expect, considering all the niggers, spics, towelheads, and Jews they got up there," I told him.

"Well, you still gotta deal with the occasional nigger and a whole lot of beaners down here—and they're just another form of spic, ain't they?" Wilbur asked.

"Yeah, you're right about that, but at least they know their place," I said, using a crumpled napkin from my pocket to wipe my damp brow and neck. "I'll say one thing about up north. It sure ain't as hot as it is here."

"Yeah, it's been hot all week, and they say it ain't gonna stop no time soon." Wilbur wiped off his own brow with his sleeve.

"I see we got company."

"Yes, sir. Over in building three. You want me to go with you?"

I shook my head. "Nah, I'll take care of it."

"All right, then," Wilbur said then went back to what he was doing.

I continued over to the third structure, past a tractor trailer, and went inside. Standing just beyond the entrance, looking very official with their hats on, were three Texas Highway Patrolmen. They all turned when they saw me, but the one in the middle with corporal stripes on stepped forward and said, "Daddy, you're back."

"How you doing, son?"

My son, Tyler, was my pride and joy. The only way he could have pleased me more was to have me a grandchild. We gave each other a big hug. When we released, I turned and shook his two friends' hands.

"Steve, Peter. How you doing, fellas?"

"Fine, sir," the Wildman brothers said in unison. They'd been Tyler's best friends since peewee football, and I practically raised them after their daddy ran off and left their momma when they were in junior high.

The three of them went to El Paso State College and played football. It was only a Division III school, but they had fun, and I loved the fact that they were so close and I could watch their games every Saturday. They even won a conference championship and went to the Division III playoffs while they were there. They came to work for me after they graduated, then they all joined the Texas Highway Patrol a few years later.

I had my own motives for encouraging the boys to pursue careers in law enforcement. Despite my incarceration, I still had my share of support in West Texas, but what most people didn't know was that I was secretly rebuilding my power base. These three boys would be at the center of it.

"Where is he?" I asked.

"He's here, Daddy." Tyler gestured toward the back of the building. "Me and the boys was just about to have a chat with him when you walked in."

"Well, son, I think I'd like to be a part of that conversation."

Tyler smiled then began to walk toward a small office in the back. He opened the door, and sitting on a chair, looking scared as shit, was Johnny Brooks.

That black bastard jumped to his feet when he saw me. "KD," he mumbled.

"How ya doin' there, Johnny?" I took a few steps so that he and I were now standing face to face. I wasn't but a few inches taller than him, but the additional two hundred pounds my body carried made it look like I dwarfed him. His nervousness amused me.

"I'm doing okay. I just wanna go home. Can I go home now?" He glanced at me for a moment, then down to the ground.

"Well, that all depends."

His lips trembled as he glanced over at Tyler and the boys.

I eased closer. "How'd that last delivery go, Johnny?"

"It went fine." Johnny nodded, his eyes still lowered. "Right on schedule."

"Is that so?" I asked.

"Y–ye–yes, sir," Johnny stammered.

"Then why the hell were you missing for twelve hours?" I slapped him.

Johnny finally looked up, trying to protect his face. "I–I di–di–didn't go missing. I made the drop on time. I swear, KD. Call the dispatcher and ask them!"

"Ya know we got GPS tracking on the trucks. The GPS went ghost for almost twelve hours after you crossed the George Washington Bridge, and you didn't answer our calls."

"I don't know anything about that," he replied.

"You don't know nothing about that?" Tyler repeated, taking off his hat and getting in Johnny's face.

"I parked underneath a bridge and went to sleep," Johnny nervously spit out. "Maybe the bridge blocked the signal?"

"Maybe you turned that fuckin' GPS off and went off the damn grid for twelve fuckin' hours to talk to the feds." I grabbed

Johnny by the collar and pulled him so close to me that the heat from my breath caught him in the face. "Don't play dumb wit' me, boy."

"I–I–I'm not playin' witcha. I swear."

"Johnny, Johnny. You do know I've taught these boys how to use police techniques to beat the shit out of someone without leaving a mark, don't you? We will find out where you were even if we have to beat it outta you," I added, which prompted the other boys to remove their hats.

Johnny's eyes were as wide as the tires of the tractor trailer outside.

"Step aside for a minute, Daddy." Tyler chuckled, rolling up his sleeves.

I glanced at Johnny and shrugged, stepping out of the way. "See, you left me no choice."

Before Johnny could reply, Tyler smacked him three times, way harder than I had. "Where the hell did you go? And you'd better not lie to me neither, you li'l prick."

"A'ight, don't hit me no more," he pleaded, lifting his hands to protect his face. "I–I–I went to get some pussy before I made the delivery in the morning. That's all," Johnny sputtered.

"You what?" Tyler asked, his face so close to Johnny's their noses were practically touching.

"I got some pussy." Johnny's eyes and voice lowered as he turned to me. "I got a little sweet young thing I been running after, and she finally decided it was time to give ol' Johnny some. So, I turned the GPS and my phone off and parked the truck across the street from her place so I could see it. I'm sorry, KD. I couldn't resist. She's twenty years old and got the prettiest set of titties you've ever seen."

I couldn't help but laugh. I released him from my grip, and he fell to the floor.

"Ha! Well, ain't that some shit?" I snickered as I wiped my forehead again with the tattered, damp napkin. "He was getting some pussy. It all kind of makes sense."

"Fuckin' on company time? Is that allowed, Daddy?" Tyler chuckled.

"Must've been some good pussy to take twelve hours, Johnny." I shook my head.

"Yes, sir, best I ever had."

Johnny went to get up off the ground, but the toe of my cowboy boot struck him in the stomach, and he crumbled back down. He had enough sense to stay down while I talked.

"That's for making my ass go all the way to New York looking for you and embarrassing myself in front of that nigger Duncan." I kicked him twice more. "Now, you listen to me, and you listen good, you worthless piece of shit. When you're making a delivery for me, you don't fucking deter from the schedule—ever—without telling us where the fuck you're going. I don't give a shit if you're pulling over to take a piss in the fuckin' woods. We'd better know about it. Understood?"

"Yes, sir." Johnny nodded rapidly like a damn bobblehead doll.

Tyler yanked Johnny to his feet. "And if that GPS ever gets tampered with again, it better be because you're dead. Because if you're not, you soon will be. Got it?"

"Oh, yes, sir, I got it," Johnny panted.

"Now, get your black ass home and get some rest. You got another run in the morning," I said.

Johnny nodded and hauled ass out of the building.

"You think he was really out gettin' pussy, Daddy?" Tyler asked as we walked outside.

"The truck was delivered on time. What the fuck else was he gonna do, go to the feds? But you keep your eye on that motherfucker the entire time he's on the road this time. I want somebody checking that GPS every hour on the hour," I said.

"Yes, sir." Tyler nodded. "I guess your meeting with Duncan didn't go so well?"

"That son of a bitch is trying to run us outta business," I grumbled. "He's talking about getting out of marijuana and forcing me to take a buyout. Some-bitch thinks he's doing me a favor."

"That's not good. The trucking company is at the center of all our plans, Daddy," Tyler said with a frown. "And we need his drugs to cover up everything else we plan on doing."

"Don't you think I know that, son? I knew that uppity nigger was gonna give me a hard time, but I didn't think his ass was gonna go this far."

"Maybe me and the boys should go up and have a talk with him," Tyler suggested.

"Nah, that ain't gonna work. You boys go up there to New York and they might send you home in a box," I said. "You see, there's one thing LC Duncan told me while I was there that's correct. This thing is about money and power."

I turned to face the boys so they could see the seriousness on my face. "We may have been going about this whole thing wrong. This has got to be handled in a way that reminds people just who KD Shrugs is and what I represent."

Roman

8

I signed the bill with a big-ass *R*, handing it back to the room service attendant. His eyes almost burst out of his head when he saw that I'd added an extra hundred dollars to the bill as a tip.

"Thank you so much, sir," he replied, giddy like a little kid. "Is there anything else I can do for you before I leave?"

"No, I think we're good, brother." I tightened the plush robe the hotel had provided, then picked up a few grapes from the tray he'd just delivered. "Oh, there is one thing. Can you recommend a place I can take my girl dancing tonight?"

He gave me a confused look, then chuckled like I'd asked a trick question. "Sir, there's only one club that anyone on our staff would recommend, and that, of course, is Wet Dream."

"Thanks," I said.

"My pleasure," he replied and slipped out the door.

I popped the cork off the three hundred–dollar bottle of champagne he'd brought up with the grapes and cheese Kandace had ordered. I would have preferred some Hennessy, but I grabbed the bottle by the neck and took a long swig.

"*Ahhh.*" I lowered the bottle, impressed. That was the first time I'd ever had super expensive champagne, and that shit was smooth as hell. I guess there really was something to living the good life. I took another swig, then picked up a glass, heading into the bedroom of the hotel suite, where I found Kandace completely naked, with her ass in the air, bent over and rubbing lotion on her ankles.

"Damn," I yelled, raising the bottle to my lips as I took in the sight. I'm sorry, but I'm an ass man. The bigger the better, and Kandace's ass was fucking huge! No exaggeration, it looked like two halves of a watermelon. Just looking at it made me so excited my dick jumped out from between the flaps of my robe.

"Like what you see?" she teased, twerking and clapping her ass cheeks like we were in the strip club.

"Hell yeah!" I was mesmerized by her bouncing ass.

"Then why don't you come over here and show me?" she said, slapping those damn ass cheeks together even louder.

She didn't have to tell me twice. I took a long swig of the bubbly, placed the bottle and the glass on the dresser, and let the robe fall to the ground. Following my pointed dick, I eased my way over to her and placed a hand on each of her bouncing hips. I let my dick slide up and down from the top of her ass to the tip of her clit.

"Come on, daddy. Stop teasing me and put it in," Kandace almost whined, taking hold of the nightstand and backing that thing up into me. It didn't take much maneuvering to slide my dick up in her soaking wet pussy.

That was one of the things I loved about Kandace. She didn't mind foreplay—hell, she loved when I ate her pussy—but dick was her thang. All I had to do was mention I wanted to fuck, and her pussy was dripping wet. I slammed my shit into her for a few minutes, and the moans and groans she made were like a crowd at an NBA game urging the home team on to victory. The louder she moaned, the harder I fucked. The harder I fucked, the louder she moaned. Kandace and I had sexual chemistry like nothing I'd ever seen, and that chemistry always led to one thing: an explosion.

"Oh shit, daddy, I'm about to cum!" she wailed.

"I know, baby. Hold on. I'm almost there," I pleaded as I continued to plow into her.

"Fuck, I don't know if I can." She shuddered.

"Fuck it, then. Let it go, baby. Let that shit go!" I screamed, and that she did.

"I'm *cummmmming*!" she shrieked with intensity, dropping to her knees. "I'm fucking cumming so good!"

I held onto her sweat-soaked body, going down to the carpeted floor with her and trying to keep pace so I could release my own orgasm, which I did within seconds. "Me too, boo!"

"Oh, yeah. Give it to me, daddy," she purred, clamping her ass cheeks down on my dick like a vise grip.

I collapsed on top of her, spent, but she didn't seem to mind. She was enjoying the afterglow of her own sexual high. A few minutes later, we were both cuddled up, asleep on the floor.

Three hours later, we pulled into the crowded parking lot of Wet Dream. The long line to get in was wrapped around the building. The night air was hot and muggy, and I didn't really feel like waiting in a long-ass line, but as soon as I put the car in park, Kandace was ready to hop out.

I glanced at the other people waiting as we walked past. It seemed to be a mixed crowd in their twenties and thirties. Most were casually dressed, but there were a few people who looked like they were about to go to a job interview instead of a nightclub. When we finally made it to the end of the line and took our spot, Kandace wrapped her arms in mine. I wasn't really into PDA, but we were on vacation, a long way from home, so I let it slide. Besides, after the way she put it on me earlier, I was seriously thinking about making her my girl.

Kandace was a stripper at a club in Hunts Point, not far from where I lived. I'd been eyeing her for a while, but she'd been dating this local drug dealer who she was faithful as hell to. He didn't know what he had and started fucking some other broad and got caught—same old story. Once I found that out, I started sending flowers and shit to her job, and eventually I wore her down and she finally gave me some ass. Like I said before, our sexual chemistry was amazing, and after that night, she started sneaking off and calling me. I'd been tapping that ass ever since, and to be honest, it wasn't just the pussy. I liked her company too.

The line slowly began to move, and after a few minutes, a large Cuban-looking guy wearing a black suit stopped by us. "What are you doing back here?" he said in a thick accent.

I didn't react, but then Kandace said, "Rome, I think he's talking to you."

Fuck, please don't tell me I look like somebody this big moth-erfucker has beef with, because he looks like he eats niggas my size for lunch, and I'm a long way from home and don't have a strap.

I exhaled, putting on a fake smile. "Standing in line to get in the club, brother. You don't have a problem with that, do you?"

"You? Standing in line to get in? Yeah, that's a problem." The man began to laugh.

I looked over at Kandace, who looked just as confused as I felt.

A few more of his buddies in black suits walked over, and they were even bigger than him.

"What is he doing in your line?" he asked one of the other men, pointing at me.

I worried that this was about to get ugly.

"I don't know." The man shrugged.

"The boss is gonna have your head for this," the Cuban man replied, removing the velvet rope from its post. "Why don't you folks follow me."

"Where are we going?" Kandace asked.

"To the VIP line, where you should have been to start with," he said.

Kandace and I glanced at each other, then happily went along with the guy. He led us past the crowded line, around the corner, and through a door marked VIP into a small, dim hallway. Loud music came through the walls, and we passed an office and a small stairwell, then finally he opened a door and we were standing directly behind the DJ booth. Bright neon lights flickered to the beat, illuminating the venue. It was a nice size, with a bar that spanned one wall, high-top tables and booths on the other, and a large dance floor in the center. It was crowded, and as I scanned the room, trying to figure out where my date and I would go, the guy snapped his fingers at one of the cocktail waitresses walking by.

"Take him and his guest to VIP and take care of them for the rest of the night," he shouted over the music.

Again, Kandace and I exchanged glances as we followed the waitress through the crowd. We got to a large booth protected by a velvet rope.

As she unhooked it, she said, "Welcome back. I'll be right back with your usual."

"Uh, thank you. I appreciate that," I said as I reached for Kandace and helped her to her seat.

"I thought you said someone told you about this place. You ain't tell me you were a regular. How often you come here?" Kandace asked.

"I don't. This is my first time here," I leaned over and whispered. "I'm guessing they think I'm someone else. Mistaken identity."

"What? Don't you think you'd better say something?" Kandace's eyes widened.

"Hell no! I'm going along with it. All this damn royal treatment they giving us? We 'bout to enjoy this shit," I told her, adjusting my chain. "They probably think I'm a rapper. You see my swag. Plus, I'm with a bad bitch."

"Bitch?" Kandace frowned and stiffened.

"I meant it as a compliment, babe. Chill." I leaned over and kissed her, and she relaxed. Seconds later, she was bouncing in her seat to the music and looking around.

"Here you are." The waitress returned with a tray holding two glasses and an ice bucket cradling a bottle. As she set it on the table in front of us, I was tempted to send it back.

"Ace of Spade!" Kandace gasped.

"Is something wrong?" the waitress asked as she opened the bottle and began pouring. "This is your usual."

"Um, how much is this a bottle?" I asked.

"It's usually a thousand dollars a bottle, with service," she replied.

"I guess we living that life tonight," I said to Kandace, all the while thinking about how fast my thirty grand was going. I reached in my pocket for my debit card. "You might as well run a tab wit' this."

"Tab? You trying to get me fired?" The waitress shook her head, pouring us each a glass of the champagne. "You know your money's no good here. My boss would kick my ass if I tried to run a tab for you."

"I am allowed to tip you, though, right?" I took a hundred-dollar bill off my roll.

"It's customary." She smiled, taking it from my hand. "Oh, and he'll be here in an hour. You might wanna get rid of your beard." She picked up the tray and left.

"What was that supposed to mean?" Kandace asked.

I ran my hand across my goatee and shrugged. "Beats the hell outta me."

My cell phone rang, and I checked the caller ID. It was Mr. Worth, my mama's next-door neighbor.

"Shit!" I was alarmed, not only because he rarely called me, but it was damn near one in the morning.

"What's wrong?" Kandace could see the concern on my face.

"I'm not sure. I'll be right back. I gotta take this," I said, jumping up and heading back to the hallway we'd come down so I could hear. "Hello?"

"Roman, it's Bob Worth from next door," he told me.

"What's up, Mr. Worth?"

"Son, they just rushed your mama to the hospital. I think it's a heart attack. You need to get over there and check on her."

"Damn! Okay, I'm on my way." I hung up without saying another word and ran back into VIP. I grabbed Kandace's arm and shouted, "Put that shit down. We gotta go now."

Kandace guzzled the rest of her drink. "Why? What's wrong?"

"My mama had a heart attack."

We rushed out of the club. My heart was beating so fast I could hardly see straight as I thought about the woman who'd given me life, now fighting for hers. I had to get home fast.

KD

9

At 6:37 p.m., the blue Cadillac pulled out of Morningstar Recycling and Scrap then headed south toward the 7-11 and stopped. The driver of the car was a middle-aged, balding white man dressed in plaid blazer and khaki pants, the kind of guy you would barely notice if he walked by. He stepped out of his car and went inside, returning a few minutes later with a plastic bag that probably contained milk or eggs his wife had asked him to pick up on his way home. In his free hand, he had a six pack of Bud Light, which he most likely planned on drinking as he watched preseason football. He got back in his car and didn't even notice that he was being followed, or probably didn't care. Men like him didn't worry about things like that, although perhaps they should.

He drove out of the city limits for about two miles, and we hung back a few cars—just enough to see him, but not enough to raise any suspicions. Like in a movie, when he passed a big old billboard off to the side of the road, a highway patrol car pulled out behind with flashing lights. I had to laugh because I was sure he was confused as hell, considering he was driving at least ten miles under the speed limit. Like the upstanding citizen he was, he pulled over right away. The patrol car pulled in directly behind him and parked.

Peter Wildman stepped out and adjusted the hat that matched his state-issued Highway Patrol uniform. Tyler, who was driving the car that I was in, did the same. They slowly approached the Caddie, Tyler on the driver's side, David on the other.

Tyler spoke to the driver, who eventually opened the door and stepped out. I couldn't hear what was said, but his expression told me he was not happy. All three men walked toward the car I was in, then Tyler opened the back door and ordered the driver to get in.

"How you doin', Herman?" I greeted him with a grin.

"KD, what the hell is going on?" Herman Cooke looked relieved, confused, and slightly pissed all at the same time. Being the president of Morningstar Recycling and Scrap and also on the board of several Fortune 500 companies, he was accustomed to being the one in control of a situation.

"Sorry for the theatrics, but I just wanted to give you a personal invite to a little gathering out at the ranch next Friday night," I said.

"Well, damn it, why the hell didn't you just pick up the phone and call me instead of doing this shit?" Herman laughed nervously.

"See, that's the thing." I gave him a knowing glance. "I tried calling, but it seems like you ain't answering your cell phone, and your secretary always seems to disconnect the call when she hears my voice for some strange reason."

"Uh, well, sorry 'bout that, but we just can't—" Herman cleared his throat.

"Can't what, Herman? Talk to me." I looked in his eyes and could see what he wanted to say, but he just didn't have the balls to say it. That was okay, though. I probably would have smacked the shit out of his spineless ass if he had said it. "Now, is it me, or have you just said fuck old KD like the rest of them?"

"It's not like that. You know I've always appreciated everything you've done for me. We're friends." He tried to smile, but it just looked fake.

"Then how is it?" I asked skeptically. "Because I'm not feeling the love anymore. Not like I used to."

Herman began to shift in his seat uncomfortably. I could see beads of sweat pop up on his bald head, but he remained silent.

"Before I got arrested, we'd go huntin' and fishin' together, and you'd ask me for favors, and in the spirit of friendship, I'd do them. Remember the time I helped you get rid a them fellas from up north who were trying to put you outta business? I covered that shit up real good, didn't I?" I leaned over a little closer to him. "I swear, it sure would be a shame if someone found those boys' remains on your property."

"Bodies on my property?" Herman's eyes went wide, and he swallowed hard.

"Oh, yeah. I forgot to tell you I buried those bodies on your property, didn't I? I mean, it's no biggie. Nobody knows where they are but me."

Poor Herman looked like he was going to shit on himself. "KD, if I've hurt your feelings in any way, I apologize. I've just been a little busy. Is there any way I can make it up to you? Why don't we go fishin' on Sunday?"

"I'd like that . . . but what I'd like most is for you to go to my get together next Friday. I think you'll find it fun."

"I wouldn't miss a party of yours. You know that, old buddy." He sounded like he was struggling to breathe.

"Good to hear that you'll be there, *old buddy*. I'll see you Friday night." I leaned past him to tap on the window to signal Tyler, who was standing outside the door. He opened it, and Herman stepped out, stumbling slightly.

Tyler and David escorted Herman back to his truck. He'd barely closed the door before he stepped on the gas, burning rubber as he sped away.

"Well, that looked like it went well," Tyler said when he returned to the driver's seat.

"It did," I agreed. "But let this be a lesson to you, son. Always plan ahead and leave yourself a way out because you can't trust anybody in this world. Except your daddy."

Rio

10

Paris and Sasha had talked me into joining them at this club I'd never heard of before, and when we pulled up, I was skeptical as hell. From the lack of a line outside, I was afraid it was one of those locals-only joints. I felt a lot better when I recognized Pierre, one of the guys on the door, and he gave me the rundown on the club. He said it was ladies' night, so there was no need to discriminate at the door. He also told me one of my good friends, Matt, and his partner were the owners. That was a good sign because Matt never did anything half-assed. The club business was like that—very incestuous. Everybody knew everybody else, from the cocktail waitresses to the bouncers to the owners.

Inside, I was impressed. The club had a rustic, chill vibe, and the music was really good. There was a nice crowd for a Thursday, but it wasn't so packed that you couldn't move around. I'd paid for a table in the VIP section, which included bottle service that we immediately took advantage of, ordering champagne and shots. Half a bottle of champagne and a few shots later, the three of us had taken over the dance floor like we owned the place. All eyes were on us, and I, for one, loved the attention.

All doubts about the place had evaporated. I was enjoying myself, and I was also glad that Sasha had loosened up and was having fun. Most times she tried to play it off and tough it out, but she was still grieving over her mother's and father's violent deaths. Out of all of us, she needed this the most.

"This spot is lit!" Sasha yelled happily when we returned to our section from dancing.

"It is," Paris agreed, leaning toward me so that we could take a selfie. We posed, and then she showed me the finished product. "This is cute."

"Aren't we always?" I said, reaching for my own phone to snap a few pics. It was vibrating, and Sebastian's name showed up on the screen with a text alert. He was a guy I'd been dating off and on—lately more on. We were supposed to be getting together the following weekend. I smiled in anticipation of whatever flirty message he had sent.

Sebastian: Really, Rio? That's how we do now?

My smile quickly faded.

Rio: Huh? What are you talking about?

I watched the three dots appear on the screen as he typed.

Sebastian: You knew I was on my way to the club and your ass just up and left? Oh, and I know you showed up here with some bitch on your arm too, you disrespectful bastard.

"What the fuck?" I said aloud.

"What's wrong?" Paris asked.

"Sebastian's jealous ass, that's what's wrong," I huffed.

"Damn, Rio, you must have put it on him." Sasha jumped into our conversation.

"I did." I smiled devilishly and rotated my hips, making them both laugh. "Well, I gotta go to the restroom, and then I might as well call his ass. I'll be back."

I made my way around the dance floor, so busy dialing Sebastian's number that I bumped into a guy near the bathroom entrance. "Sorry," I mumbled, heading into the men's room. By now, I'd called Sebastian four times, and he'd sent me to voicemail each time. On the fifth try, he finally answered.

"What the fuck do you want, Rio?"

"I want to know what hell those texts were about."

"You pretty motherfucker, don't you dare question me like I did something wrong and not you. What the fuck?" Sebastian yelled.

"First of all, I haven't done nothing wrong, so I don't know what bug crawled up that tight ass of yours, but you need to pull it out and calm the hell down," I replied. I didn't know what had him so upset. "Now, use your big-boy words and talk to me."

"There's nothing to talk about now. The time for us to talk would've been when you showed up at my club all boo'd the fuck up with some bitch, kissing and shit. Then, when my people tell you I'm on the way, you get up and leave before I can get there. What the fuck was that all about?"

I pulled the phone way from my ear for a second as if he would be able to see the crazy look on my face. "Sebastian, what the hell are you talking about? I'm not in Miami. I'm in New York." I leaned against the wall near the bathroom sinks.

"Whatever, Rio." Sebastian sighed. "Don't fucking call me no more, 'cause your ass is officially cut off."

"Wait, what?" He sounded serious. "But I didn't do shit."

"Keep telling yourself that shit," Sebastian replied. "And you and your bitch owe me a thousand dollars for that bottle of Ace of Spade. Bye, Felicia." He ended the call.

My emotions were all over the place. I was confused, angry, and most of all hurt. I really liked Sebastian. We had a good time together, not to mention he was cute, always dressed to impress, and was damn good in bed. Plus, we had a lot in common, seeing as how he was a club owner who sold and distributed drugs on the side—just like me. Even skeptical Paris thought we were a perfect match.

"That's him right there," I heard someone say.

I looked up from my phone just as some dudes approached me. I recognized the guy I'd bumped into on my way into the bathroom. He was with a couple of beefy brothas who looked like they ate steroids for breakfast.

"You sure that's him, Theo? This dude looks like he's got a little sugar in his tank," one guy said, stepping up.

"Yeah, that's him," Theo replied. "I used to play ball with his ass down by Yankee Stadium."

The angry-looking guy in the middle stepped closer, crowding my space, and then so did his two friends. If I thought about exiting, they had just made it impossible.

"I had a feeling your bitch ass was gonna show up here since your boy was deejaying. I hear you got something that belongs to me," the angry giant said.

"Obviously you're not talking to me," I said, shaking my head.

"You damn right I'm talking to you, motherfucker." He stepped so close I could smell the hot sauce on his breath. He was taller than me, standing a little over six feet, and he was built like he knew how to fight and so did his boys. "You think you could sneak around and fuck my girl and get away with it? Well, you was wrong!"

"Mister, I don't know you or your girl." I almost laughed at his accusation. "You must have me confused with someone else. I definitely ain't fuck nobody's girl, trust me. I'm on a whole 'nother team."

We were now standing face to face. I tensed up, sensing that something was about to pop off, and whatever it was, it was not going to be good. I wasn't Paris or Sasha, but I had enough training to take this guy out. However, I knew I couldn't take all three, so I was going to have do this diplomatically.

"Where is she?" he snapped in my face.

I was so busy wondering who the hell his chick was that before I knew it, his hands were wrapped around my throat, choking the shit out of me. I gasped to breathe and swung at his face in an effort to free myself from his grip. My fist connected with his jawline, but instead of loosening like I wanted, his fingers tightened. I decided to choose another course of action and kneed him in the stomach. He released my neck, and we began to scuffle.

I got in a few good blows but then he reached behind his back. It was time to get the hell out of there, but before I could take a step, he had a steel blade pressed against my neck.

"I'm gonna ask you this one more time. Where the fuck is Kandace?" He applied some pressure on the knife. The thought of it piercing my skin had me scared to death. My heart raced as I stared into his eyes and saw anger and hatred. This guy was about to kill me. This was it. This was how I was going to die—in the bathroom of a fucking nightclub in Harlem, all because this motherfucker thought I screwed some chick named Kandace. Ain't that a bitch? I always knew I was going to die in dramatic fashion, but this damn sure wasn't it.

Paris

11

I'd spent the last five minutes trading flirtatious looks with the DJ. He was the same guy I'd met a few days ago outside the jewelry story, and he was even sexier than I remembered. Good thing he waved me over, so I wouldn't have to approach him first. I didn't want to look all thirsty like some of these desperate chicks that had been coming at him all night.

"I'll be right back," I told Sasha.

"Where you going? You're not gonna just leave me here alone, are you?" she called after me as I stepped down from the VIP section.

"Trust me, I'm not going very far." I gestured toward the DJ booth.

She glanced over there and saw my intended target. "Well, then, I approve," she said.

I wasn't worried about leaving Sasha. Rio would be back soon, and anyway, her little protest about being left alone was basically an act. She was not shy at all when it came to men.

Before I could knock on the door to the DJ booth, he had opened it, cheesing. "I see you came through. That's what's up."

He gave me a hug, and I caught a glimpse of the diamond bracelet he was wearing. He may have been rugged, but he had great taste as well: two factors that attracted me. As I stepped into the DJ booth, I was surprised how much quieter it was. We could actually talk without screaming.

"I told you I might come check it out," I said, swaying to the music.

"A woman of her word. I like that." He smiled at me, displaying the shiny grills in his mouth that weren't there before. "I guess I gotta be a man of my word and get you that drink. Just hold on a sec. I gotta change this song."

He slid on his headphone and bent over his equipment. Meanwhile, I gave him the once over again. Damn, he was fine, and he had the kind of body that just screamed at a sister that he could throw it.

"I like that bracelet," I said, touching his wrist when he turned back to me. "That shit is lit. I was looking at one just like it for my brother's birthday right after I met you."

His eyes shifted, and he pulled back his wrist. He was now on alert, but I could see him trying to play it off and remain calm. "Word? Did you get it for him?"

"Nah, the place got robbed while we were there."

"Oh, for real?" He raised his eyebrows, looking both surprised and slightly uncomfortable.

"Yeah, can you believe it? It was robbed by a UPS man and a dude in some fly-ass Jordans."

We both looked down at his feet. He was wearing the same damn shoes he'd had on when he robbed the jewelry store.

"You can tell a lot about a man by his shoes." I gave him a knowing look.

"What you trying to say, ma?" He took up a defensive posture.

I couldn't help it. I laughed. "That I should get two drinks— one for coming to see you, and the other for knowing how to keep my mouth shut. What do you think?"

He let out a sigh, and his demeanor relaxed. "I think you're my kind of woman and you should get the whole damn bottle." He waved over the cocktail waitress. "So, what's your name?"

"You first, handsome."

"They call me DJ Dee, but my name's Denny. And you?"

I quickly went through my mental Rolodex of club aliases as I tried to decide which one to give him. This wasn't an ordinary thug I was talking to. Whoever he was, he had swag and style, but more importantly, he was reckless and daring. Whatever name I gave him had to show him we were evenly matched.

"I'm Princess—"

My introduction was cut short by Sasha, who rushed up to the booth. I walked over to the door, totally expecting her to block. "That's my friend. Hold on a second."

"Hey, something's up with Rio," she said into my ear. "He hasn't come out the bathroom yet."

"Did you try calling him? Maybe he slipped out without you noticing."

"Maybe, but I called and I sent him a text. He ain't answer."

"Shit." There was some sort of commotion near the back of the club. "Excuse me, Denny. I gotta go check on a friend. I'll be right back."

With Sasha right on my heels, I rushed toward the back. There was a small crowd gathered outside the men's room, all pressing together to try to get a better look. I pushed my way past all the nosy bystanders that were too afraid to go in.

"Oh my God! Rio!" I yelled as I entered, unable to believe my eyes. Rio was on the floor, bleeding. It looked like someone had kicked the living shit out of him. I rushed to my brother's aid. "No, no, no," I repeated, cradling his head.

"Is he alive?" Sasha asked, leaning down to check his pulse. "Thank God. He's got a pulse."

"We need to get him to a hospital! Somebody call a damn ambulance!" I yelled at all those stupid motherfuckers that were watching us, whipping out cell phones to take videos.

KD

12

"Looks like we got here just in time," I said as we pulled up to the hangar of the tiny airport in Beaumont. A small Cessna was parked on the tarmac, and three men and a woman walked toward it. One of the men was clearly a bodyguard or private security, and the woman and the younger man were staffers. The older man was the one I'd come to see.

"Pull up right next to that sucker."

"Not a problem," Tyler said, flashing his cruiser lights and pulling up so close that I could damn near step out of the car and onto the plane.

"Congressman," I said when Tyler opened the rear door for me to step out.

The bodyguard reached inside his blazer, but the older man, Congressman Wesley Bell of the Fifth District of New Mexico, stopped him.

"Hold on, Joseph. I know these gentlemen," Wesley said, staring at me with disdain.

I didn't give a shit. I just stared back. I'd known him almost forty years, back to when he was just plain old Wes, way before he was a town clerk, then the mayor of some backwoods town in New Mexico, and then a fucking congressman.

"Y'all go ahead and get on the plane. This'll only take a minute."

The male staffer followed his direction, but Joseph and the woman beside him hesitated.

"Go on, now. I'll be fine," Wesley told them, and they finally began walking up the steps.

Once they were out of sight on the plane, Wesley turned to me. "KD, what the hell do you think you're doing?"

"I heard you were in town, and I came by to talk a few minutes, that's all," I explained to him calmly. "Would you rather I stopped by your office?"

"Hell no! You know I can't afford to be talking to you. Not after what happened last time. That shit got you put away for years, and I was almost caught up in that mess." He shook his head angrily.

"You *were* caught up in it, and I've got the Polaroid to prove it. I just took the blame so you could get the job you're in now, *Congressman.*"

"And I used that job to get your ass out in two years instead of twenty. As far as I'm concerned, we're even."

"The fuck we are," I said in no uncertain terms. You know, it amazed me how short these sons of bitches' memories were. "I lost my job, my wife, and my reputation protecting you. More importantly, I lost two years of seeing my boy grow up. So I don't wanna hear we're even."

"Shit. What do you want, KD?" he blurted out in disgust.

"I'm having an event out at my place Friday night. I need you to make an appearance."

"I won't even be in town Friday night. I'm headed to D.C. for the next week and a half, so whatever event you're having, I can't make it." He turned to walk away.

"Now, we both know you can go and come as you fucking choose, especially since you have the use of this nice plane at your disposal." I looked at the Cessna and waved at the staffers who were peering through the windows. They quickly turned away as if they hadn't been watching us. I continued, "Now, ask yourself this: what would happen if your wife and constituents found out that you were with me that night? And that it was your idea, mister holy roller congressman?" I said with an innocent shrug.

Wesley gave me a death stare. "You son of a bitch. You know this is blackmail."

"Call it what you want, but if I were you, I'd call it an opportunity from a friend."

"You're calling yourself my friend while you blackmail me into an *opportunity*?"

"I was your friend when you left me in that warehouse alone with those three girls," I said, faking indignation. "You know how loyal I am and the lengths I'm willing to go to protect my friends. So, if you think about it, being my friend is not necessarily a bad thing. Please don't force my hand."

I could tell he wanted to run on that plane and fly away, but he was trapped, and we both knew it. I wanted to laugh.

"Now, I need you at this party. I'd like you to come as a friend, but if need be, it can be as my fucking bitch."

"And if I come to this gathering, what then? What's the upside for me?"

"How about the beginning of your gubernatorial run?"

He raised an eyebrow, and I watched as he shed all concern. That's when I really knew I had him right where I needed him. As I'd expected, talk of more political power was just the thing to get his dick hard.

Chippy

13

"LC, you need to call me as soon as possible. Rio's been hurt—*bad*."

I hated leaving a message like that for my husband, but he'd left me no choice. I'd attempted to call him twice and got no answer. All I knew was that he had caught a flight from Baltimore to Atlanta, so I supposed his phone could have been turned off. But then again, it wasn't like he was flying commercial where they make you turn them off. On a normal day, I would have cursed his ass out for ignoring my calls like that, but now I had much more serious things to worry about. My son needed me.

"Ma, I'm gonna let you out and park the—"

By the time Vegas pulled up to the hospital, I had jumped out and was halfway to the entrance of the emergency room. I heard him trying to tell me something, but I was too busy rushing inside.

"I'm looking for my son, Rio Duncan," I said to the woman at the reception desk. I scanned the crowded waiting room, looking for Paris and Sasha, but they were nowhere to be found. "He was brought here by ambulance a little while ago."

She didn't respond immediately, and I was two seconds away from going off on her when she finally looked up from her computer. "He's in the back. Have a seat and we'll call you when he's either admitted or discharged."

I fought the urge to scream. In my head, I was saying, *Bitch, if you don't take me to my son!* But I mustered up enough self-control to politely respond.

"I understand, but I'm his mother, and I need to be back there with him."

She sighed heavily, as if I was annoying her. "Look, there are already two people back there with him, and that's the limit. I don't make the rules."

I took a deep breath, reached in my purse, and pulled out a hundred-dollar bill, which I placed on the desk. "Are you sure? I think there's only one person back there. The other one left."

She looked around to see if anyone was watching, then slipped the hundred-dollar bill under the desk and into her pocket. "You have ID?" she asked.

Greedy bitch.

I handed her my driver's license, and she printed out a sticker with my name. "Curtain seventeen. Wait at the door to the left, and they'll buzz you in."

I snatched up the sticker and attached it to my shirt. A few seconds later, I was in the triage area, looking for my son.

"Mom!"

I saw Paris racing toward me with Sasha right behind her.

"Where's Rio?" I pulled them into my arms. I could see that they'd both been crying, which made me even more anxious to see my baby.

"They took him to do some X-rays. The doctor told us to wait here," Paris said, taking me by the hand and leading me into a small room made of curtains.

"Sit here, Aunt Chippy." Sasha pointed to one of the two empty chairs.

"No thanks, baby. I'm too anxious to sit," I told her. "What are they saying? Is he hurt bad?"

"They beat him up pretty bad. He was unconscious, but he woke up right before they took him down for X-rays. The doctor says he might have a concussion and a few broken ribs," Paris replied. "I'm sorry, Mom. I should have never brought him to that club."

"This is not your fault. That boy lives in those clubs." I put my arms around her as she cried on my shoulder. Seeing her so upset made me worry even more. Paris was the one child who rarely showed any kind of emotion, and she never cried, unless it was to get her way. She feared nothing and no one, but right now, she was scared.

"I should have stayed and taken care of whoever did this," Paris said.

"No, you shouldn't have," Vegas said as he walked into the tiny room. The bitch at the front desk would be going home with plenty of extra cash that day, I thought.

"We'd just be trading one mess for another. Now, can someone tell me what the hell happened?" Vegas asked.

"We were at a nightclub in Harlem, having a good time," Sasha said. "Rio went to the bathroom, and when he didn't come back, I got worried and went looking for Paris. We found him on the bathroom floor, beat really badly."

"Nobody saw nothing?" Vegas asked.

"We don't know," Paris told him. "We were too focused on taking care of Rio until the ambulance arrived. Plenty of people standing around gawking at us, but not one of them stepped up to say shit to us. I should have—"

"So, did they rob him?" I interrupted. "Is that what this was?"

"No, it wasn't a robbery. They didn't take anything from him. He still has his wallet, his jewelry, and his phone. It was something else," Paris said.

"Do you think they targeted him because he's . . . ?"

"Gay?" Sasha finished my question, shaking her head.

"Nah, definitely not," Paris answered.

"How do you know? Gay dudes is getting bashed every day," Vegas said.

I hated the way that sounded, but Vegas wasn't wrong.

Paris shook her head. "Before Rio went to get X-rays, he told us the guy kept asking about his girl. He kept saying Rio slept with his girl."

"Yeah, he did, didn't he?" Sasha chimed in.

"Family of Rio Duncan?" A young guy wearing a white lab coat and blue scrubs entered the cramped space. Vegas stepped aside to make room for him.

"Yes? I'm his mother."

"I'm Dr. Crandle. I'm treating your son."

"How is he? Is he okay? Can we bring him home?"

"He's pretty banged up, ma'am. X-rays show he has a couple of broken ribs and a sprained wrist. He also has a pretty bad concussion, so we took him up for a head CT and a couple of other tests," Dr. Crandle explained.

"So when can we take him home?" Vegas asked.

"We're going to hold him overnight for observation. We don't like to take chances with head injuries. Better safe than sorry."

"Thank you, doctor." I shook his hand.

"You're welcome. That's one lucky young man. Looks like someone tried to kill him with their bare hands, and they almost succeeded," the doctor said, placing his iPad under his arm. "He must have had God on his side."

"Yeah, well the ones who did this are gonna wish they had God on their side," I whispered to my kids after the doctor left. I glanced at Vegas, and he read my eyes, nodding his understanding. He walked out of the room to go handle his business.

LC

14

There wasn't an empty parking space at the Marriott in Columbus, Georgia. The lot was overflowing with police cruisers, SUVs, and any other law enforcement vehicle you could imagine. Inside, the Victorian Ballroom was just as crowded with the drivers of those vehicles. Men and women in various uniforms all sat at round tables in front of half-eaten baked chicken and rice pilaf, listening as Derrick Hughes, newly elected president of the National Sheriffs Association, gave his acceptance speech. Tall and broad-shouldered, Derrick had the build of a Marvel superhero and a voice as deep as Barry White's. It was obvious from the applause that erupted the members in attendance felt he was the right man to lead them.

Junior and I stood in the back of the ballroom, where we'd slipped in unnoticed. I felt a bit of pride and satisfaction as I watched the young man at the podium. Not only had he won the election in his own county in Georgia three years ago, which was no small feat for a black man, but now, he'd been voted into an even higher position of power. The Duncan family donations and political connections had helped him win the election.

Derrick and I made eye contact, and I nodded.

"Now, I'd like to take the time to introduce a man who has been supportive of our organization throughout the years. He's here to share a few words with us this afternoon. Mr. LC Duncan, Chairman of Duncan Motors. Let's give him a hand," Derrick announced.

There was some polite applause as I made my way to the front of the room and stood behind the podium.

"Good afternoon, and thank you, Derrick. It's certainly a pleasure to be here today with you all to celebrate the induction of all of your fine leaders. We at Duncan Motors know the work that you and your departments put in day after day and how dangerous it is out there protecting and serving your communities. Sadly, we also know that they don't pay your officers and staff anywhere close to what they're worth, which is why we support you the way we do," I said.

"And we appreciate it!" someone in the crowd yelled over the applause that my remark received.

"We appreciate you too." I smiled. "And we will continue to show our appreciation. But, this year, we wanted to do something a little special for you. So, each of your departments will be the recipient of a brand-new chase car, courtesy of Duncan Motors."

The applause became louder, and animated conversations broke out at a few of the tables.

"Now, these aren't just regular chase cars. These are brand-new 2020 Corvette police interceptors, completely outfitted with everything you need and more. And let me tell you, there won't be a vehicle out there that you can't catch in a high-speed chase."

A particularly enthusiastic guy in the front row yelled out, "Are you serious? Whoa!"

"Yes, I'm serious." I laughed. "Oh, and in case you're wondering, each one of these babies runs about a hundred and fifty grand, so Duncan Motors won't be covering the insurance on them. That's gonna be on y'all."

"Oh, then I'll be the only one in my department driving that some-bitch. Might as well park it in my driveway right now," a sheriff in a mustard-colored uniform yelled as laughter erupted from the officers at his table.

"I won't tell if you don't," I joked. "In addition to the cars, we would also like to continue our support of your children and widow's benevolent fund. Junior?"

Junior walked up to the podium and held up the large cardboard he carried. The audience gave a standing ovation at the oversized check made out to the National Sheriffs Association in the amount of one hundred thousand dollars.

Derrick came over and shook my hand. "Thanks for coming out, LC. We truly appreciate your support."

We did the obligatory pose with the check for a few pictures, then Junior and I returned to the back of the room while Derrick wrapped up the meeting. Many of the attendees shook my hand and thanked me personally as they exited. I'd known many of those sheriffs for years. The value of building relationships with law enforcement was a lesson I'd learned a long time ago, and ironically, I'd learned it from KD Shrugs and his cronies.

Derrick came to stand with me and Junior as the last stragglers were filing out. "LC, this was an unexpected surprise," Derrick said.

"We needed to talk—and it never hurts to have a PR moment and show a goodwill gesture to law enforcement," I told him. "Congratulations again. You should be very proud of yourself."

"Hey, I couldn't have done it without you and your family's support. Any of it."

"Well, you've always been the right guy for the job, and everyone knows it. I'm just glad we were able to help you spread the word. Let's take a walk," I suggested.

The three of us exited the ballroom out the back door to where Junior and I had parked, away from everyone else. It was empty except for one of the cooks, who stood several yards away, smoking a cigarette and talking on his cell phone. He didn't even glance in our direction.

"I'll pull the car up, Pop," Junior said, giving Derrick and me some privacy.

"So, how are things going so far?" I asked, looking over to make sure the cook was still ignoring us. "Any dissention in the ranks?"

"No, not really, thanks to those envelopes that were placed under everyone's hotel room doors. Sheriff Richards and his buddies are still a little sore that he lost, but they'll get over it. The rest of them all seem to have fallen in line." He smirked.

"Well, I'll have to see what we can do to appease Sheriff Richards and his people. Help keep them in the ranks."

"That would be appreciated." Derrick became serious. "So, what did you really want to discuss?"

"I'm concerned about one of your predecessors, KD Shrugs in Texas. I've spent the past few days talking to some of our mutual friends, and we're concerned that he's planning something, and it needs to be nipped in the bud."

"You do realize that Shrugs is done. He's a nobody, a convicted felon." Derrick shook his head as if KD were the least of his problems. "I'd be more concerned about Richards than him."

"Richards can be controlled. KD can't. He's too ambitious. He's also got friends all over the South that he's helped to make a lot of money. The kind of people who would love to see me and you in the fields." I studied his expression. "Do you understand what I'm saying?"

"One hundred percent, and I appreciate you bringing this to my attention. I'll see what I can find out and put this Shrugs in his place as quickly as possible."

"Smart man." I patted him on the shoulder as Junior pulled the car around. "But remember, we're talking about a man who's ruthless and will stop at nothing to get what he wants. You be careful."

Roman

15

After a night spent in the Miami airport, guzzling coffee and Red Bull to stay awake, Kandace and I were finally able to get on a flight back to New York. I put her in a Lyft back to her apartment and then went straight to Mercy General Hospital. As I walked through the doors, I said a quick prayer for my mother's health. I'd tried calling Aunt Coretta from the airport but got no answer. What if the worst had happened and she just didn't want to tell me over the phone?

I took a deep breath to steady myself before I opened the door to my mother's room. Other than the fact that she was hooked up to some beeping machines, she kinda looked like she was resting—better than I had imagined she would. Aunt Coretta was leaned back in a chair in the corner, snoring loudly like she'd worked an overnight shift.

Not wanting to wake them, I quietly moved the empty chair to my mother's bedside. As soon as I sat in it, her eyes fluttered open.

"Roman," she whispered and smiled.

"Hey, Mama," I said. "How you feeling?"

"Tired."

Aunt Coretta sat up. "Roman, when you get here?"

"A few minutes ago. What are the doctors saying?"

"They haven't really said nothing. Just waiting on test results." Aunt Coretta stretched and yawned.

"I'm fine, baby," Mama told me.

Looking at her, I knew that wasn't true. She was breathing heavily, even with the oxygen tube in her nose, and she could hardly keep her eyes open. Even though I knew that was probably due to the drugs they had her on, there was a slight look of worry on her face that I'd never seen before.

"You're not fine, Mama. You're in the ICU. Having a heart attack is not fine." I turned to my aunt. "I need to talk to the doctors and find out what's going on."

Mama reached over and touched my arm. "I'm sure they'll be in here shortly. They're doing rounds."

There was a tap on the door, and as if he had sensed we were talking about him, a tall, white-haired doctor walked in.

"How are you doing? I'm Dr. Ford," he said as he walked over to the bedside.

"I'd be doing better if I knew what was going on with my mother."

"Roman, don't start," Aunt Coretta warned.

"I'm not starting nothing. We've been waiting all night for answers, and nobody seems to know anything. I done came from halfway across the country to get here and still don't know nothing except she had a heart attack."

"I understand your frustration. Mr. Johnson, is it?" the doctor asked.

"Yeah."

"We just wanted to make sure we had some of her test results before we made a definitive diagnosis."

"Well, what's the diagnosis?" I asked loudly.

Dr. Ford turned his back to me and spoke to my mother. "How you feeling today, Ms. Johnson?"

"I've definitely felt better," Mama said. "Feels like an elephant done sat on my chest."

"Yes, I'm sure it does." The doctor leaned down to listen to her breathing.

I watched as he moved the stethoscope around her chest, asking her questions like I wasn't standing there waiting for him to answer the one I'd asked him.

Finally, he turned around and said, "It appears your mother suffered a heart attack last night."

"We know that," I replied, frustrated.

"Roman, please." Aunt Coretta scolded me, then turned to the doctor and apologized. "I'm sorry about my nephew's agitation. Like he said, he traveled all night, so his patience is a little thin because he needs a nap."

"I don't need you apologizing for me, Aunt Coretta," I snapped at her.

"It's fine," the doctor said. "In addition, she's in acute renal failure."

"Her kidneys?" Aunt Coretta stood and walked over to be closer.

"Yes. She's been sick for a while. She's lucky to be alive, and we're going to do everything to keep her comfortable," he said.

"So, will she have to be on dialysis?" Aunt Coretta asked.

"Honestly, I don't think right now that's an option. Her heart is very weak, and I don't believe her body would be able to handle dialysis."

"No dialysis?" I yelled. "What the fuck? My mother needs help. What are you gonna do for her?"

"Can she have a transplant?" Aunt Coretta's voice cracked, and I realized she was on the verge of crying. She and my mother were super close.

"Like I said, it's too early to—"

I cut him off. "Give her mine."

"Roman, no." Mama, who hadn't said a word while the doctor was updating us, now spoke emphatically. "I won't allow you to do that."

"I think our first goal is to let her get some rest and wait for the other tests," Dr. Ford said. "I'll be back this afternoon to check on you, Ms. Johnson." He thanked us and walked out of the room.

I looked over at my mother and rubbed the top of her hand, carefully avoiding the IV line attached to it. She'd been a good mother, a hard worker, and a great provider. She'd always been there for me, even when she shouldn't have been. Now, it was time for me to be there for her.

"I'll be right back, Mama." I went into the hallway, looking for the doctor. I spotted him at the end of the hallway, just as he was about to enter another patient's room. "Dr. Ford. Yo!"

He turned around and waited as I sprinted over to him.

"What can I do for you, Mr. Johnson?"

"I want you to do whatever you have to to give my mother one of my kidneys. I don't care what it takes or how much it costs."

He let out a small sigh like he had sympathy for me, or else he was sick of my ass. Either way, I didn't care. This was my mother's life we were talking about.

"I understand you wanting to help her, but donating a kidney is a major undertaking, medically speaking," he said.

"I don't care. What I gotta do?"

He glanced at the door to the other patient's room like I was holding him up. "Well, the first thing we have to do is run some tests to see if you're even a match."

"So, let's get to testing."

"I'll set it up for the morning. Now, go get yourself something to eat and get some rest. You look beat."

It had been damn near twenty-four hours since I'd slept, and I was definitely hungry. The dinner Kandace and I had in Miami the night before was long gone, so I took the doctor's advice and went to grab some food from the hospital cafeteria.

As I stood in line trying to decide between the dry-ass baked chicken or asking the fine-ass nurse in front of me for her number, Denny called.

"Yo, what's up? You a'ight?" he asked.

"Yeah, I'm a little shaken up, but I'm holding it together."

"Where you at right now?"

"I'm at the hospital. I'm probably gonna be here for a minute."

"You at the hospital for real? Damn, man. I mean, I heard what happened, but I thought the niggas was lying. I damn near put my hands on the dude that told me."

The nurse turned around, and we made eye contact. I smiled as she gave me a quick look up and down. Her face wasn't as impressive as her ass in those scrubs, but she was decent.

"This is crazy. You know if I woulda knew that shit was going down, I would have had your back," Denny said.

"It's cool. I ain't even tell nobody. I just came straight here." I was surprised that Denny seemed so upset about my moms. Then again, we had been friends and partners since middle school.

Denny exhaled. "He whooped your ass that bad?"

"What?" I said, thinking I'd misheard him.

"I mean, when I heard it, I figured you got roughed up a little, but you went straight to the hospital. Yo, how we gonna handle this shit?" Denny asked. "Matter of fact, don't even worry about it. You rest up. Trust, this nigga Vaughn ain't getting away with this shit."

"Vaughn? Denny, what the fuck are you talking about?" I said, hopping out of line and rushing out of the dining room.

"I'm talking about Vaughn putting his hands on you in the bathroom at the club last night."

"His hands on me? Now, you know that shit ain't happen." I almost laughed at the thought of that ever occurring. "That nigga might be big, but there is no way I'd let him put his hands on me. I'd shoot his ass first."

"But you just said you was at the hospital."

"Bro, I'm here with my moms. She had a heart attack last night, and now it's some shit going on with her kidneys."

Denny was quiet for a minute.

"Denny, what the fuck is going on?" I asked.

"Yo, man, this shit is crazy. Word on the street is Vaughn rolled up on your ass last night and fucked you up."

"I wasn't even in New York last night. I was in Miami with Kandace. That's probably why he's coming out of his mouth sideways like that, but he's about to regret it."

"Word," Denny said. "Let's take care of this nigga."

"Where the fuck you at?"

"I'm on my way to my baby mom's right now. What you thinking?"

"I'm gonna go spend a little time with my moms and then catch a catnap. I'll call you in a few hours. I got an idea that's gonna put Vaughn in his place and get my moms the money she needs for her hospital bills."

Nevada

16

I was lying across my bed, half asleep, when a chime came from my iPad. I sat up and read the notification from Instagram, letting me know that someone named KBeauty was attempting to send me a message. I had no clue who KBeauty was. It wasn't anyone I followed, so I wasn't going to accept the message without doing a little investigating. I clicked on the profile and smiled when I realized it was Kia, then immediately accepted the request.

KBeauty: I need your help!!!!

NevadaD23: You okay? What's up?

KBeauty: I'm going to fail this GED exam if I don't get some help.

NevadaD23: No you're not. I got you. What seems to be the problem?

KBeauty: Everything. I just don't get any of this math. Think we could meet up so you can help me?

NevadaD23: Meet up? Like in person?

As soon as I typed the message, I regretted it. I no doubt sounded like a lame, and Kia would think I was corny after reading it. But I was pleasantly surprised by her response.

KBeauty: Yes, in person. Not only can I get help with my math, but I also get to see your cute face.

NevadaD23: I don't know if you've heard, but I'm kinda on lock down.

KBeauty: I mean, I kinda figured something happened when you left all of a sudden the other day without saying goodbye.

NevadaD23: Yeah, my mom kinda spazzed out and made me leave, but I'll make this happen. Gimme five minutes.

KBeauty: Okay.

I hopped up and walked into the living room, but no one was there. I went into the bedroom on the other side of the hotel suite that my mother slept in. She was going through some papers in her briefcase.

"Mom?" I walked in.

"Yes. What is it, Nevada"?" She sighed, putting the papers in a folder, then into the leather bag.

"Are you going somewhere?"

"No, I have a business meeting with someone here in the suite," she told me.

That was good news to me. She might be happy to have me out of the way so she could have privacy for her meeting. I took a chance and asked, "Well, can I go to the library?"

"Library? Why? School hasn't even started, Nevada." She wasn't as eager as I had hoped.

"Mom, you know I'm in AP classes and had summer assignments."

"So, you haven't completed them? The summer is over." She shook her head and folded her arms.

"I have completed them, but there's some last-minute research I want to do, that's all. Besides, I'm about to go crazy in this suite. It's just the library. Please," I begged.

"Fine, Nevada. You can go for the afternoon, and that is it."

"Thank you, Mom." I ran over and gave her a kiss.

"I will have the driver drop you off," she stated.

I turned to walk away with a slight smile on my face, which she quickly erased for me.

"And I'll have him wait for you until you are finished. Two hours. That's it."

"But Mom, why can't I just have my phone back and I can call an Uber?" I complained.

"You don't agree? Then fine, you will remain here in the suite that you say you are so desperate to leave." She shrugged.

"Fine" I said then hurried back to my room to tell Kia.

NevadaD23: You still here?

KBeauty: Yep, you good?

NevadaD23: I'm good. We can meet up. St. Agnes Library. In an hour. Will that work?

KBeauty: On Amsterdam?

NevadaD23: That's the one.

KBeauty: See you in an hour.

As I got dressed to go meet up with Kia, something dawned on me. My mom wanted to know about me completing my summer assignments. If she was going to move me to California, then why did she care if I finished assignments for a school I wouldn't be returning to? I almost went back into the living room to ask her about it, but I decided not to jinx it. I was in a good mood at the moment and wanted to stay that way while I was out with Kia.

I arrived at the library right on time. Since I didn't have a phone to call Kia, I decided to wait for her just inside the entrance, where she could see me, but my mother's driver, who was parked out front, could not. I could feel my heart racing. Was that because I was nervous about being caught in a lie by my mom, or was I nervous about seeing Kia? I wasn't sure, but I took a few deep breaths to try to calm my nerves.

Fifteen minutes later, she still hadn't arrived, and I started to wonder if she was ever coming. I slipped my iPad out of my book bag and logged on to the library wifi to message her.

"Sorry I'm late."

Before I could type a message, I felt a tap on my shoulder, and there she was. Dressed in a cropped T-shirt, cut-off denim shorts, and sandals, she looked even more beautiful than she had the other day at the water park. It was hard not to stare.

"It's no big deal."

"Then why does it look like you're about to send me a message?" She pointed at my iPad screen with her IG profile displayed.

"Uh, I was just gonna let you know I was grabbing us a table." I shrugged as I put the iPad back into my bag. "You ready?"

We went inside the main room and found a table near the back, somewhat secluded. Kia reached into the bag she was carrying and pulled out a thick book, tossing it onto the table with a thump.

"GED preparation guide," I read aloud. "This is a big book."

"It's a big test," she said, reaching back into the bag and taking out several pens, a notebook, and a calculator.

"I see." I sat in the chair beside her. "I guess we'd better get started."

As we got to work on the subjects she was struggling with, I noticed that Kia was really focused, which made me even more curious about her. How did someone who was obviously smart and eager to learn end up without a high school diploma, working for someone like Marie?

"Here, let me show you." I slid a little closer to correct a problem she was working on. I couldn't tell if it was her hair or her perfume, but she smelled as good as she looked.

"Oh, I get it now." She exhaled loudly and sat back in her chair. "I'm so slow."

"You're not slow. You're actually very smart," I said.

"You think so?" She glanced over at me.

"My grandfather says that really smart people are ones that use their resources. You needed help, so you came to me and asked for it. You used your resources," I said with a smile. "So, just based on that logic, you're smart. And based on the work we did today, I know you're gonna ace this test." I fumbled with a pencil on the table to keep my hands busy so I wouldn't give in to the urge to brush away the piece of hair that was hanging in her face.

"I don't know about acing it, but I do feel a lot more confident. So, let's get back to work, teach." She put her hand on my arm. Unfortunately, at that moment, my stomach decided to growl loudly. "Whoa, sounds like my teacher is hungry," she said with a laugh.

"Maybe a little." God, how embarrassing. I had been so excited about the two hours of freedom my mother granted that I forgot that I hadn't eaten since breakfast.

"Why don't we grab something to eat? I'm a little hungry myself." Kia began packing up her study materials.

I looked at my watch. We'd been studying for an hour, but because Kia had been fifteen minutes late, that only left forty-five minutes before my mother's driver would be looking for me.

"I don't really have time to go anywhere."

"We can just walk over to Central Park and grab something quick from a cart. Come on. My treat." She stood and reached for my hand.

I packed up my stuff in a hurry, then wrapped my fingers around hers, momentarily forgetting everything but the feeling of our palms connecting. We were almost at the exit before my senses kicked back in.

"Wait." I stopped in my tracks.

"What's wrong?"

"Let's go out the other door," I suggested, remembering the Town Car was parked out front.

Kia looked at me funny, but then shrugged. "Okay, whatever you say."

We changed directions, slipping out the side door of the building and out into the street. She held on to my hand as we walked to the park, only releasing it to pay for two slices of pizza. The park benches were all full, so Kia found a nice grassy spot where we sat down to eat.

"This is so good," she said with a mouth full of pizza.

"It really is. I haven't had a slice in a while."

"Yeah, probably because your family has a chef making you gourmet meals all the time," she teased.

I shook my head. "Nah. Believe it or not, my grandmother does most of the cooking at our house."

"Stop it." Kia looked surprised. "Your family has all that money, you live in that huge mansion, but she has to cook? Why?"

"She doesn't have to. She chooses to," I said. "She's really family oriented, and she says this is her way of showing love to her family. And she can *cook*."

"She sounds cool."

"She is. I've learned so much from her. From all my family."

Kia's phone vibrated. She took it out of her bag and checked the message. "Guess it's time to head back. That was Marie. I have an appointment in two hours."

Reality was like a cold bucket of water over my head as I remembered where we were and, more importantly, *who* we were. Neither one of us could lounge around in the park all day. I had a mother who would kill me for sneaking around like this, and Kia had a boss who was very demanding of her time.

I stood and helped her to her feet. "Yeah, I gotta get back myself."

"I really appreciate you helping me, Nevada." She smiled at me, then stood on her toes and kissed my cheek.

"I enjoyed it," I said, blushing. I'd tutored lots of people before, but never one as pretty as Kia, and no one had ever thanked me with a kiss.

We started walking back, and Kia took my hand again.

"Can I ask you something?" I said.

"Sure. Ask away. I'm an open book."

"Do you enjoy your . . . *appointments*?" I knew it was a personal question, but this little bit of time I'd spent with Kia made me feel comfortable enough to ask it. Plus, I just really wanted to get to know her better.

Kia got quiet for a minute, and I worried that I'd insulted her. But she didn't drop my hand, and eventually she shrugged and said simply, "It's a means to an end."

I took a chance and pressed further. "And what about your family? Do they know about what you do?"

We'd arrived at the corner near the library. I was ten minutes past my curfew to return to the car, but that didn't matter to me in that moment. Kia's eyes met mine, and neither one of us moved. Then, she told me her story.

"My dad was a soldier. He died when I was ten. I don't even know if my mother is still alive, honestly."

I touched her cheek, thinking that was the end of her sad story, but the tragedy had only just begun.

"When I was twelve, my mom married a guy who was a regular at the bar she worked at in Korea. I guess she thought since he spent lots of money, he would be a stable husband. He wasn't. Turns out he was a creep, a drunk, and a perv—and an abusive one at that. He would beat and rape my mom, which drove her to drink. Then, while she was passed out, he would come in and rape me, and eventually my younger sister. It went on for a couple of years, and then we decided to escape the hell we were living in. We ran away from home."

"Oh my God," I whispered. It was kind of surreal, standing on a busy New York corner with people rushing by, oblivious as she poured out the story of all the pain she'd suffered in her life.

"A couple of weeks after we left, we were sleeping on the street, and this woman offered to take us in. But she let us know real fast that we had to earn our keep to stay with her. It turned out she had a pimp who was calling all the shots. She cleaned us up and taught us what men wanted."

"But you were only kids . . ." I said.

"Yeah," she explained with a sigh. "But it was scary out there on those streets. We thought about running again, but to be honest, it was better than being forcibly raped by my stepfather, and they did feed and clothe us."

I felt rage as I imagined Kia and her sister in such a horrible situation, which, she explained, didn't get much better after that.

"Eventually, the lady and her pimp sold us to some men who brought us to the United States and put us to work in Asian brothels. They moved us around from one shithole to another across the country." She brushed away the lone tear that fell from her eye.

"What about your sister? Where is she?"

"Probably dead. They separated us somewhere in Florida before I met Marie." Now she allowed the tears to flow freely.

"I'm so sorry," I said, wishing there was more I could say or do.

"Don't be. Marie found me a year ago, and I'm in a better situation now, and I'm grateful. I could be dead too. Yeah, I'm still turning tricks, but at least most of the money is mine." She sighed. "Right now, I'm saving my money so I can get out of this business and go to college. I want to become a private investigator."

"A private investigator? Why?"

"So I can find out what happened to my sister."

And just like that, it all made sense.

Roman

17

I hopped into the passenger's side of the Expedition Denny had purchased while I was in Miami. It wasn't brand spanking new, but it was new to him, and he was proud of it. Normally I would have commented on his ride, but not that night. I was in no mood for mindless car talk. All I wanted to do was hurt somebody the way I was hurting inside about my mom, and our next stop would be the perfect place to inflict some pain.

"You bring the bag?" I asked.

"It's right there in the back."

"Good. I can't wait to pay that lying-ass Vaughn a visit," I said, reaching for the bag. "He 'bout to make a nice donation to my mom's medical expenses."

"You sure you wanna even deal with this right now?" Denny raised an eyebrow at me.

"Hell yeah. I been wanting to rob this nigga for three years," I said, taking the ski masks and guns out of the bag. Denny and I didn't discriminate in who or what we robbed, although up until a few months ago, our primary business had been robbing drug dealers and dope boys around the city. "Why wouldn't I wanna deal with it?"

"Your mom. How is she?" Denny asked.

"She's real sick, man. In ICU right now. I might have to give her my kidney."

"Damn, I'm sorry to hear that." Denny shook his head.

"The thing is, even if they say she can have it, she ain't got the insurance to cover it, so I gotta come up with the money," I said, pumping a shell into the shotgun chamber. "Which makes robbing this motherfucker even sweeter."

Denny parked his truck in a lot down near the entrance to City Island, and a few minutes later, Li'l Al pulled up in a stolen minivan. The two of us jumped in, and Li'l Al began driving toward the building that Vaughn lived in.

The street was quiet, probably due to the fact that it was in a residential area. Li'l Al circled the block, dropping Denny off on the other street behind Vaughn's house. The plan was for me go through the front door, while Denny would sneak behind the house and go through the back. Vaughn didn't think anyone knew where he lived because he did most of his drug business down on Boston Road on the other side of the Bronx. Screwing Kandace came with more benefits than just good pussy. She knew everything there was to know about Vaughn, and now so did I.

Denny got out, and Li'l Al circled the block again, parking on the corner. I slipped the ski mask over my face, keeping low until we got the text from Denny, letting us know he was ready. At that moment, Li'l Al slammed his foot on the gas, speeding down the street and coming to a stop in front of Vaughn's place. I hopped out of the van with a shotgun in one hand and a .44 in the other and ran up the steps to Vaughn's front door. You would think my first instinct would be to kick in the door, but in my experience, these drug dealers were so cocky they never locked their doors. I twisted the knob, and voilà! The door opened.

"What the fuck?" A guy was sitting on the sofa, playing a video game when I rushed in. He dropped the game controller and reached for a Glock that was on the table in front of him, but before he could touch it, I had my .44 pointed at his face. He tossed his hands in the air, and I grabbed the gun, tucking it in my waistband.

"Oh, shit!" I heard from someone in the back, which confirmed that Denny had entered as well.

"Where the fuck is Vaughn?" I barked at the dude on the sofa, who now looked like he was trying to think of his next move.

"Fuck you," he said.

"Man, that nigga don't pay you enough to be a fucking hero," I warned, stepping close enough to hold the barrel of the shotgun at his knee. "Now, talk or get capped. I don't got no time for a whole bunch of back and forth."

"He's upstairs," the dude finally said as Denny entered with another one of Vaughn's guys.

"Get over there on the sofa," Denny commanded.

I began to ease my way to the staircase.

"Yo, cuz, be careful," Denny said.

I nodded my head as I ascended the staircase slowly. For the first time since we'd entered the house, I was nervous. I arrived at the only room with a closed door and pulled the trigger of the shotgun. The wood cracked as the blast splintered it damn near in half. I'd read somewhere that shots fired, whether they hit someone or not, disoriented people, and instinctively they went to the ground. I wanted whoever was on the other side of that door to be disoriented as hell.

"Ahhhhhhhh!" A woman shrieked as I stepped inside the room and pulled the trigger again. She grabbed hold of the blanket and held it tight against her.

"The fuck?" a naked Vaughn yelled from the floor, where he was scrambling to get up.

I stepped closer and held my gun to his face.

"Wake up, motherfucker!" I yelled. "Where's the fucking stash?"

"Ain't no fucking stash, nigga. I got some cash on the dresser. Take it and get the fuck out!" Vaughn said with a look of disgust.

"Fuck that chump change. Where's the stash?" I asked again.

"Fuck you. I told you ain't no stash!"

I suddenly noticed his black and swollen eye and remembered what Denny said about the other night, when Vaughn said he supposedly beat my ass in the club. I hit him in the face with the barrel of one of the guns. "You stay lying, huh? I hope you realize it's about to cost you your life and hers."

"No!" The girl screamed and flailed her arms around, no longer concerned with covering herself with the blanket. "I'll tell you where it is. Please don't kill me."

"Shut the fuck up, bitch," Vaughn growled at her, and I hit him in the face again, harder this time.

"You know where it is?" I asked the girl.

"Yeah, it's in the room across the hall in the back of the closet," she said.

I took off the duffle bag that was hanging across my chest and handed it to the girl. "Go and put everything in it into this bag. Every fucking thing. You understand?"

Her hands were shaking as she took the bag from me.

I pointed the other gun at her. "And if you try anything funny, after I kill his ass, I'll kill you, too."

The expression on her face said it all. She understood that I wasn't playing. "I swear, I won't do anything funny."

"You got two minutes to get across that hallway and back in here. Don't make me have to come looking for you," I warned her.

"You won't." She scrambled out of the room.

"Traitorous bitch," Vaughn panted as sweat poured down his face and mixed with the blood.

"Shut the fuck up." I stepped toward the doorway and yelled, "Yo, you good down there?"

"Yep!" Denny yelled back.

"A'ight, strip them motherfuckers down. We 'bout to roll out in about a minute and a half!"

"I hope you know you ain't getting away with this shit." Vaughn moaned. "You must not know who the fuck I am."

"I know exactly who you are. That's why I'm here and not at your little corner spot where everyone else thinks you keep your stash." I pointed my gun to his shriveled-up dick and laughed. "And from the looks of things, I understand a lot more now too."

"Baby girl, you got ten seconds to get your black ass back here!" I warned. "Ten, nine, eight . . ."

My countdown got down to three by the time she ran back into the room. The empty duffle bag was now full.

"Here, here. That's everything, including his guns," she said.

"Put that shit on the dresser in it too." I nodded toward the cash and jewelry Vaughn had pointed out earlier. "And those keys and phones."

She followed the instructions and dumped the items into the bag, then gave it to me. I slipped it back onto my body.

"Good job. Now, bring your ass. And you too, tiny dick," I commanded.

Vaughn hesitated like he wanted to try something with his naked, unarmed self, but he got moving once I fired a warning shot into the dresser behind him. I shoved him and his girl into the little bathroom in the hallway.

"Hey, bring them up here," I yelled to Denny.

Denny escorted the two dudes from downstairs, who were naked now too, and I waved the gun in the direction of the bathroom. "In you go."

They slow-stepped it, but they understood they had no choice but to go in there with Vaughn and his woman.

"Now, don't y'all get freaky in there, okay?"

"Fuck you," one of the dudes said.

I closed the door and lodged a chair underneath the doorknob. It wouldn't hold them long, but long enough for us to get the hell outta there. We ran out of the house and into the waiting minivan. We barely had the doors shut before Li'l Al took off down the street.

"You get their phones and keys?" I asked Denny.

"Hell yeah, I did."

"Cool," I said, taking my mask off. "Wanna hear something crazy?"

"What's up?"

"That nigga Vaughn's face was already fucked up. He really did get into a fight with somebody."

"Word? Well, he gave as good as he got, because I heard the other dude left the club in an ambulance," Li'l Al added.

"What? And y'all thought that was me?"

"Hey, that's what everybody was saying," Denny replied.

"This shit is wild." I shook my head.

A text came in from my aunt, telling me my mama was up and asking about me.

"I don't know what the fuck is going on with that shit at the club, but I ain't got time to worry about it right now. Take me back to my moms."

KD

18

"Hey, KD."

I walked into the reception area of Building 6 on my property and was greeted by the smiling face of Elizabeth Martin, a pretty brunette with perky breasts and a fine ass. She was one together woman, and I was hoping to fix her up with Tyler one day. They would have some pretty-looking grandkids for me.

"How ya doing, Lizbeth? I heard you needed to see me." I removed my hat and took a seat in front of her desk.

"Yes, sir, I sure do," Elizabeth replied in the sweetest of Southern accents. "Tyler had me run some tests on the young ladies you're planning to have at your party."

"Yeah." I nodded, realizing that she would never have called me over personally unless it was important. Real important. If she said what I thought she was fixin' to say, I was going to kill Peter Lee. My party was in a day, and the last thing I needed was a bunch of diseased prostitutes. I needed those girls to be as clean as the board of health and ready to work. I'd already spent a small fortune on catering and remodeling Building 3.

"Give it to me straight, Lizbeth. How bad is it?"

She chuckled. "Not bad at all. There are a few girls I'd exclude, but the reason I wanted to speak to you is because I discovered something interesting."

I sat up in my chair. When Elizabeth had something interesting to share, it usually meant dollars signs for old KD. "Like what?"

"Four of the women are prime candidates for us to bring in house, and two may fill an immediate need."

I raised an eyebrow. "You're not shitting me, are you? You sure about that?"

"Yes, sir. I was surprised myself, so I double checked." She handed me a piece of paper, which I scanned, even though I didn't know what the hell I was looking at.

"Would ya look at that?" I could already hear the cash register ringing.

"What do you want to do?" Elizabeth asked.

"I'm gonna go talk to their pimp, that's what I'm gonna do. Then I'm going to sit down with these young ladies and make them a job offer—one that I don't think they'll be able to refuse considering the lives they lead." Smiling broadly, I placed my hat back on my head as I got up from my chair.

She came around her desk and hugged me. "You're a good man, KD Shrugs. I wish I had met you when you were younger. We could have had a good time."

"We sure could have." I laughed. "But these days, I live vicariously through my son. You and Tyler would make a fine couple."

"Maybe, but he'd have to ask me out for us to know. I think your boy is scared of me," she said lightly.

"Well, I'm gonna have to unscare him," I replied, heading for the door. "I'll be back in touch about those girls directly. Going to take a ride out to see their boss."

Hours later, I walked into my dining room, where Tyler and the Wildman boys were standing. The four women Elizabeth had told me about were seated around the table. Two were beaners from South America, one was a Chinese, and they were all pretty. The last one was a black girl with the biggest set of tits on her I'd ever seen. That little negress made my dick hard just looking at her. I had a thing for big-titty black girls. I wouldn't marry one, but I'd fuck one in a minute because the pussy was always outstanding.

"What the hell, Tyler? You didn't tell our guests they could eat?" I asked, staring at the untouched plates of food. "I spent a lot of money on this shit."

"I told them, Daddy." Tyler shrugged.

"Well, damn, y'all must not be hungry. From what Lee told me, y'all ain't ate since this morning. Is the menu not to your liking?"

The four of them sat there staring at me like I had two fucking heads, which irritated the hell out of me. I was not in the mood for games.

"Look, Lee done told me that you all speak English, so let's stop playin' around. Y'all eat up."

"We are not here to talk or eat. We are here to fuck. That's what we get paid for," the beautiful black girl stated boldly. Her accent sounded kinda French, and it was sexy as hell. "Talking will just get us beat."

"Not here it won't," I said. "You've been brought here so I can talk to you gals about an opportunity." I sat in the empty seat closest to her.

She seemed to be their spokeswoman, so I directed my conversation to her. "What's your name?"

"Celeste."

"That's a right pretty name," I told her, reaching for some of the roast and potatoes on the table. "Celeste, my name's KD. Where you from?"

"Haiti."

I leaned closer to her. "That's over there near the Dominican Republic, ain't it? Y'all had a terrible earthquake a few years back, didn't ya?"

"Yes," she replied, looking surprised that I knew anything about her country. "I lost my mother, father, and sister."

"I'm sorry to hear that. Tyler lost his momma a few years ago too."

"Thank you," she replied, shooting a quick glance at my son.

"Tyler, you boys sit down and eat. Stop hovering over our guests like they're some kinda prisoners."

The boys sat down and dug into the food as the ladies watched.

"Eat up, Celeste. It ain't poison," I said.

"What kind of opportunity?" Celeste asked. Once she picked up her fork, the other girls did the same. There was no doubt she was the leader of the group.

"An opportunity to come and live here and be a part of our organization. I want to take you from living at the bottom of the barrel and bring you here to live at the farm and be treated first class."

I motioned for Patrick, who was wearing an apron and helping the cook, to bring over a tray of lobster tails. He placed one in front of each of us. The ladies stared at their plates like they weren't sure what to do with the tails.

"Make sure we get some of that drawn butter to dip it in, Patrick. What's lobster without butter, right?" I winked at Celeste, and she smiled.

"You got that right," Tyler said as he reached over to help one of the beaners snap her lobster tail open.

"I bet you ain't eating fucking lobster over there at the Horseshoe or any of the other hellholes you been to," I said to Celeste before stuffing a biscuit in my mouth.

"No, we 'ave not," she admitted in that sexy accent of hers.

"So, how'd you like to be able to eat like this every day and send some money home to Haiti?" I looked around the table at each of the girls. "A thousand dollars a week to start with. How does that sound?"

The other three women looked excited—no longer pretending that they couldn't understand English—but Celeste shook her head. "That would be nice," she said, "but we've heard these claims before. Our families have not seen a dime, and we are beaten if we question it."

I motioned for Tyler to get my briefcase from the other side of the room. When he brought it to me, I opened it and took out four stacks, totaling a thousand dollars each, and tossed one in front of each of the girls.

"I know when they brought you here to the U.S., they probably told you plenty o' lies. So, here you go. A good faith gesture to show you that I ain't bullshittin'. And there's plenty more where that came from," I told them.

Celeste still wasn't convinced. "And what about the man that we work for now? How will we explain all of this to him? He's a very evil man."

"Yeah, maybe, but he don't wanna fuck with me." I looked her straight in the eyes. "Besides, that's already been handled, and all your belongings from his place are on the porch. I was pretty sure you'd accept my offer. Now, was I right or not?"

Celeste looked at the other ladies for a minute, but no words passed between them. Then she picked up the stack of bills, placing it in her bra. She nodded at them, and they did the same, snatching up their money real quick.

"And now what happens?" she asked.

I picked up a bottle of wine and poured some in her glass. "There's four of us and four of you. I'm sure we'll figure out something before the night is through." I raised my glass for a toast. She picked hers up and clinked it against mine, revealing her dimples when she finally cracked a smile.

Nevada

19

My eyes constantly went from checking the time on my phone to checking the entryway of the library as I sat at a balcony table, losing my mind. Kia had said to meet her at 11 a.m., but it was already 11:26. Being late seemed to be a habit with her. Dammit, where the hell was she? I had something really important to talk to her about.

A wave of relief came over me when I saw her walk in the far entrance to the left. She looked like a high school kid in her T-shirt, ripped jeans, and sneakers, with her hair pulled back. I waved, and she headed up the stairs toward me.

"Hey, hope you're not mad that I'm late. The trains were a mess." She placed her coffee and book bag on the table, then leaned over to give me a hug. She smelled amazing, and if I was mad, I couldn't be anymore. "You been here long?"

"Nah, not long at all," I lied.

"Good. Now, I have a ton of questions I need help with." She pulled her GED book out of her bag and turned to me.

I just gazed at her silently.

"What?" She moved a few hairs from in front of her face. "What? Do I have something in my teeth?"

I shook my head. Despite the importance of what I wanted to talk to her about, I was suddenly nervous and tongue-tied.

"Well, what is it then?"

I took a breath. "First, I don't want you to get mad. Okay?"

Her eyes met mine. "Mad about what?"

"About this." I opened my laptop and maneuvered it so that she could see what was on the screen—a copy of her passport. "I hacked into Marie's computer and pulled your file."

"Oh." Kia sat back and stared at me. She looked a little taken aback. "Why would you do that?"

"To help you find out what happened to your sister."

She turned to the screen. "But Marie doesn't know anything about my sister."

"I realize that," I replied. "I used the information from your passport and backtracked it to the date and entry point that you entered the U.S."

"And what did you find?" I couldn't tell if she was mad or impressed, but at least she looked curious.

"That there were a hundred other girls that entered the United States via San Francisco from Korea that day. Some of them were students, but most were brought into the country under an old GI war babies clause. Your passport was issued under that clause. From what I've read, they use fake adoption agencies and stuff like that to get underaged sex workers into the United States, then disperse them throughout the country."

"Yes, I remember that day. They told us not to speak English to anyone, only Korean, and if we told anybody that we had family or that we were prostitutes, they would beat us."

"Beat you?" I repeated loud enough to get some stares from others in our section.

"Yes, I've been beaten many times, Nevada," she said sadly.

"Marie doesn't beat you, does she?" I whispered.

She shook her head. "No, Marie isn't holding me captive like these people did. I'm free to come and go as I please. She's my boss, not my master. She's also a good person, Nevada."

"You don't know how glad I am to hear you say that."

"I can see it on your face," she replied, then turned back to my computer screen. "Now, what else did you find out about my sister?"

I took a deep breath. "Well, actually, I think I found her. Is this her?"

I pulled up the photo of the young woman I'd discovered.

She leaned closer and studied the photo for a second, and I watched her shoulders slump with disappointment. "No, that isn't my sister."

"Are you sure? It has to be. She's the only black and Asian girl in the same age range that came into San Francisco that week." I felt deflated. I had thought for sure that was her sister.

"Nevada, my sister isn't biracial. She's fully Korean." Kia looked like she was about to cry. "I appreciate you trying to help me, though."

"Hey, I'm sorry." I felt like crawling under the table. "I know you probably think I'm an idiot."

"No, you're my friend, and you tried to help me, and I really appreciate it." She leaned on me.

"I still think I can find your sister. I just have to pull all the entry records for South Korean nationals entering the country the same day as you," I explained, and Kia lifted her head. "I'm just going to need your help to identify her."

"I can do that." She was surprisingly upbeat. "Okay, let's do it."

"There is one thing, though," I said, kind of backtracking.

"What's that?"

I looked around to make sure no one was eavesdropping, and then leaned in close to whisper, "I have to break into Homeland Security to do it, and it's . . . a felony."

She looked a little scared.

"I can mask my IP and all that stuff—it's how I got the picture of the other girl I thought was your sister—but there's a chance they might detect me and track us here to the library. I'm not saying it will happen, but I have to warn you."

"I don't want to get you in any trouble, Nevada."

"I'm just a kid. Not much they're going to do to me with all the lawyers my family has. But you're nineteen. They'll use you as a scapegoat and make it seem like you manipulated me. I'll take the blame, I swear I will, but I can't promise what my mom will do. She's a pretty influential woman when she wants to be."

She took a second to think, and then asked, "How good are you at this? What's our chances of getting caught?"

"Less than fifteen percent. We're not breaking into the Pentagon, and there's probably a hundred computers on the library's server right now. I can make it look like it's one of them."

"Those are pretty good odds . . . and it's not like I've never been arrested before." She put her hand on my forearm and gave it a little squeeze. "Let's go for it. Just don't take too many chances."

"Ah, sure." I turned back to my laptop and began typing. Her comment about being arrested almost threw me off my game, but a few minutes later, I was searching all entrants into the

United States via San Francisco the day of Kia's arrival. "I'm in, but we only have about ten minutes before they realize we're in their system. Now it's up to you."

I slid my computer over, and Kia stared at the screen as I typed commands to scroll through the entrants.

She was about five minutes in, and I was getting nervous; then she let out a little yelp and pointed at the screen. "Oh my God, Nevada, that's her. That's my sister, but that's not her name."

I took a picture of the screen with my phone and quickly exited the site, relieved to be done with the hack.

"So, what do we do now?" I could hear her excitement.

"We do a nationwide search on Mi-Cha Lee." I began entering the information from her sister's passport. Several hits came up in my search, but all of them were for much older women.

"Nothing," I said. "dammit."

"It's okay. She's probably dead," Kia whispered sadly.

"I refuse to believe that," I replied. Then a thought came to me. I slapped my forehead for not having thought of it sooner. "Hold up. Didn't you just say you'd been arrested?"

She nodded.

"For prostitution?"

She nodded again, this time with her head down like she was embarrassed.

"Hey, stay with me here. I'm not judging you. I think I'm on to something," I reassured her.

She looked up.

"Did your sister get arrested too?"

"Yes," she said, a glimmer of hope in her eyes. "In Colorado and Florida during vice raids."

"Let me check something else," I said, going into a different database and doing another search. My mind was moving as fast as my fingers, which flew across the keyboard.

A few minutes later, I turned the computer around and showed her an unflattering mugshot. "Is that you?"

She gave me a look that said, *you know it is.*

I turned the computer back to myself and began typing.

"Look at this. This woman was arrested the same day as you in Broward County, Florida for prostitution. Her name isn't Mi-Cha. It's Myesha. But she's in the same age range, and she's Asian. She may have given them a fake name."

"That's what they told us to do. Let me see." Kia slid closer to look at the mugshot of the beautiful Korean girl. She gasped and covered her mouth. "That's my sister."

I continued to type and found four more arrest records in Florida, all of them after Kia and her sister had split. I showed them to Kia.

"So, is she still in Florida?" she asked.

"I'm not sure. She was bonded out the next day. She hasn't been arrested in Florida since."

"They may have moved her out of state," Kia said, deflated.

"Where did they take you after Florida?" I asked her.

"Georgia, South Carolina, Maryland, then D.C. They never kept us in one place more than a week or so. We worked mainly in Asian massage parlors and motels. Sometimes they'd rent us out to American brothels for a week or two at a time," Kia explained. "She could be anywhere."

"But at least we know she's not dead."

"This is true." Kia nodded.

"We're going to find her, Kia." I held her hand. "If I have to do a search on every state and county in America, we are going to find her. I'm not giving up."

She looked at me with tears in her eyes. "Thank you. I'm truly grateful that you did this for me, Nevada. I truly am. You've lifted a lot of the burden off my shoulders. No one has ever been this nice to me and not wanted anything."

She slowly leaned toward me, and I felt my body doing the same. I closed my eyes and held my breath.

"Nevada Duncan!"

I jerked my head away from Kia and looked around. My mother was walking toward us, her face a deep shade of red, and everyone in the library was staring.

"Uh, hey, Mom." My voice cracked slightly, and I released Kia's hand.

"Well, at least you're really at the library this time. What are you doing? Who is this?" She looked at Kia.

"Um, this is Kia. She's my, uh, I'm tutoring her," I said as I nudged Kia subtly under the table.

"Hi, Miss Duncan." Kia smiled.

I groaned and shook my head. "Zuniga," I whispered.

Kia quickly corrected herself. "Uh, I mean Miss Zuniga. So nice to meet you." She reached out her hand, but my mother looked down at it and wrinkled her nose up like it was diseased or something.

"She goes to your school?" My mother asked me.

"Yeah."

Her eyes went to Kia, and she looked down her glasses judgmentally. "Then why does she have a GED book in front of her?"

KD

20

One by one, the guests began trickling in, all men. Some looked excited to be there; others, not so much, despite the open bar, seafood buffet, and good old-fashioned Texas BBQ. Even the reluctant ones perked up, though, when thirty or so of the finest women money could buy strolled in wearing silky attire that left little to the imagination. From that point on, it was a fuck festival.

"Well, Daddy, you've got a happy crowd, and they all showed up," Tyler said as we watched from the warehouse catwalk. Most of our guests had disappeared into private rooms we'd built just for this occasion.

"Hell, I knew they'd all show up, son. I had no worries at all about that. They know better than to turn down an invite from KD Shrugs. The real question is are they gonna buy into what we're selling?" I gestured with my eyes to an apparatus hanging in a corner near the ceiling. "You got all the cameras working?"

"Yes, sir."

"Including the ones in the tents and rooms?"

"Every single one of them."

"Good. Some o' these fellas won't be hard to convince at all." I pointed to a group of men in the corner, huddled around a table. "It's those fools right there that we have to pull out all the stops on."

"Why aren't they talking to the women?" Tyler asked, staring down at them.

"Because they're smart. They've seen their share of scandal, and they don't want no part of it unless there's something in it for them. They came here for one reason, and that's because

I asked them to." I elbowed him and adjusted the black velvet cowboy hat and vest that I'd bought for the occasion. "Come on. Let's get down there and show these some-bitches what the future holds."

We proceeded down the catwalk to mingle with the guests.

"Good to see you made it, Harold. Herman. Jensen. You too, Congressman Bell," I said to the four men in the corner of the room, huddled around a bar height table. "I hope y'all are having a fine time. Y'all need a refill?" I motioned for a statuesque redhead whose nipples damn near covered her perky breasts. "Honey, these fellas need a drink—and some special attention."

"No problem." She smiled flirtatiously and opened her sheer blouse a little wider so they could get a full view. "What would you gentlemen like?"

"Nothing," Herman said, lifting a half full glass. "We're fine."

She gave them a disappointed look and walked away.

I looked at the other two and said, "You boys gonna let him speak for you and spoil your fun? I'm sure you want *something*."

"I can speak for myself, KD," the congressman replied, glaring at me. "I wanna know why the hell we're here."

"To get your dick sucked, Congressman. What the fuck's it look like?" Why was it always this arrogant prick giving me the hardest time when it was his ass who would benefit the most?

"KD, I'm a United States congressman now." He leaned in and spoke seriously. "I don't get my dick sucked in front of five dozen people."

"You know, I didn't even think about that—considering all the times I've seen you get your dick sucked over the years," I whispered back. "But I can set something up for you a little more private if you'd like."

"I'd rather get down to the true nature of our business," he replied.

"All right then, suit yourself. I figured I'd let you enjoy yourselves first, but if you prefer business before pleasure, I can understand that too. Why don't we go for a walk, gentlemen?"

"This better be fucking good," Wesley grumbled.

"This is gonna be better than good, trust me." I smiled as I led them through the crowd and out the door. We all loaded onto a golf cart then drove to another, larger building a half mile farther on the ranch.

"What the hell is this?" Harold asked.

"This, boys, is Building Six. Everything I was trying to do before I got locked up and more," I said, punching a keypad and opening the door to the building.

"Good evening, Mr. Shrugs." Elizabeth greeted me with a smile when we stepped inside. She was wearing a white lab coat, sitting at a desk and typing into a computer. "How's your party?"

"Evening, Lizbeth. It's goin' great. These here gentlemen are guests. I brought them over to show what we have going on."

Elizabeth nodded politely. "Nice to meet you, gentlemen."

"Come on, fellas," I said as we walked past. "That's Elizabeth. She's our head nurse and nutritionist. She kinda helps me run the place along with a few other key people."

"Nurse? Nutritionist? What for?" Jensen turned back to look at her again.

"If you stop looking at her tits and come on, you'll see," I told him.

I opened the next door we came to and walked in. The large room looked like a state-of-the-art fitness center. Women of various ethnicities were using the ellipticals, treadmills, rowing machines, and weight benches throughout the room. A trainer walked throughout the mirrored room, giving instructions to the mixed group of ladies who all wore black shorts and T-shirts with ID wristbands.

I led them through that room without comment and took them into a smaller room, where another group was in the middle of a yoga session. The girls turned and greeted me happily.

"Señor Sheriff!"

"*Meester* KD!"

"*Ni Hao!*"

I waved. "Hello, ladies. Don't let us disturb you."

Out of nowhere, Celeste jumped up and ran over to me, breasts flopping everywhere. She grabbed me tight, pushing those huge tits up against me.

"Mister KD," she said in that sexy-ass accent, kissing me on the cheek. "You are the greatest man I have ever met."

"Well, thank you, darlin'. I think you're pretty special too," I replied, and she ran back to her yoga mat. I turned to see the four men behind me wearing looks of confusion and concern.

I whispered, "Sorry. They act like I'm a celebrity 'round here. You know how the moolies and spics can get. Hero worshipping."

"KD, what the . . ." Old Herman could not finish his sentence.

"Come on, fellas. There's a lot more to see," I said.

We went back through the gym, where the hero worshipping continued. Then I showed them the makeshift dorm rooms with bunk beds, and the game room that had board games, video games, computers, and books.

"What the fuck is this, a college dormitory?" Wesley finally asked.

"The body can't work out twenty-four/seven. It's got to relax and regenerate," I replied without answering his question.

We entered a large kitchen, and I introduced them to the chef, who was in the middle of preparing dinner.

"Chef Gaines, what's on the menu, sir?" I clapped my hand on his shoulder.

"Well, sir, tonight we're having Cornish game hens, sweet potatoes, carrots, and corn." He smiled proudly.

"Make sure they get some greens too," I said.

"Yes, sir. We make sure they eat salad twice a day, along with their vitamin supplements."

"Good, good. Keep up the good work there," I said, then led the men into the dining area. The women in this space were like the others—all various ethnicities, same attire, and enthused to see me. I concluded the tour by showing them the spa-like bathrooms and sauna, small swimming pool, and a medical exam room.

"Well, boys, what do you think so far?" I asked when we returned to the front of the warehouse and headed toward Building 5.

"Looks like you've created a goddamn Club Med for the fucking immigrants and niggers. That's what I think," Jensen spat, shaking his head in disbelief. "Why not just give them guns and have them kill us all? It'll be faster." His reaction didn't surprise me considering he was a grand dragon for the Louisiana KKK.

"Relax, Jensen. Have a little faith." I chuckled. "I haven't completely lost my mind. I can promise you that."

"KD, you made me fly all the way from DC to show me this? Hell, you're treating these motherfuckers better than the

Democrats, and they can't even fucking vote." Wesley had a scowl on his face.

I laughed loudly. "Gentlemen, obviously y'all don't see the value of what I'm doing here."

"And what the fuck is that?" Jensen asked, not amused in the slightest.

"More importantly, what the fuck does it have to do with me?" Wesley demanded to know.

"It has everything to do with you, Congressman. You're the one who inspired this whole damn thing. You just don't see the big picture yet, but you will once you enter Building Five," I said smugly, looking up at the building across from us. "Wesley, you're not just going to be governor of New Mexico if you come on board and work with us. Your ass might just have enough political clout to become President of the United States. And the rest of us will be laughing our way to the fucking bank in the process."

Vegas

21

"You know she's pissed, don't you?" Sasha asked as we walked to my Bentley truck. My sister Paris had just had a meltdown because I wouldn't take her with us to the Bronx.

"She'll get over it," I replied. "She's way too unpredictable and too damn emotional for something like this. We're not trying to kill anybody, just get our point across."

It had already been an emotional day, with Rio coming home from the hospital after his attack. But I'd just gotten a call from my guy in the Bronx with info about who was responsible for Rio's beatdown, so I needed to check it out. With Junior and Orlando out of town, I asked Sasha to take a ride with me to watch my back. Paris, who was equally capable, had heard where we were going and got offended that I didn't ask her.

"Sasha, honey, I'm going to sit up front."

I heard the voice before I turned around and saw my mother, along with Paris, sashaying across the driveway toward the truck. My mom jumped in the front passenger's seat, and Paris smugly walked around and got in behind the driver's seat.

"What are you doing?" I asked.

"We're going with you." My mom looked over at me as she reached for her seatbelt and pulled it across her chest. "You did say you were going to confront Rio's attackers, didn't you?"

"Yeah, but . . ." It was one thing to put Paris in her place, but my mother was a different story. "Don't you want to be taking care of Rio?"

"Your brother is fine. London and Harris are there if he needs anything. Now, stop playing around and drive, Vegas."

I shook my head. "Did you talk to Pop?" I asked.

"Yes, I talked to him a little while ago, and I told him what happened. He's on his way home from Atlanta. At least he better be." The aggravation in her voice was obvious, which wasn't a good sign for my father.

She asked me, "Have you spoken to Nevada? Does he know what happened?"

"No."

"Why not? You know how close he and Rio are. You need to tell him."

"He's already dealing with a lot right now with everything going on between me and his mother. I don't want to give him anything else to worry about," I said with a deep sigh.

"What do you mean he's dealing with a lot? What the hell is going on between you and Consuela now?"

"He's got baby mama drama," Paris laughed from the back.

"Shut up, Paris," Ma snapped before I could get it out. "Vegas?"

"Consuela is tripping."

"What do you mean? You told me you were going to talk to her about the mix-up with the girls going to the water park." She sounded so aggravated.

"I tried, but she's making demands I ain't willing to entertain."

"What kind of demands?"

"She says she's gonna take Nevada back to California if I don't stop seeing Marie," I told her.

"What? She can't do that," Ma snapped.

"That's what I say, but that's the threat."

"That's one bold woman, Vegas. You need to do something about this," Ma said, raising her voice.

"Ma, I tried." I shook my head. "Nevada has tried. Sometimes you just have to wait for Consuela to cool down."

"Vegas, two nights ago, I almost lost my son. I refuse to lose my grandson. This family is everything to me, and I will not just sit back and allow it to be destroyed because you can't keep your women straight," she said forcefully. "I recognize this is your business, but this is my family, and I will not have it torn apart from the inside."

"I understand that, Ma, but what do you want me to do?" I pleaded, not wanting to upset her any more than she already was.

"I'd like to speak with her."

"If you think you can get through to her, have at it."

"I will." She folded her arms and sat back in her seat just as we turned into the neighborhood where we were headed.

I pulled over to the curb and leaned past her to get a better look at the house.

"Are you sure this is it?" she asked.

"This is the address he gave me. Says the guy's name is Vaughn Holmes."

"Okay, then what are we waiting for?" She reached for the door handle, but I stopped her.

"I don't know about this, Ma. I don't think Pop would approve of you doing this, and he darn sure wouldn't want me to let you do it."

"And what am I supposed to do? Wait on him? Do you really think this is at the top of his list of priorities right now?" she asked.

Although she made a good point, I didn't want to throw my father under the bus. Instead, I tried to reason with her. "Why don't you just let me and the girls handle this? These are street cats, and it could get real dangerous. I can't let nothing happen to you."

"Honey, I think you've forgotten this is not your mama's first rodeo. Whoever this piece of trash is, he doesn't pose a threat, and I ain't scared." She reached into the large Chanel bag on her lap and pulled out a shiny .44 magnum and held it up with a reassuring smile. Before I knew it, she had opened the car door and was stepping out.

I quickly hopped out too. "Ma, wait. You can't go in there by yourself. Jesus."

"You're right," she said, continuing her walk toward the house. "Paris, Sasha, you girls come on."

My sister and cousin jumped out and followed her.

"You're welcome to come too if you'd like, Vegas."

I took a deep breath and sighed, trudging behind them. The women in my family could be so damn difficult sometimes.

Paris

22

I jumped out of the car with Sasha and followed my mother up the steps to the house. I was too stubborn to look back, but I was sure Vegas was following us, and I'd bet money he wasn't happy about it. Oh, well. That's what he got for trying to leave me out the fray. If he had let me go with him and Sasha in the first place, I never would have told my mom they were going after Rio's attackers. Vegas and I were going to have words about it later. Of that, I was certain.

"Do we have a plan?" Vegas asked when my mom reached the top step.

"Of course we have a plan," she replied, knocking on the door like she was there for a friendly little visit.

Sasha, Vegas, and I just kind of looked at each other. I mean, this was a drug dealer's house. In these situations, Vegas or Junior would usually break down the door, or Sasha would pick the lock, or I'd climb through a window. We'd do anything but knock on the door. And they say I'm reckless.

As crazy as it sounds, a woman about my age answered the door. I tensed up, ready to start shooting, but she seemed harmless enough.

"Can I help you?" the girl asked. She glanced at my mother, but her eyes studied me and Sasha. If she was like most chicks, she was just concerned about us stealing her man. We had that kind of effect on women.

My mother put on this sweet, proper voice. "Yes, dear, does Vaughn Holmes live here?"

She nodded, still staring at me and Sasha. Bitch had no idea. We didn't want her man; we were there to whip his ass for what he did to Rio.

"Can I speak to him?" Mom smiled sweetly.

The woman turned back to the inside of the house and yelled, "Vaughn, some lady at the door for you!"

"Who the fuck is it?" he yelled back.

"Who are you?" she asked.

"I can introduce myself," my mother said, pushing her aside so she could enter the house.

The girl screamed, and at that point, Vegas, Sasha, and I didn't have any choice but to follow right behind my mother, weapons drawn. By the time we entered the living room, there were three men standing there, and one had a gun pointed at my mother. Amazingly, my mom just stood there like she didn't have a care in the world.

"Which one of you is Vaughn?" she demanded to know.

"Who the fuck is asking?" the man with the gun growled.

"Your worst fucking nightmare if you don't lower that gun from my head and tell me what I want to know. Don't you have any respect for your elders?"

"Fuck that shit. Motherfuckers ain't just gonna keep rolling up in here like they invited guests. This my motherfucking house. Now, tell them to lower their guns or I'm gonna blast your ass some new holes for your earrings."

"You do, and it will be the last thing you ever do," I told him, pointing my gun at his head.

"Fuck you, bitch," he said, getting excited. "I don't mind dying as long as she goes with me." Tough talk, but I didn't believe him, and I don't think my mom did either.

"Paris," my mother said calmly.

"Yeah, Mom."

"If this son of a bitch doesn't get this gun out my face in the next ten seconds, I want you to shoot him. You know where, right?"

"Mm-hmm. Sure do." I took aim.

"Now, baby, please don't kill him. Just shoot him. I might want to ask him a few questions when this is all over." My mother smiled at the guy we all suspected was Vaughn. "Young man, if you don't want to be shot, you might want to lower that weapon."

"She shoots me, and I'm gonna shoot you." He turned the gun sideways, pushing it closer to my mother's face. He had no idea how easy he was making this.

"I don't think so," my mother replied, leaning to the side just as I pulled the trigger.

Vaughn screamed like a little bitch. The bullet went into his shoulder, paralyzing the nerves that controlled his fingers. He spun away from us in the opposite direction, dropping his gun, which Vegas snatched up.

Like it was just another day, my mom bent over and swept off an armchair with her hand before taking a seat. Crossing her legs, she gave me an approving nod and a smile. I can't begin to tell you how good that made me feel. Making my mother proud wasn't a daily occurrence for me.

"Now, maybe we should start over. Which one of you is Vaughn?" Mom asked, taking out her piece and looking at the other two men side-eyed. They glanced at each other, then turned to their heads toward their wounded friend.

"You bitch-ass motherfuckers!" Vaughn shouted

"A'ight, Vaughn. Now that we've established who you are, she's about to ask you some questions, and if you're smart, you'll answer them truthfully," Vegas said.

Vaughn looked at her furiously. "I ain't saying shit. Fuck you and that old-ass bitch!"

"Call her a bitch again and I'll kill you myself!" Vegas back-handed him so hard it echoed in the room. Everyone else in the room, including me and Sasha, flinched. That shit hurt for sure. Probably broke a few teeth, too.

"Fuck." Vaughn grunted.

Vegas yanked him up from the ground and threw him onto the sofa.

"You motherfuckers sit down with him," I yelled, pointing my gun at Vaughn's crew. They wasted no time sitting their asses on the couch where Vaughn was busy bleeding.

"All right, let's try this again. This time, let's be a little more respectful," my mom said.

Believe it or not, this guy actually looked like he wanted to continue being defiant. Things got even crazier when the front door creaked open and a tall, cute, muscular guy about Vegas's age stepped in, followed by two other men. They didn't hide the fact that they were all wearing shoulder holsters under their jackets. The four captives on the sofa looked somewhat relieved to see them. In fact, the one who was shot actually jumped up like he was being rescued.

"Man, Big Pat, handle these motherfuckers before I do," Vaughn yelled, holding his shoulder. "They don't realize who the fuck they messin' with."

"No, motherfucker, you don't know who you messing with," Big Pat said to Vaughn as he walked over to where my mother was sitting. He kneeled down and kissed her cheek. "Hey, Mrs. D. I didn't know you was gonna be here too. You looking lovely as ever."

"Thank you, Pat. It's so good to see you." She smiled, then turned her attention back to the people in front of her. "I was just about to have a little chat with Vaughn, but he doesn't seem to want to play nice. He was acting up so much I had to let Paris shoot him."

Vaughn's eyes widened. "Big Pat, man, I don't know who the fuck these people are. They just came busting up in here—"

"Shut the fuck up, nigga. You don't need to know who they are. Just know they're the ones who put me on, and you betta tell them whatever the fuck they wanna know," Big Pat snapped.

Vaughn didn't say anything, but his silence was enough for Pat, who turned to my mother and said, "Go ahead, Mrs. D. They not gonna give you no more problems."

"Thank you." Mom smiled at him then turned to Vaughn. "Now, the first thing I'd like to know is why did you attack my son?"

Everyone on the sofa looked confused by her question. Vaughn looked over at Pat, then back at Mom, and said, "Who is your son?"

"His name is Rio."

Once again, he looked over at Pat, then my mother, but this time he looked truly confused.

"Lady—uh, ma'am—ain't nobody touched your son. I don't even know who he is. I swear."

"You were at the club the other night and had a fight with him in the bathroom," I snapped at him, itching to pull the trigger again.

"I had a fight, but it wasn't with nobody called Rio. Dude we was fighting name is Roman, and he had it coming," he tried to explain.

"Why? Why the fuck did he have it coming?" Mom growled angrily. She looked like she was about to shoot him in the other shoulder.

"Because he was fucking my girl, that's why!" Vaughn spat back. "And he's been fucking her for weeks."

"What? You said you ain't fuckin' with her no more!" the girl snapped, swinging wildly at him until Vegas pulled her off.

"Well, my son is gay." My mother took out her cell phone and showed them a picture of Rio. They all fell back silently in their seats. "So, him being with your girl or any other girl is out of the question."

One of the guys said, "That do look like the guy in the bathroom, Vaughn. Remember we was laughing about Roman dying his hair purple?"

"Shut up, Theo. It was you that said it was him in the first place. I ain't never met that nigga Roman," Vaughn mumbled.

Mom stared at them for a minute while she put the pieces together. "You mean to tell me that my son was laid up in a hospital for two days because of a mistaken identity? Over some girl?" She had her gun in her hand, swinging it around wildly as she spoke.

"Yeah, kinda. It was on accident," Theo replied humbly.

"I'm going to put this away before I use it." She sighed, biting her lip as she stared at the gun, then slid it back in her bag. I could see the anger and frustration on her face. If that had been my son, Jordan, I would have shot them all the minute I walked in the house. I had to give it to her; my mom really had it together.

"Pat!" she yelled.

"Yes, ma'am." Pat stepped closer as my mother rose from her seat.

"Me and my family are going home. I have to make dinner before my husband comes home." She gave him a hug, then looked him in the eyes. "I trust you and your friends can handle these gentlemen to my satisfaction."

Damn! I had never realized it, but my momma was a real gangster.

Pat glared at the them, slamming his fist into his palm like he couldn't wait to start delivering the pain. The four people on the sofa jumped.

"Oh, yeah. We'll handle them all right."

"Thank you, but please don't kill them. A short hospital visit will be fine," she said—and on that note, my mother walked out with us following behind. I could hear Vaughn and his friends pleading for mercy as I shut the door behind me.

KD

23

By the time the sun rose, I was already showered, dressed, and pouring myself a cup of coffee. I'd always been an early riser. There was something about sleeping past 6 a.m. that made me feel lazy. If the sun was up, I should be too. Besides, I had too much planning and preparation for my upcoming event to be lying in bed.

"Morning, Daddy." Tyler came into the kitchen wearing his bathrobe and slippers.

"Morning, son. What time you boys get in last night?"

"I guess about two, two thirty. We stopped off at the Horseshoe and had a couple of beers."

"And some pussy," I added with a laugh.

He laughed too. "Well, yeah, we got some of that too. Who says no to free pussy? Peter Lee got a new batch of girls for you and asked me and the boys to come over and try them out. I couldn't say no to that."

I chuckled. Damn boy was just like his old man, loved to fuck.

"So, were they mostly beaners? I ain't pay that Chinaman to bring me beaners," I snapped. Being close to the border, it was easy for Lee to get Mexicans and Central Americans, but I needed a higher class of whore for my business.

"No, mostly Asian, but he had a few black ones too. There was one black girl with big titties that looked like your type, Daddy."

"How big?" It was early, but the boy had my attention. "As big as Celeste?"

"No, sir! That Celeste has some of the biggest titties I've ever seen." He shook his head.

My face lit up at the thought. "Me too, and I been around a lot longer than you."

We both had a good laugh.

"Lemme go get dressed. It's almost time for work."

I stood at the kitchen window, looking out at the fields. When I heard a car door slam around the side of the house, I put down my coffee and left the kitchen. I needed to see who the hell was at my house at this time of day.

I picked up my .38 just in case, then opened the front door and stepped onto the porch to see an El Paso Sheriff's Department cruiser parked alongside it.

"What the hell are you doing on my damn property this early?" I growled. "You're lucky I didn't shoot you."

"Morning, Sheriff—uh, I mean KD." A tall, lanky man in an El Paso Sheriff's uniform approached me. I recognized Roscoe Thomas immediately. He'd started out with me back when I was the sheriff. He was actually pretty lazy, which was a big part of why I'd helped him get elected. I didn't want anyone I couldn't keep under my thumb snooping around my place or my businesses. Tyler had wanted to run for sheriff of El Paso a few years back, but he was much too valuable to me as a highway patrolman, where he had jurisdiction all over the state, so Roscoe was the next best thing.

"We just came by to say hello and make sure everything's all right out here. That's all. How y'all been?" Roscoe put one foot on the bottom of the porch and leaned on his knee.

"We . . ." I echoed, looking over the yard. I hadn't noticed the other two police cars parked over by the trucks, or the four other men—two black and two white—all wearing police uniforms I didn't recognize. I didn't appreciate seeing them now, especially on my property. Two of the men were over by the tractor trailers parked on the side of the house. One of the black guys took out his phone and took a picture of all the license plates, while the white guys took pictures of the buildings.

I rushed over to the side of the porch and leaned over the railing. "Hey, what the fuck are you doing? You get the fuck away from there right now!" I turned back to the sheriff. "Roscoe, what the fuck is going on?"

"Calm down, Mr. Shrugs. We're just here for a friendly visit," the other black guy said to me. His voice was deeper than any I'd ever heard, and from his mannerisms, I could tell he was the one in charge.

"Mister, I don't know who the fuck you are, but unless you have some kind of warrant, I suggest you get the fuck off my property."

"Um, KD, this here is Sheriff Derrick Hughes from Fulton County, Georgia," Roscoe said.

"Fulton County, Georgia?" I scowled. "You're a long way from home. That's almost a twenty-hour drive."

"Yes, sir." Hughes gave me a prideful smirk as he stepped onto the porch. "Nice to finally meet you, KD. I made the trip just to see you."

"If you're from Georgia, why the fuck are you all the way out here in El Paso, Texas? And more importantly, why are you at my place?" He towered over me, but I was determined to let him know that I wasn't intimidated. I tried to eyeball him, but he was one big-ass nigger face to face.

"We're here because some mutual friends of ours sent me to check on you—take you to breakfast and make sure you understand how things are gonna go from here on out," he said bluntly. "You see, I'm also the newly elected president of the Sheriffs Association."

Well, fuck me. They really did elect a nigger.

"Boy, the chances of us having mutual friends is slim to none. Which are about the same chances of me sitting down to eat with your black ass," I snarled.

"Well then, I guess I have to explain it to you right here and now." Hughes took a step closer, smiling at me all nice and polite. He was one confident nigger. "If you want these trucks of yours to continue traveling cross country without being disturbed or pulled over every ten miles, then you'd better start playing ball with everybody. And I do mean everybody."

"You listen to me, boy," I said through clenched teeth. "I don't know who the hell you think you are, but I'm the last person on earth you should be threatening. You ain't even from 'round these parts, so I suggest you get your black ass back to Georgia and get back there fast. And tell whoever these mutual friends are that if they got something to say, they better come do it themselves, because I know where all the bodies are buried, and I have no problem digging them up." I spat on the ground, just barely missing his shoes to make my point.

I expected Hughes to back off, but instead, he took another step in my direction and smiled as he bent down to whisper in my ear. "No, *boy,* you listen to me, and you listen closely, because that good ol' boy bullshit is over. This ain't a threat like you think it is. It's a warning."

The screen door opened, and Tyler walked out, standing toe to toe with the nigger sheriff.

"Everything okay out here, Daddy?"

Hughes looked him up and down. "You must be Tyler. Nice to meet you." He tipped his hat. "You gentlemen have a fine day, you hear?"

I stood and watched as he stepped off the porch and whistled for the other three men. They climbed into their cars, one with Georgia plates and the other with Arkansas plates. Roscoe started walking toward his own car.

"Roscoe!" I yelled at him.

"Yeah, KD?" he asked just as he was about to get in.

"Don't bother putting your name on that ballot come reelection time. You wouldn't wanna waste your time and money for something you're gonna lose. Now, get the fuck off my property."

Roscoe looked like he was thinking about replying, but then he must have realized there was no point in trying to reason with me. He got into his car and drove off in the same direction as the other vehicles.

"What was that all about?" Tyler asked.

"That, son, is a great big pain in the ass that appeared out of nowhere." I watched the out-of-town sheriff's vehicles kick up dirt as they headed down the private road and off my land. "A pain in the ass I suspect was sent by LC Duncan."

Roman

24

The volume of the television was as high as it could go, but it was still difficult to hear—not that I was paying attention to the random HGTV show on the screen. I'd convinced my aunt to leave for a little while, promising that I'd call if there was any change in Mom's condition. There hadn't been. She was still asleep. Seemed like she was sleeping most of the time. I wasn't sure if that was good or bad.

"Man, that's crazy," Denny said. He'd been sitting with me for a while.

"What?" I turned to see what he was talking about.

"They paid like a hundred grand for that house and sold it for like almost three hundred?" He pointed to the television hanging in the corner of the room.

"Yeah, because they pretty much made a whole new house," I told him.

"I'm saying, you know how much profit they made just by adding some paint, hardwood floors, crown molding, and a farm sink?" Denny looked like he was deep in thought as he counted on his fingers.

"Did you say farm sink?" I tried not to laugh. "Nigga, what the fuck you know about a farm sink?"

"I'm just saying, maybe we in the wrong business. Maybe we need to be flipping houses," he argued.

"Sounds good. Lemme know when you get that general contractor license. Matter of fact, lemme know when you figure out what a farm sink is for real," I said, laughing.

"You can laugh all you want, but that's where the money is."

The fact that Denny was serious made this conversation even more humorous to me.

"It's plenty of boarded up places in the neighborhood I'm sure we can get for cheap," he continued. "We can do this, Rome."

"Slow ya roll, Nipsey Hussle. We ain't ready to buy back the block just yet," I said.

"Mr. Johnson?" A short, older white woman knocked before she walked in with a middle-aged black woman.

"Yeah?" I sat up.

"Hi, I'm Rebecca Naples with hospital billing, and this Nadine Walker from City Hospital Hospice Care. We came to talk to you about your mother." She spoke softly.

"Hospice?" I got a sick feeling in the pit of my stomach.

"Yes sir, the hospital social worker sent me up here," Walker answered. "Your mother's condition . . ."

I glanced over at my mother, who was still asleep, then back to the lady. "Can we talk about this somewhere else? I don't wanna do this here."

"Of course. I understand. We can go into the waiting room down the hall."

"Hey, man," I said to Denny.

"I got Ma. Go do what you gotta do. I'll be here with her," he told me.

I followed the ladies into the small room with FAMILY CONFERENCE on the door.

Entering the room, I blurted out, "My mother ain't going into no hospice."

They sat, then Naples began speaking in the same soft voice. "Unfortunately, Mr. Johnson, your mother is uninsured, and the charges for care are excessive. We can't continue to care for her here. She's too sick."

"Do you know how crazy you sound, lady? She's too sick for you to take care of her? That's bullshit and you know it. Y'all greedy asses is just thinkin' about the money, not about what's best for my momma."

She opened up her mouth to start talking, but I kept going, raising my voice to drown out whatever she was trying to say.

"First of all, I know she's sick, but she's gonna get better. Dr. Ford is tryin'a set up her kidney transplant. So she ain't leaving here," I finished forcefully.

"I'm sorry, but that's hospital policy. My hands are tied due to her current state of health and the outstanding bill she already owes."

"How much is the fucking bill?" I yelled. "I'll pay it."

They gave each other a nervous glance.

"Mr. Johnson, like I said, it's quite expensive," Naples said.

"She's not leaving here, and she damn sure ain't going over to City Hospital. Now, how much is the fucking bill?" I glared at her.

She reached into the folder she was holding and handed me some papers. "It's about forty thousand dollars."

I looked down at the itemized bill. I knew it was probably gonna be high as hell, but I damn sure wasn't expecting it to be that high.

"Shit," I said, much quieter now.

The bitch from billing looked like she wanted to say "I told you so," but instead she just nodded.

I straightened my spine and said, "Listen, I'm gonna pay this shit, but I can't pay the whole thing today. I can get you fifteen, maybe twenty by the end of the day, the rest by the end of the week, okay?" I folded the papers and stuck them in my pocket. "I said okay?"

Naples nodded. "If you make that substantial of a payment, that will buy you a little more time."

"A'ight, I'ma go home and get the money now. So go ahead and schedule my mom's kidney transplant." I stared her down to make sure she understood I wasn't asking her, I was telling her.

"You may want to speak with Dr. Ford regarding your mother's transplant." She stood up, and now her voice wasn't quite so sweet. Maybe she wasn't used to being told what to do.

"Do you know where he is?"

She looked at her watch. "He's probably still in his office. His rounds start in about fifteen minutes."

"Bet." I rushed out to find Dr. Ford's office. There was no way I was gonna let them kick my mother out and take her to the worst hospital in the state. The care at City Hospital was so bad that people called it The Morgue. Patients were known to go there with a little cough and end up dead. I didn't care how much it cost or what I had to do. My mother was staying where she was.

"Mr. Johnson, come in," Dr. Ford welcomed me in when I found his office and knocked on the door. "Ms. Naples called and told me you were headed down here. What can I do for you?"

I wondered what she'd said about the way I went off on her, and I reminded myself to stay calm with the doctor. I didn't need him to get pissed off and take it out on my moms.

"I wanted to know about the transplant for my mother. I'm ready," I said.

"There's a small problem with that, Mr. Johnson."

"Please don't tell me it's the money." I fought back the urge to curse his ass out. Did anyone around here give a shit about anything but getting paid?

"Well, that too, but that's not my department." He stopped talking and stared at something over my head like he was afraid to make eye contact.

What the fuck was going on here? His vibe was making me nervous.

"Doc, what exactly is the problem, then?" I asked.

"Unfortunately, my problem is you're not a match."

It took me a few seconds to speak because I just kept repeating his words in my head: *You're not a match. You're not a match. You're not a match.*

"I'm not?" I blinked. "Are you sure?"

"Yes. I'm positive."

My emotions were all over the place, and I couldn't think straight. I'd heard what the doctor said, but he had to be wrong. There was no way he could be right. There was some sort of medical mistake—hospitals made stupid-ass mistakes all the time. Maye some dumb motherfucker in the lab mixed up my blood sample with someone else's.

"Nah, that ain't right." I shook my head to try to clear it.

"I'm sorry, Mr. Johnson."

"Run the test again."

He shook his head and gave me a sympathetic look. "We've run the test several times. The results are not going to change."

"How can that be? I'm her son." There was a buzzing in my head, and I felt kinda like I might pass out.

"Genetics are funny. They don't always fall where we think they should," Dr. Ford said. "I know this is painful, but I'll speak with the hospital administration and get your mother added to the transplant list as soon as possible—provided you're in good standing with the billing department. But, Mr. Johnson, either way, like I said, this is a very expensive long shot."

At least he was working with me. "Hey, Doc, how much does an operation like this cost?"

"We're talking over two hundred thousand dollars, and that's not including the medication she'll be required to take afterward. It's a huge financial undertaking."

"Shit, you got that right," I said, stunned by the numbers. "You just do what you gotta do. I'll come up with funds," I told him. "Even if I have to rob a bank."

He laughed, and I joined in, even though I was dead-ass serious.

When I got back to my mother's room, she was still asleep, and Denny was still glued to the TV watching run-down homes get fixed up.

"What's up? Everything good?" he asked as I paced the floor.

"Yeah, I just had to get some stuff straight with her bill," I told him. I wasn't ready to say anything about the genetic test, because as far as I was concerned, that was just some fucked-up mistake that I would sort out later. For now, my only focus was getting my mother back on her feet.

"She needs this surgery, but real talk, I ain't got the money to pay for it right now." My voice was low because even though my mom was knocked out, I didn't want her overhearing our conversation.

Denny leaned forward, his voice just as low as mine. "Yo, we still got that shit from the other day. That's something."

"Yeah, but that probably ain't gonna be enough to cover it."

"Listen, bro, your mom's been more of a mother to me than my own. You ain't in this by yourself. Whatever we get, for however long we get it, it's yours until she's better."

I looked over at the guy who'd been my best friend since elementary school. He always had my back, and now he had me damn near in tears. I swallowed hard, trying not to show the emotions I was feeling.

Denny walked over and dapped me up. My voice cracked as I said, "Thanks, bro. I love you, man."

"I love too, bro."

Rio

25

"Okay, Rio, you can do this." I told myself as I popped a Xanax, which the doctor had prescribed for anxiety. What I really needed was a line of coke. "You can do this. You're a Duncan."

My ribs were healing and my bruises were fading, but inside, I was terrified. Every time I heard a male voice, I would jump, scared that I was about to get beat down again. I couldn't keep living like this—hence, the reason I was parked outside a house in City Island, trying to gather my nerve. I'd been staring at the house for the past ten minutes. No one had gone in or out, and the only light came from the first-floor front windows.

I reached for the door handle, preparing to step out of the car, but I felt my heart rate instantly increase. "Man up, Rio. You know you wanna do this," I scolded myself. I'd been thinking about doing this ever since I got home from the hospital a week earlier.

Grabbing a black bag from the passenger's seat, I riffled through the array of weapons—knives, nunchucks, pepper spray, a small baton, taser, handcuffs, and a gun. I opted for the gun, which I slipped under the back of my shirt. Gathering my courage, I finally got out of the car and crossed the street.

"Who is it?" a female voice yelled over the blaring TV when I banged on the screen door.

"Uber Eats," I said, praying that they even delivered in this area.

She snatched the door open. "I didn't order no—"

I grabbed her by the hair and pushed my way inside, whipping out my gun.

"Who the fuck is it?" a man yelled.

I turned to see a guy hopping into the living room on his one good foot. The other foot was in a cast, and he was holding a crutch. One of his arms was in a sling. Dude was fucked up—and from the look on his face, he was pretty shocked to find me standing in the living room.

"Get your hands up." I pointed the gun at him.

"Man, just shoot me, 'cause there ain't no way you gonna get me to raise my hands as much pain as I'm in," he said.

"We don't want no fuckin' trouble," the woman announced when I let go of her hair and shoved her toward the hop-a-long dude.

"A little late for that. Do you know who I am?" I asked hoppy.

"Yeah, you that crazy lady's son. Rio."

"Exactly. Now, where the hell is Vaughn?"

He pointed to the room he'd hobbled out of, and I motioned with my gun for them to move. I followed them into the kitchen where there was, believe it or not, a hospital bed and an even more fucked up man. He had two broken arms, and his leg was in a cast, propped up in the air. The cervical collar around his neck made it impossible for him to turn his head and look at me, so I walked around the table into his line of sight. His face was so fucked up it looked like something out of a horror movie.

"I came here to fuck you up, but it don't look like you can get anymore fucked up unless I break your other leg," I said, making sure he could see my gun.

"Wh th hl . . . gth fck uh!" The man sounded like he was speaking gibberish.

I playfully hit his leg with my pistol, and surprisingly, the girl came running to his side. She stopped abruptly, though, when I pointed my gun at her.

"Leave him alone! They wired his jaw shut!"

"I ain't gonna touch his ass," I told her with a smirk. "Like I said, I came here to fuck him up, but now I almost feel sorry for him. Karma really is a bitch, huh? She always comes to collect what's owed when you least expect it. And if she won't, my momma sure as hell will." I laughed for the first time since they'd put me in the hospital—maybe because I now had visual proof of how much my family really loved me. I didn't have to be worried about anything because they always had my back. God, I loved being a Duncan.

"So, who exactly is this guy Roman, and where can I find him?" I asked.

I was really curious about the guy who supposedly looked so much like me that I got my ass beat over his drama. And let's not forget the fact that I'd found out a few days ago that someone who looked like me ran up a $5,000 tab at my favorite South Beach hotel. I had some questions for this motherfucker, whoever he was.

Vaughn looked at his girl, then at the other guy, who was leaning against the doorway.

"Let's not everyone speak up at the same time!" I pressed down on Vaughn's chest bandage.

"Aahhhrrrgh!" He growled through clenched teeth.

"Damn, you see that nigga can't talk!" hop-a-long yelled.

I raised my gun. "Then somebody better talk for his ass, or you'll be sipping a juice box for six months right alongside him."

"All I know is he used to live over there by Yankee Stadium with his momma. They stayed in this orange brick townhouse with a big-ass mural of all the New York rappers on the side of it, but he been moved out from there."

"His mother still live there?" I asked.

"I guess. Me and him ain't been cool since we played ball back in high school."

"If you really wanna find him, find that bitch Kandace. She can tell you all about him," the girl volunteered. Vaughn rolled his eyes at her, and I could see that she'd struck a nerve.

"And where does Kandace live?" I asked.

"Hell if I know," she replied. "But her ass works at that strip club Dreams over in Hunts Point."

"Okay, then. Lemme leave you folks to your misery and go pay her a visit." I turned to leave, feeling redeemed and confident. "Believe it or not, I like strip clubs."

KD

26

"KD, this is some of the best fried chicken I've ever had," Patrick mumbled with a mouthful of food. "And the fried okra puts my momma's to shame."

"That ain't shit, boy. Did you taste the catfish yet?" I shoved a forkful in my mouth, savoring the flavor of the well-seasoned fish. He shook his head, and I handed him a packet of hot sauce. "Put a little of this on it and give your taste buds a treat."

He popped a piece of the fried fish in his mouth.

"Good, ain't it?" I glanced over at him from my seat in the passenger side of the truck, but he didn't say a word. The boy was too busy grinning like he was getting his dick sucked. I couldn't help but laugh, reaching for another forkful of fish to stuff my face.

As good as that food was, I still kept one eye on the restaurant we were parked across the street from, in case Sheriff Derrick Hughes and his merry band of nigger-loving sheriffs decided to come out. We'd used Tyler's friends in the highway patrol as our eyes and ears and finally caught up to Hughes right outside of Dallas. They'd stopped at Geraldine's Café, one of the best soul food restaurants in Texas. The tiny place was a popular spot for highway travelers who came from all over for the soul food and homemade pies. After watching the four lawmen be seated, I had sent Patrick in to pick us up some supper.

By the time we finished our peach cobbler, it was dark, and I was stuffed. Hughes and his men were walking out of Geraldine's around that same time. When they reached their vehicles, Hughes stuck his hand out and shook the hands of the two officers from the car with the Arkansas plates. Then they climbed into their vehicle and exited the parking lot.

Hughes, who had another twelve-hour drive, stretched his long body then opened the door of his sedan and got behind the wheel. The other sheriff slipped into the passenger's seat. We watched them pull out and head in the opposite direction of their colleagues, prompting me to send a text.

I waited a good ten minutes before we followed, taking the same road as Hughes. There was only one road that made any sense to travel if you were headed to Georgia, so we took our time. Twenty-five minutes later, on an isolated strip of highway, we saw the flashing red-and-blue lights of the highway patrol. We pulled up behind the patrol cars, staying in the truck until Steven and Peter Wildman approached us on the passenger's side. I rolled down my window.

"They give you boys any problems?" I asked.

"They weren't happy about us pulling them over, but once Steve explained to them that they were in Texas and had no jurisdiction, they surrendered their weapons and let us take them into custody." Peter chucked, and so did his brother.

"I bet that Barry White–sounding motherfucker was about bust a damn gasket when you told him he was under arrest for impersonating an officer," I said, joining in on their laughter. "I'm surprised he didn't resist."

"Oh, he thought it about. Until I pulled out my weapon and made it clear I was about to make him a statistic," Steve snickered. "That's when his partner started talking about lawsuits and how they were gonna own Texas."

"All the while handing over his weapon," Peter said. "I almost felt sorry for them. You know, them being law enforcement and all."

"Where are they?"

"Handcuffed in the back of their car. You wanna see them?"

"Oh, I sure as hell do," I told them in no uncertain terms. I had to make sure that the Wildman boys had done the job because this was the first time I'd ever had them do anything on my behalf without Tyler being involved. He didn't like it, but I'd made my son stay behind in the El Paso area to write tickets so he had a rock-solid alibi. "I wanna make sure that damn nigger knows who's behind this shit."

Steven opened the door for me to get out. I left Patrick in the truck, and we walked around to the passenger's side of the Fulton County Sherriff's car. I opened the door, and Hughes let me have it with that deep-ass voice of his.

"Shrugs, you son of a bitch, I hope you liked prison, 'cause when I'm finished with—"

"Boy, you ain't gonna do shit!" He couldn't finish his sentence because I pulled out my pistol and shot his ass in the chest two times.

Seeing what I did, Steve opened the rear driver's side door and pumped two into his associate. I closed the car door with a satisfied smirk.

"Collect their cell phones and make sure they're dead," I told Pete as I walked to the back of the car.

I waved at the flatbed truck that was approaching with its flashing yellow lights. It pulled up next to me. Johnny Brooks was behind the wheel.

"I need that car on this flatbed in the next five minutes, Johnny. Can you do that without fucking it up?" I asked.

He turned and looked at the car, then back to me. "Yes, sir. No problem."

"Well, hurry the hell up then. Let's go."

He lowered the ramp, and Pete slowly drove the car onto the bed of the truck.

Once it was loaded on and chained down, Johnny looked at me and smiled wide enough that I could count his gold teeth. "Was that fast enough, KD? I told you it wasn't gonna be a problem."

"Well, good for you. I'll buy you a damn ice cream cone when we get back to El Paso. Now, cover that damn thing up with a tarp and secure it good. We don't want the world to see what you're carrying."

Johnny quickly did as he was told, just as I knew he would. That's why I had brought him along. He wasn't the brightest man I'd ever met, but after the last time he fucked up a run, he knew damn well he'd better follow directions this time.

"Now, you listen to me and listen good," I said when he came back over to me. "I want you to take this car over to the scrap yard at Magnolia Recycling. You know where that is?"

"Yes, sir."

"I've already called Herman, so he'll be expecting you. When you get there, I want you to put this fucking car through the compactor twice—no, make it three times. Ya hear me?" I grabbed Johnny by the collar so he understood how serious I was.

He started nodding quickly.

"Good. Now, git." I pushed him toward the truck.

He didn't waste any time hopping back into the flatbed and pulling off just as fast as he'd pulled up. I got back into the truck with Patrick and we headed back toward El Paso, while the Wildman boys headed to Louisiana to dump the cell phones in the swamp. I checked my watch, satisfied by all that we'd accomplished in less than fifteen minutes. I had to laugh, wondering what LC Duncan would think if he knew I'd just made his nigger sheriff and his police car disappear without a trace.

Chippy

27

I squared my shoulders and said a quick prayer as I approached the door, reminding myself to remain calm, even though I knew it would be difficult. I knocked softly. After a few moments when no one came to the door, I knocked again, this time slightly louder. I was just about to leave when the door finally opened.

"Grandma!" Nevada tossed his arms around me in a hug so tight that we both nearly fell over.

"God, I have missed you," I said, hugging him just as hard. I had missed our daily routine ever since Consuela had taken him out of my house. When he was with us, I was in charge of getting him to and from school and all his various activities, so we spent a lot of time together. Now his absence left a hole in my heart. I loved that boy so much. LC had said it many times, but he really was our future—which made it even more important that I completed my mission successfully.

I stepped back to get a good look at him, and my eyes filled with tears. Rio may have been my baby, but Nevada was my heart.

"I missed you too, Grandma," he said sadly.

"My goodness. I do believe you've gotten taller."

Nevada laughed. "Funny. I've only been gone two weeks."

"I know, but it feels like forever." I peered at him a little closer. "There is something different about you, though."

Nevada smoothed his finger across his top lip, where there was a faint, thin line of hair. "Well, I have been growing a mustache."

"Yes, I can see that," I told him, squinting to see his imaginary mustache. "Well, can I come in?"

"Yes, of course. I'm sorry." He stepped out of the way, and I entered the hotel suite.

He whispered, "Grandma, can you talk some sense into my mom? She's taking me to California tomorrow."

"Your father told me. That's why I'm here," I whispered back.

I looked around, a little surprised by how unkempt the place was. Either the hotel housekeeping staff wasn't very good, or Consuela was a hot mess. I knew it wasn't Nevada, because he kept his room at my house orderly and clean.

"Where's your mother?" I asked.

"She's in her room getting dressed."

"Nevada, did you order room service again?" Consuela walked out of her bedroom and stopped dead in her tracks when she saw me. "Chippy . . ." There was no doubt from the tone of her voice that she was surprised by my presence, and not pleasantly.

"Hello, Consuela," I said politely.

"I didn't know you were coming." She glanced at Nevada, picking up a few things from the sofa.

"Oh, I was in Manhattan and thought I'd stop by to see Nevada. I'm sorry. Should I have called first?" I purposely put her on the spot. I wasn't Vegas or Nevada—she couldn't bully me.

"No, of course not. You're his grandmother. You're always welcome," she said with fake cheerfulness. "Please, have a seat." She gestured to the sofa.

I sat down, and Nevada sat next to me. She cleaned off an armchair and sat across from us.

"So, what's this I'm hearing that you're going to be attending school in California?" I addressed my question to Nevada, but I was looking directly at Consuela.

"He's going to attend Simi Valley Prep," Consuela answered for him. "It's one of the best boarding schools in the country."

I took a moment to let her words sink in, then I unleashed my attitude. "Boarding school? He's not living with you?"

Consuela's eyes darted to Nevada. Obviously she knew at that point we were about to have words. "Nevada, leave your grandmother and me alone so we can talk. Go finish packing."

"But, Mom—" Nevada started to object, but I shook my head at him. His protests subsided just as quickly as they started. "Yes, Mom," he said, then gave me a hug and exited the room. He trusted me to handle this.

"You know, Consuela, when Vegas told me you were taking Nevada west, there wasn't really much I could say. You're his mother. A child should always be with his mother."

She nodded as if she thought I was done, but that was far from the last thing I had to say.

"But what the fuck is this shit about boarding school?"

She flinched a little but recovered quickly, firing back with plenty of attitude of her own. "I'd rather have him in boarding school than around Vegas's whores."

One, two, three . . . I counted to myself to keep from screaming at her.

"So, this isn't about Nevada. This is about Vegas."

"Sins of the father," Consuela said with a shrug. "I've asked Vegas not to have my son around his whores time and time again, but he refuses to listen."

"Are you talking about Maria?" I asked.

"*Sí, la mayor puta,* Maria."

I knew exactly what the word *puta* meant. It was any ugly slur in any language, and one I didn't like to hear any woman use against another.

"Consuela, you're being unfair. You know how much Vegas loves his son."

"Vegas isn't fit to be a father to my son," she said matter-of-factly.

It took everything in me not to haul off and smack her for that comment about my son.

"Unfit? You know that's not true. You brought Nevada to our home so he could be with us. You knew he needed to be with his father," I said. "Before you brought him to us, that poor boy was living from boarding school to boarding school and anywhere else you decided to drop him off. You never spent one Christmas, Easter, or Thanksgiving with him. For the past three years, we've done nothing but provide stability and love because we are his family. There is nothing unfit about my son or my home."

She softened her tone just a little. "I'm sorry, Chippy. I was not talking about your home. I thank you for opening your home and all that you've done. But I must do what's best as a mother."

"Oh, please. You're doing what's best for yourself," I snapped angrily.

Consuela slid to the edge of the sofa. "Don't blame this on me. It's your son's fault."

"He has more than his share of blame, I'll admit that, but you're not innocent in this either," I told her.

"Me? What did I do?" Consuela stood up, indignant, but I knew it was an act. We were cut from the same cloth, Consuela and I. "He's the one giving him condoms and trying to make my baby into a man too fast."

I stood and walked over to her, placing a hand on her shoulder. Our eyes met.

"I understand, Consuela. I'm a mother too, remember? It's hard watching your child grow up sometimes. You want to protect them. It's your instinct. But Nevada's not a baby anymore. He's a young man. He needs his father, whether you like it or not. And we both know Vegas wouldn't do anything to hurt him."

"What do you want me to do, Chippy? Allow him and the *puta* free will with my son?" Consuela frowned. "That whore will never raise my child."

"First, I want you to stop calling her that. Every time you refer to Maria as a whore, you're teaching Nevada to disrespect women. You expect Vegas to be a good example for Nevada, but what about you?"

Her face softened. "Oh."

"Second, you're his mother—nobody else. And I'll fight Vegas, Marie, and anyone else if they try to say different," I stated forcefully. "I'm not playing that shit."

She blinked a few times, looking surprised. "Thank you," she said.

"You don't need to thank me. But you and my son need to figure this shit out and get it together. That boy is the future of both of our families, and you are his parents. From now on, you stay at our house, not in a hotel, and I don't care if Vegas likes it or not. He's going to have to deal with it because you are family." I could see that she was finally listening and accepting what I was saying. "Oh, and another thing. There will be no more of this talk about California and boarding schools. That won't be happening. Forget about Vegas. I am the one who won't allow it. Do you know how selfish that would be of you to haul him off to California and dump him in a boarding school while you're off jet-setting to work? Let's face it, Consuela. We all know that as much as you love Nevada, you are one hell of a businesswoman—a successful one—and you won't allow anything, including being a mother, to stop you from handling your business." I stared at her and allowed my words to settle into her mind for a moment.

"Now, it's Labor Day weekend. Enjoy your time with your son. Talk to him and explain why you're concerned about him having a condom. But I expect him to be back home in time for school Tuesday morning."

Consuela took a deep breath, straightened her back, then nodded her head once. "Fine. But I don't want that wh—" she hesitated. "I don't want that *woman* near my son."

"You have my word." I was relieved that she agreed to my demands, but I wasn't finished. "One more thing."

"What is it?"

"Do you mind coming with me and my grandson to lunch?"

"I'd be honored," she said with a smile that looked genuine.

"Nevada!" she called out. When he didn't answer, she yelled again. "Nevada!"

After another few seconds of silence, we both went to his room. She knocked loudly, but still no answer. Consuela opened the door only for us to discover that the room was empty. Two drawers were emptied and left wide open, and there was no sign of his laptop or knapsack.

I turned to Consuela. "Where could he have gone?"

Roman

28

"Well, well, well, if it isn't the guys with the coconuts for balls. I wasn't expecting to see you two anytime soon. I thought you'd be on a beach drinking piña coladas and strawberry daiquiris after your last score." Lex smirked when we walked into the hardware store, but his eyes didn't leave the bag Denny had slung over his shoulder. "So, who'd you hit this time, Jacob the Jeweler?"

"Funny, Lex, but you ain't gonna be making jokes once you see what we got." Denny patted the duffle bag.

"Is that so? Well, let's see what you got." Lex motioned for us to follow him into the back.

Inside Lex's office, Denny unzipped the bag and took out the jewelry we'd gotten from Vaughn and his people. Lex picked up each item, examining them one at a time. He didn't look pleased.

"I hope this ain't all you boys got, because right now you're looking at about eight hundred bucks."

"Eight hundred? Are you crazy?" I yelled.

"Hey, you can take this fake shit back if you want to." Lex shrugged, pushing it toward Denny.

At the sound of the word *fake*, I groaned. "That cheap motherfucker Vaughan been wearing fake shit this whole time."

"No worries." Denny nudged me. "That's not the only thing we brought."

"Let's see it. What you got?" Lex inquired, peering over to see what else Denny was about to pull out.

"What do you think of this?" Denny removed the brown plastic-wrapped bricks from the bag and carefully placed all four of them on the desk.

Lex looked over at me, wide-eyed. "Tuh, you should've started with these instead of the cheap-ass jewelry."

Denny laughed. "We saved the best for last."

"I can see that. Where'd you get them?"

"None o' ya business. How much you paying?" I asked.

"Depends on what it is and the quality," Lex said, reaching into the drawer and pulling out a small pocketknife, which he used to slice the plastic on one of the packages. He used the knife to scoop a pinch of the white substance, placing it on his tongue. He stood up straight, looking impressed. "Hmmm, heroin."

"It's good, huh, Lex?" Denny looked like he was about to go over the table.

"How much?" I repeated.

"We're about to find out," Lex told us as he reached into another drawer, taking out some kind of testing kit.

We watched as he took another sample of the heroin and put it in a small glass vial, then shook it before holding it up to the light. The vial was now a bright blue.

"Fuck me. This is some primo shit. I've never tested anything so pure."

Denny leaned over and whispered to me, "We must've caught 'em before they cut this shit."

"That's why that motherfucker ain't have no cash. He just scored," I whispered back.

"Okay, fellas, I can give you sixty-five hundred a ki," Lex said with a big grin.

"You said this shit was primo, superb!" I reminded him.

"Hey, take it or leave it. You got another buyer, go right ahead."

Surprisingly, Denny leaned over and started putting the bricks back in the bag. "Fuck him, Rome. I'll step on this shit a couple of times myself and take it down south and let my cousin sell it for us. We'll make ten times what he's offering. He's forgetting we ain't broke no more."

"Lex, listen, my mom is sick and needs surgery. I ain't trying to be out their slinging dope, but if I have to, I will. So, what's your best offer?" I asked. Last thing I wanted to do was spend the next month worrying that one of Denny's cousins would get busted and dime on us. Plus, I need the money for my mom's transplant.

"Sorry to hear that," Lex said, not taking his eyes off the dope. "I'll tell you what. I'll give you a grand for the fake jewelry and eleven grand per ki. That's the best I can do."

I knew we were being taken advantage of, but at this point, I didn't have a choice. Dr. Ford had already said that if the transplant was a go, it would cost in the hundreds of thousands. Even with Denny giving me his share, what Lex was offering wouldn't put a dent into that amount, but it would at least be a start. The hospital wasn't gonna do shit without a down payment.

"Just give us the cash," I snapped.

Thankfully, Denny didn't protest.

After we'd exchanged the goods for cash, Lex looked me in the eyes and said, "Listen, I'm sorry your mom is not well. But if you guys are looking for a big score, I may have one for you."

"How big?" I pushed.

"It pays a hundred grand a piece."

"Get the fuck outta here. A hundred thousand a piece?" Denny almost dropped his money.

"Yep."

"And what do we have to do for this hundred grand? Rob the White House?" I asked.

"Cute." Lex laughed. "No, there's a truck coming in from Texas. Y'all get me that truck, you get a hundred grand each, no questions asked."

"For a truck? What the fuck is in the truck?" I asked skeptically.

Lex glared at me then shook his head. "For a hundred grand a piece, do you really care?"

"Maybe," I said. "This just sounds a little bit too good to be true. What's the catch?"

"The catch is that the guys who own the truck will kill your asses and mine if they catch us. Any more fucking questions?" Lex stared at us. When we didn't give him an instant response, he waved his hand in disgust.

"You know what? Maybe I was wrong. Maybe you two aren't the guys for the job. Maybe your coconuts are just plain old walnuts."

"Our nuts are just fine. It's the bullshit that—"

"Say less," Denny whispered, touching my arm as he cut me off. "You forgetting your mom needs that money for her operation."

"He's got a good point," Lex added.

I was still unconvinced, but they were right. I needed the money.

"When and where do we find this truck?" I asked.

Lex smiled. "So, does this mean you want the job?"

I glanced over at Denny, already knowing what his answer was. I said, "I still have to think it over, but for now, yeah, we want the job."

Rio

29

I went by Dreams and every other strip club in Hunts Point, but I couldn't find anyone named Kandace. Lots of chicks with stage names like Candy Cane, Brown Sugar, and Honey, but Kandace must've been her government name, because no one had ever heard of her. So, the next morning, I went to plan B and wound up riding up and down the Grand Concourse, looking for an orange building with a mural on the side not far from Yankee Stadium. After hours of searching, I finally found it on a side street.

I walked up to the front door, trying to look casual in spite of my nerves. I pressed the doorbell and waited for a few seconds, then knocked when there was no answer.

"Roman?" There was an older man walking up the stoop next door, holding a bag of groceries. This shit was getting creepy. He obviously had me confused with Roman, but at least now I knew for sure I was at the right house. "What're you doing?" he asked.

I turned my head to look at him, and my hood slid back a little.

He squinted. "What the hell is going on with your hair? Is that purple?"

I thought about taking off, but the guy seemed harmless enough. The house seemed empty, so I wouldn't get any information from anyone who lived there, but maybe if I played along like I was Roman, the old dude might tell me something useful.

"Yeah, uh, I decided to try something different," I said.

"Mm-hmm, that's different all right." He laughed as he held up a bunch of keys and jingled them in the air. "One thing hasn't changed, though. You been locking yourself out since you were in third grade."

"Yeah, you're right." I couldn't believe my luck. This guy was coming up the steps with his key to unlock the door. At that moment, I made the decision that I was going inside.

"There you go," he said.

"Thanks."

He picked up his bags. "When you go back to the hospital, let your mama know I'm praying for her. She's a good woman. And your aunt too."

"I will. Thanks again." I stepped inside and closed the door behind me before he could try to talk my ear off.

It was dark and quiet inside, but I still felt the need to yell out, "Hello?"

There was no answer. The old guy had said Roman's mother was in the hospital, so I guessed that was why the house was empty. I clicked the light switch on the wall near the doorway, revealing a tidy little living room. Someone clearly loved this place, even if the stuff in it was outdated. The hardwood floors were worn out but clean, and the floral sofa and TV console had to be at least twenty years old.

There were some framed photos on the TV console, so I walked over to get a better look. I picked up one picture of a lady and a little boy, and then nearly dropped it when I saw the resemblance. I didn't recognize the smiling woman, but the little boy, who looked to be about three years old, could have been me. It was really eerie, like seeing myself in some alternate universe. My hand was shaking a little as I put the picture back and picked up another one. It was a photo of the boy sitting in front of a Spider-Man birthday cake with a candle in the shape of a 9. I looked at one photo after another, each highlighting lifetime events that, if had I not known better, could have been my life—minus the prom. This shit was getting creepier by the second.

At the bottom of the shelf was a large photo album. I would look through it later, but I wanted to explore the rest of the house first. There were two bedrooms that were obviously occupied by women, based on the perfume bottles and jewelry in there. I skipped over those rooms and kept searching. At the end of the hallway, there was another bedroom, the one that I'd been hoping for: Roman's room. There was an unmade bed, a single dresser, and a closet. I guess Vaughn's buddy was wrong. Roman did live here.

I started with the closet first. He had the typical collection of Nike shoe boxes and Timberland boots. Hoodies, oversized jackets, and jerseys hung in the closet. This dude may have looked like me, but he damn sure didn't have my taste in fashion. Not one single dress shirt in sight. *Typical thug.* And what was with the cheap-ass Axe body spray? I would never. How the fuck anyone had confused me with this fashion-challenged loser was beyond me.

I closed the closet door and was about to start rummaging through the dresser drawers when my phone vibrated.

"Hello?" I whispered.

"You must be somewhere you're not supposed to be if your ass is whispering." It was Sebastian. Thanks to Paris and Sasha, who felt sorry for me, we were talking again. They'd convinced him to check out the video from his club, and when he saw the wack outfit and hideous shoes the guy was wearing, he realized it wasn't me. He knew I'd never be caught dead wearing something like that.

"So, what are you doing?" he asked.

"I'm inside this fake-ass motherfucker's house." I walked out of the bedroom and sat down on the floral sofa as I talked with Sebastian.

"In his house?" Sebastian hissed. "The doppelganger? How?"

"I broke in, that's how," I snapped back.

"What? Why?"

"Inquiring minds want to know," I replied, picking up the photo album I'd found earlier.

"And what'd you find out?"

"You're not gonna believe this shit. It's gonna sound crazy."

"Crazier than your ass breaking and entering? I don't think so."

"Oh yeah, crazier than that." I took a deep breath and admitted out loud the thought that had been stirring in my head ever since I entered the house and saw those pictures. "I think this guy's my brother." There. I'd said it. I still couldn't believe it, but I'd said it.

"Rio, you're trippin'."

"If you saw the pictures of him that I saw, you'd understand that it's possible. Haven't you ever seen *Sister, Sister* with Tia and Tamera? It's possible, Sebastian."

"You're reading way too much into this over a couple of pictures."

"Maybe, but I look more like this guy than I do Paris—hell, anybody else in my family, honestly. And you know that's always been a running joke in the Duncan household: Rio's adopted." I started flipping the pages of the photo album. More pictures, certificates of promotion, sports awards, report cards. This guy's momma must have saved every scrap of paper that had anything to do with him.

Sebastian was still skeptical. "Everyone has a doppelganger. You've just found yours."

"I hear you, but being in this house, this room, I can feel something, some type of connection. I can't explain it." I flipped the page and saw a picture of Roman and the woman at his high school graduation. "Wouldn't it be crazy if this woman was my mom and Roman was my brother?"

"Rio, are you on drugs or what? You need to hurry up and get the hell outta there before you get caught."

"You're right." I stood up from the sofa. "I'm just gonna be a little bit nosier, and then I'll get out of here."

I went back into Roman's room and opened the top drawer of his dresser to snoop around. In among his socks and underwear there were a few condoms, a couple hundred-dollar bills, and a shiny .44. I pushed aside a pile of socks and found an envelope that was kind of yellow from age. I pulled a paper out of the envelope and was rendered speechless.

"Rio, you still there?" Sebastian asked.

"This can't be true. Is this shit for real?" I said. "Sebastian, I think my life is officially over."

"What? What's going on?"

"Me and him have the same birthdate," I mumbled.

"Get the fuck out. How is that even possible?"

"I don't know, but it says it right here in black and white on his birth certificate. Roman Marcus Johnson, date of birth February eighteenth, 1993. Mother, Margaret Wilma Johnson. No father is listed."

I felt like I couldn't catch my breath.

"Shit! Rio, are you okay?"

"No," I said on the verge of tears. "Sebastian, I'll call you later." I didn't wait for an answer before I hung up. I didn't know what the hell was going on, but I didn't want to talk about it anymore.

Feeling too numb to think straight, I closed the drawer and turned to leave. On my way out, I slipped the birth certificate in the pocket of my hoodie—for what reason, I wasn't sure.

"Rio, you need a drink or several." I took one last look around the little living room and then left the house, nearly bumping into a woman who was heading up the walkway.

"Hey, Rome." She stopped right in front of me, blocking my path. "Uh, hey, babe."

I kept my head down. "Uh, hi."

"What the fuck did you do to your hair?" She frowned, touching my purple 'fro. To be that bold, she had to be the infamous Kandace.

"Dyed it," I said.

"I see. But why?" Her lip curled, and she looked at me as if I had done something wrong.

I was instinctively about to snap my neck and ask the bitch what the hell her problem was and tell her that I probably paid more for this dye job than she had paid for her entire outfit, but then I remembered who I was supposed to be. "I lost a bet." I flipped the hood over my head and went to walk past.

"Well, maybe it's not so bad. In fact, I think you look cute." She grabbed my arm and turned my body toward her. "Maybe I'll dye my hair purple too."

"That'd be nice," I replied, trying to step around her.

"Hey, where you going? I came over here to check on how your mother's doing and to see if there's anything I can *do* for you before I go to work."

Her hand caressing my crotch made me jump back. "Whoa."

She frowned again. "Roman, what is wrong with you?"

"Nothin'. I got a lot on my mind with my moms in the hospital is all." I tried to play it off with what I hoped was a thug effect. "I'll holla at ya later."

"Damn. All right, but can a sista at least get a kiss before you leave?" She stepped closer and put her arms around my neck, puckering her lips in anticipation.

I swallowed hard. *You can do this, Rio. It's just a kiss. Pretend it's Sebastian,* I told myself as I closed my eyes. I leaned toward her, but dammit, I just couldn't do it.

"What the hell is going on with you?" she asked when I pulled away from her. "Are you cheating on me?"

"No, no, I ate some garlic knots and my breath is kickin'. I'm sorry, but I just can't do it to you, for real," I said, then brushed past her and rushed to the street.

"Roman!" she called after me.

"I'll holla!" I waved as I sprinted around the corner to my car. At that point I got in the car feeling a wave of uncertainty and anxiousness. I hated that feeling, and the only thing I could think of to get rid of it was a very expensive bottle of tequila.

KD

30

I opened my eyes just as we passed by the WELCOME TO LOUISI-ANA sign. It had been a little over a week since the disappearance of the nigger sheriff, and things had been surprisingly quiet. Roscoe had stopped by, along with a couple of his deputies, to tell us the news and ask if we knew anything about it. I suspected old Roscoe was afraid that if he came alone, his ass might be the next to disappear. Of course, we told him we didn't know nothing. Tyler and I both had strong alibis, with him on duty there in El Paso and me on the ranch with forty of my faithful employees as witnesses. So, with that behind me, it was time to move to the next phase of my plans.

"You remember how to get to where we're going?" I asked.

"Yes, sir." Patrick took the exit, then turned down an obscure road. He took his time as he maneuvered the car through the thick trees and brush along the way.

We seemed to be far away from civilization, until finally, a faint light appeared. We followed that light for about a mile, until we entered what appeared to be a parking lot in the middle of nowhere. Patrick stopped the car, and we got out and began walking toward it. As we got closer, I could hear loud chanting.

"White power! White power!"

We finally arrived at a clearing that was occupied by a large group of men, all clad in white sheets, gathered around a huge, burning cross. Patrick walked closer to the crowd, while I stayed back in the shadows near a grove of trees and a white Cadillac. Leaning against a tree, I watched and listened as one of the men, whose red robe made him stand out in the sea of white, gave a rousing speech.

"They like to tell us we have white privilege!" he yelled. "Well, brethren, I'm here to tell you that they're damn right! We have privilege because that's the way God wants it. The white man is meant to be the ruler over all creation. And with the support of our great President Donald Trump, we will take back what's ours. We will make America white again!"

The crowd went fucking crazy, and I even found myself inspired by his words, clapping and whistling in agreement.

"Now, I want you all to raise your hands and pledge your allegiance to our beloved Klan," he said, and every white-sheeted arm rose up as they loudly professed their loyalty to the KKK.

He wrapped up the meeting by saying, "God bless white America!" and slowly, the crowd of men dispersed. They climbed into their cars, pulling off their hoods and robes, and driving back to their nice, respectable lives. If they were anything like the Klan members I knew back in Texas, there were probably some highly influential people beneath those hoods who would use their power to keep the darkies and illegal aliens in line in their communities.

"Nice turnout, Harold." I said when the red-robed speaker approached the Caddie.

He nearly jumped out of his robe. Even with his hood on, I could see the fear in his eyes. "Jesus Christ, KD. What the hell are you doing hiding in the damn bushes?"

"I was just sitting back here, enjoying the gathering. That was a damn good speech, too. I gotta admit, I was a little nervous when I found out they'd up and made you Grand Wizard. I figured your being a circuit court judge and all would've made you a little soft. But you're doing a fine job."

"Well, thank you for the vote of confidence," he said warily. "Now, I know you ain't come all this way out here to observe my leadership skills, so tell me why you're here. You having another one of those parties?" He sounded excited. "Folks are still talking about that last one."

"Glad you enjoyed it. Maybe we'll have another one around Christmas. Let me talk to Tyler."

He seemed to relax a little, removing his hood and going to the trunk of the Caddie to get a few beers from a cooler. He handed me one. I popped the cap and took a long swig.

"Thanks. That hit the spot."

"No problem. There's more if you want 'em." He took a swallow. "So, what's on your mind? I've known you long enough to know when something's troubling you. You look like you could piss vinegar."

"I've got a situation I could use some help with," I said humbly.

"KD, we've always been friends. You know if there's anything I can do for you, all you gotta do is ask. What seems to be the problem?"

He leaned against his car as if I was about to give him a grocery list.

"I need a badass who's not afraid to get his hands dirty. Someone who will follow orders and not ask a whole bunch of fucking questions."

Harold laughed and pointed at the stragglers leaning against their cars with their white robes still on, drinking beer and shooting the shit. "Take your pick. Half of these boys are ex-military or former law enforcement with an axe to grind. Pay them right and they'll serve you well."

"No, I've got enough trigger-happy country boys on the payroll. What I need is someone special who can operate up north, in places like New York City, without getting lost, frustrated, or overwhelmed," I explained.

Harold chuckled, looking excited. "I got just the boy for you." He turned to a red pickup truck that was surrounded by five or six men. "Hey, Pee Wee, go fetch your cousin Slick for me."

"Sure thing, judge." Pee Wee, who lived up to his name at no more than five foot four, ran off into the darkness. He returned with one of the meanest-looking jarheads I'd ever seen. He was at least a foot taller than Pee Wee, 290 pounds of pure muscle, and he wore a crew cut and a scowl that made him look like he might rip your damn head off.

"Slick, this here is KD Shrugs, a good friend of mine from El Paso," Harold said.

"Nice to meet you," Slick said in this gruff voice that made him appear even meaner.

"Slick here is from New York City and presently looking for work."

"Is that so?" I grinned. "What type of work do you do, son?"

"Bounty hunter. I used to work for a bail bondsman in Queens until he hired a spic to replace me for half the money." You could hear the bitterness in that boy's voice from a mile away. "I was in the Marines for three years before that, but I was dishonorably discharged for beating my nigger sergeant's ass." He said that shit with such conviction I wanted to salute him.

"So, you're a bounty hunter, huh?"

"Yes, sir, a damn good one," he replied. "But I'll do just about anything if the price is right. I got a baby on the way."

"That's a very responsible way of looking at things," I replied, but my next question would determine whether we could work together. "So, Slick, would you kill a man if I asked you to?"

He hesitated, staring at me as if I'd opened a whole new can of worms, which I did. "No, sir, I would not kill a man—not unless it was self-defense."

I glanced over at Harold, a little disappointed, until Slick finished his response.

"But niggers, spics, and Jews aren't men, so killing one of them is like deer hunting. Far as I'm concerned, it's open season."

That boy didn't even crack a smile, but I did. Matter of fact, I laughed my ass off. "Slick, my friend, you're hired. How's a hundred grand a year sound?"

"Sounds real good. When do I start?"

"Right fucking now."

Nevada

31

"Thanks," I said to the Uber driver as I climbed out of the back seat of his Honda Accord.

The last week had completely sucked, other than sneaking off to tutor Kia at the library a few times. My mom and dad were still at each other's throats, and each day was looking more and more like I was going to end up in a boarding school. Well, if I was going to be forced to leave New York, I was going to make the best of the time I had left, not locked up in the hotel like a damn prisoner. Luckily, Mom and Grandma had been so busy arguing about my fate in the living room that they hadn't heard me slip out the back door of the suite.

As I stared at the entrance to the building where I'd been dropped off, my phone began vibrating in my pocket. I didn't bother checking it, because I already knew it was my mother. She'd given it back to win favor in her argument with my dad, but it didn't work. I was mad at both of them—especially her. She was the one trying to send me off to boarding school.

I took the phone out of my pocket and hit the IGNORE button, but she just called back two seconds later. I was tempted to block her but couldn't bring myself to be that disrespectful.

The phone chimed with a text message on the screen.

Mom: Where are you? Call me right now and tell me where you are. Don't make me call the police.

I knew she didn't mean it. My mother hated the police more than she hated my dad's girlfriend—and she hated Marie with a passion. But in case my sudden departure from the hotel had upset her enough to contact the authorities, I sent her a quick response.

Nevada: I'm fine. I went to see a friend. This whole boarding school thing is stressing me out! Just give me some space. PLEASE!!!!

I hit the SEND button then turned off my phone.

I walked toward the entrance and paused, not knowing whether I should ring the bell. My slight dilemma was solved when the door suddenly opened and a man walked out, bumping into me.

"Oh," was the closest thing I got to an apology as he continued past.

I grabbed the door before it shut and walked inside. Looking around, I was surprised by what I saw. Marie's place was called the Hellfire Club. I'd expected to see a room full of naked women carrying trays of drinks and giving lap dances like you would see in the strip clubs on TV. In my mind, I'd always pictured the Hellfire Club as a slightly sleazy place with red lighting. Instead, the entrance looked more like the lobby of a nice hotel, with soft jazz coming from surround-sound speakers. There were guys sitting around in leather armchairs, smoking cigars and drinking whiskey that was brought to them by super-hot waitresses. The women wore tight dresses and stiletto heels, but no one was naked.

No one seemed to notice me as I went into the bar area, which turned out to be closer to what I had been expecting. Men sat around small tables as waitresses dressed in sexier, see-through lingerie brought them drinks. One woman, wearing a short kimono, took a man by the hand and led him up a nearby staircase. As he followed behind her, he lifted the back of her robe and smacked her on the ass. She giggled and turned around, so he loosened the belt and fondled her breasts. I watched as they groped each other for a few seconds before finally making their way up the steps. There was no question where they were going or what they were about to do.

"What the hell are you doing here?"

I felt a hand on my shoulder and turned around. I had to tilt my head up to look at the huge man grimacing at me.

"I keep telling you young motherfuckers to stay the fuck outta here. After the last warning I gave you and your little friends, I thought you would've learned a lesson. I guess not."

"I . . . I've never been here before. I'm looking . . ." I stammered.

"Yeah, I see your horny ass looking. But after I blacken your eye, you ain't gonna be able to see nothing."

I winced as he began dragging me toward a nearby door. "Wait! You don't understand."

"Bubba! What are you doing?" Kia called out. "Let him go."

I was able to turn my head just enough to see her rushing toward us.

"I'ma let his little ass go right after I fuck him up one good time," Bubba told her.

"If you do, you may as well kiss your job goodbye," Kia told him. She looked so much older in her sexy clothes and heavy makeup. "Do you know who this is?"

"Nope," Bubba said. "And I don't care."

"This is Vegas's son, Nevada. You care now?"

"Vegas? Marie's Vegas?"

She nodded, and the man released his grip.

"You owe him an apology," she said, pulling me toward her.

"My bad, little man. I didn't know. But real talk, your ass is underage, so you can't be in here. It's bad for business. Scares away the regulars." Bubba nodded toward a couple of people who were looking over at us.

"Come on, Nevada." Kia pulled me by the arm, and I followed her into the kitchen and up a back stairway.

After several twists and turns down a few more hallways, we finally got to her room. She closed the door behind us, then motioned for me to sit on the bed. I slid off my knapsack and looked around at the small room. Aside from the distinctive Asian-themed decorations, it looked like a regular bedroom with a queen-size bed, a dresser, and a vanity covered with makeup and perfumes. It didn't necessarily look like a place where Kia entertained strange men for a living.

"You okay? What are you doing here anyway?" she asked.

"We were supposed to meet at the library this morning, but you didn't show up or answer my DMs. I hope you're not upset about my mom. She's just being overprotective."

"Aw, that's cute." She smiled sweetly. "No, I'm not upset. I was doing an outcall, and my client wanted more time."

"I wish you would have let me know. I really was worried." I shook my head and stared at the floor, feeling like a fool.

"I know. I'm sorry. But I can't use my phone during a date. It's a big no-no. They're paying for my time."

I hated that she called what she did a date.

"Besides, you should have never come here. This place isn't for you."

"Is that a crack at my age?" I asked.

"No." She walked over to the bed and sat down next to me, taking my hand. "It means you're the only friend I have outside these walls, and this place has a way of corrupting people. I don't want that for you." She looked intensely into my eyes. "I want you to stay away because you're my light at the end of the tunnel, Nevada. Every time I look at you, I see there is a way out of this life. If you become part of it, I'm trapped."

"Wow, that was deep." I didn't know what else to say. I had no idea she felt that way about me.

"That's was kind of deep, wasn't it?" She laughed, and so did I.

There was a knock on the door. Kia placed her finger over her lips to tell me to stay quiet.

"Yes?" she called out.

"Hey, Ki." It was Danielle. I recognized her loud voice right away. "One of your regulars is downstairs."

"Okay, I'll be right down," Kia replied.

"You better hurry. It's that nerdy guy Bob, the one you said is a big tipper."

"Tell him I'll be right there, Danielle. I gotta clean up my room."

Danielle left, and Kia said to me, "I have to go down there, and you gotta get outta here." She leaned over and kissed my cheek, and as usual, I blushed. "And I meant what I said about you staying away from here."

"Yeah, I know, but I had to see you. I'm leaving tomorrow," I said sadly, lifting my head so that our eyes met.

"Your mom is really sending you to boarding school?" Kia asked, and I was shocked to see her eyes fill up with tears.

"She thinks she is. But I'm not going to California tomorrow," I said defiantly, and I meant every word. "I'm going to Texas."

Kia looked confused. "What's in Texas?"

"Your sister."

KD

32

"Oh, shit. Yeeeeeeah. Oh, yeah." I moaned as I watched the brim of my Stetson rise and fall in front of me. My eyes rolled back in my head and my legs tensed up as I gripped the side of the bed until my knuckles turned white. I was sweating so profusely that my hair must have looked like I'd just stepped out of the shower.

"You like that, Mr. KD?" Celeste asked, lifting my hat from her head so I could see those beautiful full lips expertly suck on my dick.

I couldn't even answer the Haitian beauty for fear that if I did, it would bring the euphoria I was feeling to an end. The rhythmic motion of her mouth had me on the verge of exploding. I leaned back slightly and began thrusting my pelvis as I erupted with a prolonged growl, not caring that I sounded like a wounded animal.

"Fuck, that was good. I mean damn good, girl." I panted, wiping the beads of sweat off my face. My heart was pounding so fast that I could barely catch my breath. Once again, she'd proven my preference for dark meat to be a sound and fulfilling choice.

I heard a knock on the bedroom door and glanced at her like she might be expecting someone—'cause I sure wasn't. I knew one thing: somebody was looking for a foot up their ass.

"Who is it?" I shouted.

"It's me," I heard Patrick shout back.

"What do you want, boy?" I growled angrily. "I'm gettin' my dick sucked!"

"I understand that, KD, and I apologize. Normally I'd never disturb you while you were getting your dick sucked, but we got company. Important company that just rolled up." Patrick was a dope, but at least he knew not to announce any names in front of one of the girls.

"All right, I'll be right there." I sighed, tapping Celeste so I could sit up. "Hand me my britches, brown sugar."

A few minutes later, I had sent Celeste out the back door to Building 6 and was stepping into my living room, pulling my suspenders over my shoulders. I was greeted by Congressman Wesley Bell sitting on my sofa.

"Afternoon, KD." Wesley gave me that fake-ass politician smile that told me he was up to something. "That was a fine party you gave the other night. I especially enjoyed the tour. It brought a lot of things into perspective. I appreciate you bringing me on board."

"Cut the bullshit. What the fuck do you want?"

Patrick handed me a much-needed beer, and I sat down on my recliner, taking a long swig.

"I have someone important I want you to meet. Someone that could change both of our lives significantly."

I could tell from the seriousness in his tone that whoever this person was, the congressman respected or feared him, or perhaps even both. I was all ears and open to talk to whomever about whatever, but I wasn't gonna be intimidated by anyone.

"All right. You know I like game changers. Set it up." I gave him an approving nod.

"I already have. He's outside." Wesley raised his phone to his head and spoke into it. "Could you please send him in?"

Well, this was going to be interesting. I watched cautiously as Wesley stood and my front door opened.

"Come on in," Wesley said to a man in his late fifties with salt-and-pepper hair and a clean-shaven face. He was well dressed in an expensive suit and Italian shoes that said he either oozed money or was a conman.

"Leo Greer, this is KD Shrugs, the man I was telling you about."

"Nice to meet you, Mr. Shrugs." Leo held out his hand.

"Same here." We'd never met, but I knew who Leo Geer was, and I knew why Wesley had brought him. Leo Geer was one of the twenty richest men in the country. He'd inherited Save Smart Dollar Stores based in Hartford, Connecticut, from his old man. Leo was swimming in money. He was also one of the biggest contributors to the Republican Party, funding some of the most powerful Super PACs. I had no doubt as to why Wesley was so far up his ass.

"Have a seat," I said.

Leo sat down next to Wesley. "Well, I'm sure our fine congressman here has told you about my situation."

"Actually, I haven't," Wesley cut in. "I thought I'd let you tell him yourself so he can get a better understanding."

"Mr. Geer, before we get started, there is one thing I know for a fact. Nobody comes to the farm unless they have a problem, are looking for a problem, or they need help solving a problem. You're a long way from Connecticut, so which one of those categories do you fit into?"

He leaned back in his chair and shot a glance at Wesley. If he was offended by my directness, I didn't give a shit. That's the way we did things down here in Texas.

"Mr. Shrugs, I have a problem, and from what I hear from the congressman, you're the only one who can solve it." He sounded humble, and for a man with that much money and power, that said a lot.

"What kind of problem is it?" I asked.

"It's similar to the problem you solved for me a few years back. From what I could see last week, you're already set up for it," Wesley said.

I hung my head and exhaled dramatically. "That's a very expensive problem you have there, Leo."

"Money is no object when it comes to a child. I've been turned away from more people than you can imagine. Time is not my friend. You're my last hope."

A smile crept up on my face. "Well then, you've come to the right place. Do you have any paperwork or specifications you'd like to share? It sure would speed up the process."

"I think this will give you everything you need." He handed me a computer jump drive.

"Good, good. I like a man that comes prepared. How'd you like a tour of our facility? Give you an idea of what we do out here at the farm."

Leo glanced at Wesley, smiling hopefully. "Of course. I'd love a tour."

We exited the house and jumped on the golf cart parked out front. They climbed on the back, while I got behind the steering wheel, and we headed toward Buildings 5 and 6. I noticed the concerned look on Leo's face as we pulled up in between the buildings.

"This is it?" he asked.

"You were expecting maybe the Taj Mahal?" I rolled my eyes, glancing at Wesley. He had better not have brought me some uppity Northerner who was gonna look down his nose at me.

"Trust me, Leo, things aren't always how they appear. You're going to be surprised," Wesley murmured as they followed me to the door to Building 6.

"Afternoon, KD." Elizabeth was sitting at her desk, wearing a lab coat.

"Afternoon, Lizbeth." I stepped aside so she could see our guests. "I'm sure you remember the congressman from the last time he was here."

"Of course. Welcome back, Congressman." Elizabeth smiled.

"And this here is Mr. Greer. I'm gonna give him a tour. He's interested in using our services." I handed her the jump drive. "Why don't you get started on this and see if we have anything in house that may be useful for him? And could you let Dr. Baker know we're here? We'll be heading over to Building Five from here."

Elizabeth slid the jump drive into her computer. "Soon as I run this through our data base, I'll let Dr. Baker know to expect you. We should have some answers by the time you finish your tour."

"Thank you, Lizbeth." I waved for the fellas to follow me. "Come on, boys. Lemme show you around."

Down the hallway, I showed them the spa-like amenities before heading to Building 5, which housed the lab, infirmary, and medical office. Dr. David Baker was waiting for us when we arrived. Technically, he wasn't a doctor. He'd lost his medical license a couple of years back for writing illegal prescriptions. But I overlooked that small infraction and hired him on the spot. He was perfect for what I needed at the farm.

"How you doin', doc?" I said. "This here is Mr. Leo Greer. And I think you know Congressman Bell. Did Lizbeth tell you we were coming?"

"Yes, she did. And I do believe we have found the perfect match for Mr. Greer. Elizabeth is doing some last-minute tests right now. Would you all like to check it out?" Dr. Baker asked.

I turned to Leo. "Well?"

He tried to hold back a smile. "Sure."

We followed Dr. Baker into a medical examination room, where Elizabeth was drawing blood from the arm of the Chinese girl who'd been at my house the night I met Celeste. She had only been on the farm a short time, but she'd already gained considerable weight.

"How's it looking, Elizabeth?" Dr. Baker asked.

"Better than can be expected, doctor. So far, everything's a go. I'm going to run her blood again just to make sure, but she's healthy and disease free." She turned to Leo and gave him a smiling thumbs up. He looked like he was about to get emotional.

After thanking Elizabeth and Dr. Baker, we left the building and returned to the golf cart.

"See there, Leo, I told you KD would come through," Wesley bragged, patting him on the back.

"I know. I just can't believe it. I can't wait to tell my wife." Leo wept openly now, grabbing hold of me tightly. "Thank you, Mr. Shrugs. Thank you."

I let the man have his emotional moment, then removed myself from his grip and drove the golf cart back to the house, where his car and driver were waiting.

"So, what's next?" Leo asked as we stepped off the cart.

"Well, next you decide if you'd like to purchase our services," I told him. "If you do, then it's five million. You pay two up front, and the rest upon delivery. I'd also like an unnamed favor for myself, redeemable whenever I see fit—and your word that you'll help my friend Wesley here get elected as the next governor of New Mexico."

"I'll have the money wired later today, and you don't have to worry about Wesley. He's already cut his deal for bringing me here."

I glanced at the congressman, who just stood by the cart smugly while Leo handed me a card.

"My cell phone number is on the back. When you need that favor, just pick up the phone and I'll have your back."

I smiled like a Cheshire cat. Having a favor from a man like him was gonna come in mighty damn handy. "Well, that'll be just fine. I'll be sending a truck up north in the next few days. Make sure your people are ready."

"Oh, they will be. You just make sure that damn truck is there," he replied.

"It'll be there. I guarantee it," I stated with certainty, dollar signs dancing in my head. I was so damn happy I felt like I needed my dick sucked again.

Rio

33

I woke up hungover and overwhelmed on a sofa in the basement of my Soho night club. I'd had the place remodeled into a man cave/office for those late nights when I was too tired or too drunk to go home. It also came in handy on those special nights I needed a little privacy. Shaking my head and stretching to get rid of the cobwebs, I spotted my cell phone, an empty bottle of tequila, and Roman Johnson's birth certificate on the glass coffee table. The birth certificate brought back a flood of memories from yesterday, most of which I would have loved to forget. But that wasn't gonna happen.

Sitting up, I checked the time on my phone, ignoring the ton of missed call notifications and text messages I'd received. Shit, it was almost four in the afternoon—not unusual for me, but way past when I had planned on getting up. I dragged my ass to the bathroom to relieve myself, then stripped and got in the shower.

I'd spent half the night drinking tequila, thinking about whether Roman could really be my brother, and the other half calling every hospital in the Bronx, looking for a patient named Margaret Johnson. I finally found her at Mercy General Hospital, where a friendly operator who didn't seem to give a shit about patient privacy informed me that she was in the Critical Care Unit. I planned on paying Margaret Johnson a visit as soon as I got myself something to eat to get rid of my headache.

When I got to Mercy General, my heart was pounding. I had no idea what I would say to this woman when I found her. And what if Roman was there in the room with her? Was I ready to face him yet? I was so damn nervous I swear there was a chance I would fall out and have to be admitted to the hospital myself.

I pictured myself being put in the room right next to Margaret Johnson's. How fucked up would that be?

The door to her room was slightly ajar, so I paused outside, holding my breath and listening for any voices inside the room.

A nurse walking by said, "Mr. Johnson, you can go ahead in. She's in and out of sleep, but she's been asking for you. Your aunt said she'll be back in the morning."

Holy shit! This woman thought I was Roman. But now it was safe to assume that Roman wasn't inside that room. That thought calmed my nerves a little.

"Oh, thanks," I said, then pushed open the door and stepped inside Margaret Johnson's room. It was small, with a couple of weird chairs that probably pulled out into an uncomfortable bed, and a television. In the middle of the room, lying peacefully in the hospital bed, was the woman that I'd come to see. She was surrounded by machines and monitors that were connected to her through all kinds of tubes that snaked out from under her blanket. I eased closer to her, studying her face to see if she bore any resemblance to me.

Her eyes fluttered open, and she smiled. "There's my Roman."

I opened my mouth to speak, but nothing came out. She lifted her hand and reached for me. I stared for a moment, then put my hands in hers. This was it, the chance I'd been waiting for to get answers to the questions that had been swirling around in my brain ever since I found that birth certificate. Was this woman my birth mother? Was I adopted? Or even worse, had I been abducted from her at birth? If so, had she been looking for me? And where was my birth father? There was no man in any of the pictures at her house, and no father named on Roman's birth certificate. Was he dead? In jail? A deadbeat? I had so many questions, and the answer to any one of them threatened to upend everything I thought I knew about myself.

We held hands for a few seconds, but then her smile faded.

"You're not my Roman," she said, pulling her hand back and gazing at me. "Your hands are way too soft." She stared at me a while longer. "You . . . you're one of the other babies."

"Yes." I didn't really understand what she meant by "other babies," but I didn't want her to stop talking, so I pulled one of the chairs closer to the bed and sat down. I took her hand again, caressing it gently. "It's all right. I'm Rio."

She gasped, indicating that she recognized my name. "Rio. I always loved that name."

Oh, shit. This was really happening. My stomach became tied up in knots.

"Rio," she repeated then closed her eyes like she was done talking. Her breathing slowed, and within seconds, she was asleep again.

No, no, no, no! I screamed in my head, willing her to wake up. I needed answers, but this woman couldn't stay awake long enough to talk to me. What the hell was I going to do now?

Roman

34

"Man, let's go," I said to Denny, who was dozing off in the front passenger's seat, much like Li'l Al, who was knocked out against the driver's side door, snoring. We'd been waiting in the warehouse district of New Rochelle up in Westchester for Lex's mystery truck, but the only thing that had shown up were a couple of hookers and their johns.

"What? Nah, we can't leave," he said. "Ain't no way we gonna walk away from this easy money. Money that you need."

"Man, I'm sick of sitting here. It's four in the fucking morning. We been here all night." I exhaled in frustration, tapping Al's shoulder to wake him up. "Yo, start the car. Let's get outta here."

"Huh?" Li'l Al sat up and looked around. "It's here?"

"No, it ain't here. We leaving," I told him.

"Hold up, Rome." Denny sat up and looked out the back window. "You hear that?"

I turned in the same direction, but I didn't see or hear anything. "I don't hear shit except my stomach telling me it's time to go get something to eat. Let's get the hell outta here."

"Nah, for real. You don't hear that?" Denny asked. "It's getting closer."

Al cracked his window and listened.

"Yo, Rome, he's right." Li'l Al pointed. "Here it comes."

"I told you," Denny said excitedly, grabbing his mask and putting it over his face.

I glanced in the rearview mirror and still saw nothing. Then I turned all the way around in my seat and squinted. Sure enough, I saw something flash in the distance, coming toward us.

"Are those headlights?" I asked.

"Get ready. Let's go," Denny said.

"Wait. We need to make sure that's the truck we're supposed to cop."

"It's gotta be. Ain't no other damn truck out here. Not at this time of the morning."

I grabbed my own mask and gun in preparation, then we sat in complete silence and waited for the large tractor trailer to drive past us. Sure enough, it was blue with Texas plates. It was the damn truck. As it maneuvered a few feet away from the warehouse, Denny and I slipped out of the van and crouched down in the darkness, moving swiftly toward it. Li'l Al waited in the van, same as always, until we signaled. We'd perfected our method of approach over time: Denny always covered the passenger's side, while I focused on the driver's side. It wasn't the first time we'd jacked a truck, but this was our first time doing one of this nature. All of them required patience and precision.

I waited for the perfect moment to make my move. As soon as I heard the engine cut off, I stepped on the small bar at the bottom of the truck, grabbed the door handle, and yanked it open.

"Give me the keys, bitch!" I growled.

The driver, a black dude in his thirties, was taken by surprise. "What the fuck?"

I had to use one hand to steady myself on the cabin of the truck, but with the other, I pointed my gun in his face. At that same moment, the passenger-side door opened, and Denny hopped in.

"You heard what the man said. Give him the fucking keys, or we can just take them ourselves after we kill your ass."

I knew Denny wasn't gonna shoot him, but he sure as hell sounded convincing.

"Man, shit." The driver reluctantly took the keys out of the ignition and handed them to me, then held his hands up, shaking his head. "I'm telling y'all, you don't wanna do this. This ain't no regular truck, and this ain't no regular shipping company. These crackers will kill your asses."

"And I'm telling you to shut the fuck up," Denny said.

"Where's the fucking GPS?" I asked.

"What?" The driver frowned.

"The GPS, nigga. Don't act like you don't know what the fuck I'm talking about. Where the fuck is it?"

He reached into an open compartment above him and pointed at a small black box. "It's bolted in."

"We know." Denny reached into a bag around his chest and pulled out a ratchet set, then began going to work on the GPS.

"Hand over your wallet and your fucking cell phone," I demanded, pushing my gun up against his skull. He didn't waste any time reaching into his pocket and giving them to me. "Good. Now, get the fuck out the truck."

I kept my gun aimed at him as I hopped to the ground and watched him climb out. Denny came around to the driver's side, handing me the GPS, which I smashed on the ground with the guy's phone, stomping them until they were a useless pile of plastic and glass. The driver had dropped down and curled into the fetal position, practically inviting me to kick his ass. But I didn't have time for that shit. I yanked him off the concrete and shoved him toward the large container connected to the back of the truck.

"What's your name?" I asked.

He remained silent.

I was tempted to punch him in the head, but I suppose I was feeling generous, so I decided a verbal threat would do. "Look, you're already having a bad day. Would you like to add a bullet in your head to it?" I pressed the gun a little harder into his back. "Now, what's your fucking name? And remember, I already got your wallet, so ain't no sense in tryna lie."

"Johnny Brooks," he said.

"Okay, Johnny, open this bitch up!" I commanded.

"I–I–I can't," he stammered.

"Why the fuck not?" Denny came closer and pressed the barrel of his gun against Johnny's temple.

"It's got some kinda digital safe attached to it. You gotta have a code. I don't have the code."

Denny looked it over and nodded his head. "He ain't lying. This shit is high tech as hell for a beat-up old truck like this."

I glanced over at Denny and motioned for him to come beside me. With my gun still pointed at Johnny, we had an impromptu meeting to discuss the situation.

"What's the hold up? Let's get the fuck outta her," Denny whispered.

"Before we go, I wanna know what the fuck is in that damn truck. Think about it. If Lex is offering us two hundred grand, whatever's inside's gotta be worth a couple mil. We might be playing ourselves and getting the short end of the stick. You know how Lex is."

Denny shrugged. "I hear ya, but we might not be able to get rid of whatever the fuck is inside like Lex can. Let's just get the fucking truck to Lex and get our money, man."

I walked back over to Johnny. "What's in the truck? And don't fucking lie!"

"I . . . I don't even know. My boss don't tell me shit. I just pick up and drop off. That's it. But he's fucking crazy, and if y'all don't kill me, either way I'm still a fuckin' dead man, and so are you," Johnny said, hunched over and clenching his stomach.

"What do you think is in it?" I peered at him.

"I honestly don't know, but the only way to describe it is contraband," he said.

"What the fuck is contraband?" Denny asked.

"The kinda shit you don't report to the police when niggas like us steal it from you," I explained, then signaled for Li'l Al. He raced over and took the keys from me, then climbed into the truck. I snatched Johnny away and tossed him to the opposite side so he wouldn't get run over. Then, Denny and I ran to get into the van.

"Watch your back!" Johnny shouted after us. "Those crackers are gonna kill us all!"

"What the hell is he jibber-jabbering about?" Denny asked.

"Nothin'. Call Lex and tell him we got the truck," I told Denny as we waited for Li'l Al to turn the truck around to follow us.

"And tell that Israeli bastard that we don't want a hundred grand a piece anymore. We want two hundred grand."

Denny turned and looked at me. "You sure about that?"

"I'm a man with balls the size of coconuts," I said, imitating Lex's accent. "Of course I'm sure."

KD

35

I woke up to the sound of the damn rooster crowing and Tyler fucking the hell out of some broad in his bedroom, which surprised me. He usually didn't bring those heifers home. Ah, what the hell. It was his house too, and he was a grown-ass man, so he could fuck whoever he wanted.

I got out of the bed and took my morning dump before heading to the kitchen to put on a pot of coffee. While I was waiting for it to brew, I took out some taters, some eggs, and a slab of that thick country bacon for Patrick to cook for breakfast. I usually enjoyed my first cup of coffee while reading the *New York Times* on my tablet to see how the fake news had smeared our great president, but before I could even pull up that liberal piece of shit, I was hit by a notification that damn near gave me a heart attack.

"Shiiiiit," I mumbled, looking down at my tablet again to make sure my eyes weren't playing tricks on me. It only took me a second or two to realize they weren't, and I hauled ass to the back of the house.

"Tyler!" I burst up into his room. I'd caught the boy on the downstroke, but I didn't rightly care—at least until I saw that he wasn't just fucking some gold-digging piece of white trash. He was fucking . . .

"Lizbeth!"

"Hey, KD." Elizabeth covered herself, but she didn't look embarrassed. In fact, I think she was kinda glad I knew they were fucking.

"Daddy, what is wrong with you?" Tyler yelled.

"I'm deeply sorry to have walked in on you two like this," I said in my sincerest voice, "but Tyler, our truck's gone missing. The damn GPS is off again."

"You mean the truck going to New York and to that Greer fella in Connecticut?"

"That's the truck."

"Fuck, Daddy!" Tyler climbed out of bed and found his boxers, slipping them on. "Did you call Johnny?"

"No, but I'm gonna call his ass right now." In my haste to tell Tyler, I hadn't even thought about calling Johnny. I pulled my phone out of my pocket and found his number in my contacts. The fucking thing went straight to voicemail.

"I'm gonna kill that black son of a bitch," I grumbled.

"You think he's out getting some pussy again?" He glanced over at Elizabeth and tried to clean it up. "I mean . . . going to see that woman again? Sorry, Liz, I've got work to do."

"Don't be. You boys handle your business. Me and you have plenty of time to have fun in the sheets." She got out of that bed naked as the day she was born and kissed my son like a damn movie star, then smiled at me, making me blush. God, I loved that gal. She picked up her clothes and headed to the bathroom.

"Tyler, as far as Johnny's concerned, I don't give a shit if he was getting some pussy or not. That don't change the fact that we told him not to."

"What we gonna do now?"

"I don't rightly know. But we got to get that shipment to Greer." I looked down at my phone again. "It's six thirty here, which mean it's eight thirty in New York. The first drop-off is nine o'clock. I guess we sit here and pray. If we're lucky, he'll be making the drop in thirty minutes."

"And if not?"

We call Slick and tell him to kill that son of a bitch Johnny," I said directly. "'Cause I'm gonna be out six million dollars. Five from Greer, and another million from the delivery to the people in New York."

Vegas

36

"Fuck!"

It was a miracle I didn't break through the sheetrock—or worse, hit a stud and break my hand—when I pounded the wall in the hallway. I'd just flipped out on Consuela's selfish ass after she came to tell me that Nevada hadn't come back to her hotel suite. He'd been gone all night. I was usually better at keeping my rage in check, but my son's disappearance had me on tilt, and it was better to hit the wall than to hit Consuela. Truthfully, though, I knew I shouldered some of the blame myself. I should have been over there checking on him every day.

"It's gonna be okay, son. This isn't your fault," Pop said as if he knew exactly what I was thinking. I hadn't even realized he'd followed me out of the room.

"Then whose fault is it? I'm his father. I should have gone looking for him yesterday when Ma came home and said he left the hotel."

"We didn't know he'd run away then," Pop said calmly.

"We would have if Consuela had called to say he didn't come home last night, instead of waiting until noon. My son's been missing for twenty-four hours."

"I know, Vegas. Kids run away from home, but they usually come back. Are you forgetting that you ran away when you were fifteen?" he reminded me. "Was that my fault?"

I turned slowly toward him. "Yeah, actually, it was your fault. You blamed me for stealing parts for my car when it was that sheisty-ass parts manger you had working for you."

He chuckled, lowering his head. "Yeah, that was my fault, wasn't it? That guy was robbing us blind."

"You damn right he was, and you blamed me." I didn't want to, but I laughed. Once again, my old man had used humor on me to lighten the mood.

He placed a hand on my shoulder. "We'll find him. I promise you that."

He gestured for me to follow him into his home office, where he went straight to the bar and poured two large drinks. He handed me one, then sat down at his desk. "Drink this. It'll help calm you down so you can think straight."

I gulped down half of the smooth liquor, then took a seat in a chair in front of his desk. "I really should've checked up on him more. I just didn't want him to see me and Consuela fight all the time."

"We're not going to worry about what could've been done. Right now, we're going to focus on what you're gonna do once we find him. And again, we *are* going to find him," Pop emphasized. "I've got Junior pinging his phone. We should know something soon."

"Thanks, Pop," I said, finishing off my drink. "I guess we should go back in there with Ma and Consuela." I moved to stand up, but he shook his head to stop me.

"Let your mother deal with her for a while. There's something we need to talk about."

"What's that?" I settled back in the seat.

"You, of all my children, have always been your own man. But moving forward, there has to be some sort of resolution between you and Consuela. She's not the type of woman to be ignored." Pop spoke in that do-as-I-say voice he used when he was making a demand, not a suggestion. "Sometimes a man has to make sacrifices for his family. You need to do this for your son."

"Are you suggesting I sleep with her?" Obviously, my mother had told him what Consuela wanted. I guess they really didn't keep secrets from each other.

"It's not like you never took one for the team before. Hell, you spent five years in prison for a crime I committed."

"That was different."

"Was it? You went to jail because it was the best thing for the family. You gonna tell me that sleeping with your son's mother to keep Nevada from running away again or being shipped off to a boarding school isn't just as worth it?" He was dead serious, and I hated to admit it, but he made a good point.

"I can't believe we're having this conversation."

"I can't believe we didn't have it when she first showed up at the house with him a few years back. We all have our idiosyncrasies, Vegas. I've been where you're at with Donna and Lou."

I stared at him, waiting for him to elaborate, which he didn't. So I asked, "Did you sleep with Aunt Donna to keep the peace? Because I know she offered it to you."

"Hell no!" Pop said adamantly. "But that was different. The circumstances were different."

"How? How was it different?" I was not about to let him off the hook. This had been a source of contention between us for years.

"You're not afraid of Consuela or Marie. I love Chippy more than life itself, but I'm also afraid of her."

I chuckled my understanding. "Ma can be a little scary, can't she?"

"You have no idea. I've woken up to a gun in my face more than once." Pop said it so sincerely that I didn't think he was exaggerating. I'd have that image in my head for a while.

"Now," he continued, "back to my grandson. Vegas, Nevada only has two years of high school left. We're not talking about a life sentence. I know it's been a few years, but Consuela's not an ugly woman."

"No, she's not, but can you hear yourself?"

"Loud and clear. The question is, do you hear me?" He leaned forward, looking me in the eyes.

"I do." I couldn't believe I was even considering what he was saying. "What about Marie? What the hell am I supposed to tell her?"

"You're a smart man. I'm sure you'll think of something."

My phone rang with an unfamiliar number. I answered it without hesitation, thinking it could be Nevada.

"Hello?"

"Vegas, man, it's Johnny." His speech sounded slurred.

"Johnny Brooks?" I could feel Pop watching me.

"Yeah," he confirmed. "I need to see you, brother. Can . . . can we meet up?"

"I'm handling something with my son right now, Johnny. Let me hit you back after I deal with this."

"Vegas, you . . . you don't understand. This is important, man. I really need to talk to you," Johnny pleaded.

"J, you been drinking?"

"A little. But only because of what's happening. I need to see you, man."

I liked Johnny, I really did, but I couldn't deal with his drinking at the moment. "I'm sorry, man, but I gotta take care of this thing with my son."

"Aw, damn. A'ight, handle that. But when you finish, man, hit me back. Please. It's life or death." Johnny hung up.

I held my phone for a second, totally confused by our conversation.

"That was Johnny Brooks?" Pop asked.

"Yeah," I said. "He's drinking again."

"That's too bad. He came by the shop a few weeks ago, looking for you. I offered him a drink, but he turned me down. Said he'd been sober for a couple of years."

"Well, he ain't sober now. What'd he want, anyway? Money?"

"No. He said he had a good job. We were supposed to talk, but he saw fat-ass KD Shrugs and hauled ass out of there."

What the hell was KD Shrugs doing in New York and at our shop? I wondered.

"If I didn't know better, I'd think KD and Johnny knew each other," Pop said.

"They do. I helped Johnny get a job with Tyler when he got outta rehab," I told him.

"Tyler Shrugs?" Pop raised his voice.

"Yeah, he was calling around, looking for reliable drivers to drive shipments across the border. Johnny was sober at the time, so I thought it was okay. He's been driving with them for over three years."

"Dammit." Pop exhaled hard. "I wish you had told me this."

"What's wrong? I knew you didn't want Johnny driving for us, so I sent him down there with Tyler. What's the big deal?"

"The big deal is KD Shrugs and his cronies may represent the biggest threat to our business that we've ever seen."

"Pot-belly KD Shrugs? He's not even a sheriff anymore." I shrugged. "How's he gonna hurt us?"

"He's not a sheriff, but Tyler's moving up the ranks of the Texas Highway Patrol fast. With his father's guidance, which could be more dangerous."

"So, what's his problem, anyway?"

"KD doesn't like that we've been calling the shots the past few years when it comes to distribution on the East Coast and in the South. There was a time when that was his job, and we had to bow down and kiss his ass to move product."

"Fuck that redneck bastard and his Barney Fife son," I said, starting to get pissed off.

"I feel the same way, but don't sleep on him. He's had a taste of power, and we both know how intoxicating that can be. He's been putting together a war chest, using some secret business that a lot of our friends are concerned about. With Trump in the White House, all of a sudden KD's gaining political favor."

"What kind of business?"

"I don't know, but whatever it is, it's a moneymaker. He's been using our marijuana shipments and protections as a Trojan horse to move it."

I glanced over at my father. I hadn't seen him look so worried since my Uncle Larry escaped from the nuthouse two years ago. He wouldn't admit it, but he was more concerned about this shit than he was about Nevada.

"Do we have a plan?" Pops had taught me to have a plan and a backup plan. I'd been in situations with him where even the backup had a backup plan.

"I shut down our weed operation in hopes that it might slow him down, but he has other clients. It also might just have pissed him off and made him more determined. I've also been work-ing with the new president of the National Sheriffs Association, Derrick Hughes out of Fulton County, Georgia," Pop said. Something in my old man's voice didn't sound right.

"Derrick's a cop, but he's a good brother," I replied. "So what's he gonna do for us?"

"He took a few other sheriffs down to have a talk with KD. The sheriffs from Arkansas and Tennessee made it home just fine, but Derrick and Sheriff Andy Wilkins from Augusta never made it back. They vanished—along with their car."

"What the fuck happened to them?" This was not good at all.

"Nobody knows. Their cell phones were found in the swamp near Shreveport."

"And you think it was Shrugs?" I asked, though I already knew the answer.

"I know it was KD Shrugs, and so do the other sheriffs. We just can't prove it. But I'll get to the bottom of it. I hired someone to find out what he's up to. We should know something in the next day or so, but . . ." He paused when there was a knock on the door. "Come in."

Junior walked in with a frown on his face.

"You ping my son's phone?" I asked him.

"Yep, but nothing came back. Either Nevada's battery's dead, or he's turned off his phone." Junior took a seat next to me.

"Okay," Pop said. "Now I'm worried."

Rio

37

I was exhausted in every way possible: mentally, physically, emotionally. I'd stayed in Margaret's room the entire night. Most of that time, she drifted in and out of consciousness, or maybe she was just sleeping. Hell, I didn't really know. Either way, she wasn't alert. Her hand held mine the entire time, and when I shifted slightly to remove my fingers from hers, her eyes fluttered open.

"No, don't leave me," she whispered. "Not yet."

"I have to go . . . Miss Margaret." I was still unsure of what to call her. I mean, despite the recent revelation, I didn't feel comfortable calling her Mama or anything like that. Those epithets were reserved for the woman who'd raised me.

"Can you come back tomorrow? Roman will be here, and I'd like for you to meet . . . your brother," she pleaded. "I'm dying. I know I am. Please, I need to tell both of you."

"Tell me now," I said.

"Tomorrow, with Roman," she whispered and drifted off again.

It wasn't much information, but she had at least acknowledged that Roman was my brother. No more wondering about that.

I slipped out of the room when she was finally in a deep sleep, and I spent the ride home struggling with this new reality. Who was I? At one point, I reached for my phone to call the one person that I usually told everything, but I put it down when I realized this wasn't something I could say to her over the phone. This news would affect Paris too, and I had to give it to her face to face.

I pulled into our driveway and parked behind a black SUV that I didn't recognize. Inside, I heard my parents, along with Junior and Vegas, talking in the living room. Then I heard Consuela's voice and realized it must have been her car outside. Even if I was ready to talk to my parents about Roman Johnson, now wasn't the time.

I was about to make a beeline upstairs to my room when Paris appeared.

"Where the hell have you been? I been calling your ass forever."

"Sorry. I had to take care of something important. I had my phone on Do Not Disturb."

"For the entire damn night?"

"I said sorry, Paris." I turned to leave, but she snapped at me.

"Look, I saw Sebastian's little IG post saying his heart is in New York, but just because y'all are fucking again doesn't mean you get to ignore your family. There's important shit going on, you know."

I glanced toward the living room, where I could still hear everyone's voices. "I know. I have something important to tell you too."

"Not as important as the fact that Nevada's been missing since the day before yesterday," she said.

"That ain't funny, Paris." She always said stupid shit just to get me riled up. She knew how close my nephew and I were.

"I'm not laughing, Rio. Serious shit, he's run away. That's why Consuela's here." Paris tilted her head in the direction of the family room.

"What the fuck's going on? Why would he run away?" I put aside Roman, Margaret, and any other bullshit that was clouding my mind. Nevada was my little man.

"Everyone seems to think it's because he didn't wanna go to boarding school," she replied. "Not that I could blame him."

"This is fucked up." I turned and headed toward the family room with Paris hot on my trail. "I thought Mom was supposed to talk to Consuela about that."

"Apparently not before Nevada went ghost."

They all turned to look at me as I strode into the room.

"Rio, have you heard from Nevada at all today?" My mother walked over and touched my arm, her face full of worry.

Vegas stood up from the sofa. "Is that why you been ignoring our calls? I swear, Rio, if you know where my son is, you'd better tell me."

"I haven't talked to him in a couple of days," I told him. "You know if I did, I'd tell you."

"Can you think of anywhere he'd be?" my mother asked.

"I told you he's probably with that girl," Consuela snapped. She was trying to play hard, but her red eyes were evidence she'd been crying.

"And I keep asking you what girl you're talking about, Consuela." Vegas shook his head.

"It was the girl at the library," she barked back at him. "He said they went to school together, but she was studying from a GED book. How many times do I have to tell you this?"

"Does this girl have a name?" Dad asked.

Consuela folded her arms and shrugged. "I don't . . . I can't remember."

"Have you all checked his social media? Maybe there's something there. A picture of the girl?" I took out my phone and pulled up Nevada's Instagram. "What'd she look like?"

"She was pretty. Black mixed with something, probably Asian," Consuela replied.

Vegas and I locked eyes, confirming we were both thinking the same thing.

"You think?" I asked Vegas.

He nodded.

I looked down at my phone and began scrolling until I came to the photo from the day we went to the water park. I walked over to Consuela and showed her the screen. "Is this her?"

"Sí! That's the girl he was with at the library. You know where she lives?"

I looked over at Vegas. I didn't want to say anything that might make things worse. Consuela could fly off the handle pretty easily, and this information wouldn't sit well with her.

"I know where to find her," Vegas said.

"You do? Where?" Consuela asked.

He didn't answer right away, probably trying to figure out a way to handle this without mentioning the M word.

"Vegas?" Consuela said. "What are you not telling me?"

He took a deep breath. "She stays at Marie's."

Consuela narrowed her eyes at him. "What did you say?" I could hear the rage simmering in her voice.

"She works for Marie," Vegas admitted.

And why the hell did he do that? Consuela jumped up and started cursing in Spanish, her arms flying everywhere like she wanted to punch someone.

"Shit," my mother muttered under her breath.

Pop moved quickly in front of Consuela in an effort to defuse the situation before it exploded.

"The important thing is we know where she is. Vegas, you and I are going to head over there to talk to her. Your mother will stay here with Consuela to coordinate things. Rio, you check Nevada's desktop computer to see what you can find," Pop instructed. "Paris, go get Sasha and head out to the house in the Hamptons. Maybe we'll get lucky and he's out there. Junior, go have a talk with our friends at the Port Authority and make sure Nevada hasn't purchased a ticket out of town. And ping his phone again."

"No!" Consuela shouted. "I am not staying here. I am going to that bitch's place and burn it down if she doesn't give me my son."

My mother stood up. "No, you're not. You're going to do exactly what LC said because you don't want your son to hate you. You want him to come back here and hug you. To say he's sorry and that he loves you. You go over there and humiliate him, and he may never speak to you again. He's not a little boy anymore, Consuela. It doesn't matter how much we want him to be."

Consuela didn't reply, but Ma's speech did take some of the steam out of her. She sat back down, glaring at Vegas the whole time. Pop reiterated his instructions, and we all quickly disbanded without further questions, happy to leave my mother to deal with a pissed off Consuela.

I was halfway up the stairs headed to Nevada's room when my phone rang.

"Hey, Sebastian. Look, I'm in the middle of a crisis. Can I call you back?"

"Yeah, sure, but I been thinking about this situation you're in, and there's something you should think about before you go running around telling everybody about this Roman guy."

"And what's that?" I really didn't like that he was trying to dictate what I told my family.

"Your mother was pregnant with twins, right?"

"Yeah."

"You and this Roman look identical, right?"

"You tell me. It was your people who thought he was me down at the club," I shot back.

"Rio, that's not fair. I didn't—"

"Look, I told you I have a lotta shit going on here right now, and I'm really stressed out. Just get to the point, Sebastian," I said.

"Fine. What if Paris was switched at birth? What if she's the one who may not be a Duncan?"

He was making my head hurt. "Do you know what you're saying?"

"Hey, you know I like Paris. That's why I'm telling you to slow your roll and think this through before you go telling anyone about that birth certificate. This could seriously change your family dynamic and fuck some things up in a big way."

I paused for a second as his words settled in my mind. His theory actually made some sense, and that scared the hell out of me. Paris had always been my twin, my second half, my best fucking friend. What would happen to her—to us!—if all of a sudden she wasn't a Duncan?

"Rio, you there?" Sebastian snapped me out of my nightmarish thoughts.

"Why did you have to put that shit in my head?"

"I'm sorry. I just thought it was something you should think about before you tell Paris about Roman." He paused. "Shit, you didn't tell Paris yet, did you?"

"No, I didn't tell Paris yet."

"Tell me what?"

I froze at the sound of her voice, then turned around slowly. Paris was standing right behind me. I pulled the phone away from my ear and stared at her. DNA or not, she was still my sister, and I loved her. The last thing on this earth I wanted to do was hurt her, and by revealing the secret about Roman, I would hurt her deeply. Being a Duncan was important to me, but it was everything to Paris. Losing that identity would be the equivalent of me ripping out her heart with my bare hands.

"Sabastian wants us to come down to South Beach next month for his birthday party." It wasn't a lie. He had asked us to come, just not during this conversation.

"Tell him I'm there. I could use a little fun in the sun."

"Yo, Sebastian, I'll call you and we can finish this conversation later," I said into the phone and then ended the call without a goodbye.

"Is that what you needed to tell me earlier?" she asked as we headed down the hall.

"Yeah, that was it," I said before ducking into Nevada's room to search his computer for clues.

Vegas

38

"Hey, baby, has anyone heard from him?" Marie greeted me with a hug and wrapped her arms around my neck. The deep frown lines in her forehead let me know that she was just as worried as I was.

"No, not yet," I said as Pop and I followed her into her office. When we walked inside, I was surprised to see Bubba, the head of security, waiting. He was normally posted where he could monitor who went up and down the spiral staircase that led to the suites.

"Hey, Vegas."

"Bubba." I nodded, then turned to Marie. "Did you talk to Kia?"

"Well, before we get to that, Bubba has something to tell you," Marie said.

My attention went back to the giant of a man. "What's up?"

"Your son was here the other day, Vegas. But I swear I didn't know who he was when I caught him." Bubba looked down.

"Nevada was here?" My voice escalated as I turned to my fiancée. "And nobody said anything to me?"

"I just found out about this ten minutes ago, sweetheart," Marie explained. "Apparently he came by to see Kia."

"Where is this girl?" Pop demanded.

"She's not here," Marie said. "No one has seen her since Nevada disappeared. Bubba checked her room right before you got here. He found their phones and your son's laptop. They're in her room."

"Go get it!" I yelled, glancing at Pop. That was Nevada's doing. He knew we'd be tracking his phone and internet use. Obviously, he wasn't going to make this easy. "And go get Danielle. No way she doesn't know where Kia is."

Bubba moved faster than I would've expected. He returned a few minutes later with the electronics from Kia's room. Danielle was with him.

"Young lady, where is my grandson?" Pop asked immediately.

"Huh? I don't know." Danielle shrugged. "I didn't do anything. Am I in trouble?"

"Not as long as you're telling the truth," I said, the threat evident in my tone. "Now, where the hell are Kia and Nevada?"

"Seriously, I don't know where she went," Danielle said, sounding annoyed by the questions.

"Danielle, listen. This is not a game we're playing. We need to know where the hell they are. Now ain't the time for you to be trying to hold on to girl code or whatever the hell it is y'all do," I warned. "You need to tell me what you know."

Danielle's eyes went from Marie to me. "I don't know nothing, Vegas. I swear to God. I didn't even think she was with Nevada. I thought she was somewhere with Bob."

"Damn, you right. Bob didn't show up today, didn't he?" Bubba chimed in.

I turned to Marie. "Who the fuck is Bob?"

"He's Kia's biggest client," she said.

"Biggest? That's an understatement. He tips her more than it costs for the date. Everything she has, Bob gave it to her: bags, shoes, jewelry, hair, makeup, you name it. Whatever she wants, she can have. I should've snatched his nerdy, cornball ass when I had the chance. If I knew then what I know now." Danielle shook her head. "He wants to marry her."

"Biggest as in every day, sometimes twice a day," Marie clarified.

"What's his phone number? I need to talk to him," I told Marie. "As a matter of fact, give me his address too. I can go find him myself."

"Vegas, I can't give you my client's private information." She said it like it was a ridiculous request.

"What do you mean, you can't? This is my son we're talking about! Your future stepson."

"My clients expect confidentiality. It's the mainstay of my business. I can't just go around giving you their addresses and numbers."

"You think I give a shit about some pussy-paying mother-fucker's privacy right now? 'Cause I don't! This is my son we're talking about, Marie! Now, either you give it to me, or give me back that fucking ring on your finger." I stepped toward her, and Bubba went into defense mode and jumped to Marie's side.

"Calm down, Vegas," he warned.

I almost felt sorry for poor Bubba. Big as he was, he knew he couldn't take me. Hell, I'd taught him a few take downs. "You better sit your big ass down, Bubba, 'cause it's a long way to the floor."

"Bubba, please sit down," Marie told him.

I felt Pop's hand on my shoulder. "Let's all just calm down for a second. Marie, how about you call this Bob guy now while we're here? That way you can still maintain his privacy."

Marie looked at me like she wanted to slap me as she sat down at her desk and started typing into her computer. I guess I'd embarrassed her in front of Pop and her employees. I tilted my head back and exhaled. Snapping on my fiancée wasn't my intention, but she needed to learn that when it came to my son, she was either with me or against me.

She picked up the phone and dialed a number, then put it on speakerphone so we all could hear. The first call she made went straight to voicemail, but thankfully, the second call was answered.

"Copy Hut." A woman answered.

"Uh, hello, I'm looking for Bob Jessup. Is he available?" Marie said.

"He's not here. Can I take a message?" From her girlish voice, I could tell she was a younger employee.

"My name is Marie. I needed to talk to him about a large order for my business."

"I'm sorry, miss. Bobby is on vacation with his girlfriend," the woman said.

"Good for him. I didn't know he had a girlfriend."

"I know, right? Neither did we." The young woman tried to contain a laugh. She sounded like the type that loved to gossip. "Is there anything I can help you with?"

"No, he was the one who thought up the idea. Where did they venture off to? He's not answering his cell phone."

"I don't know exactly, but when I talked to him, he was excited because he'd just left the Dr. Pepper museum. Bobby loves Dr. Pepper. It's his favorite soda." She giggled.

"Okay, well, thank you so much," Marie said. "When I talk to Bob, I'll be sure to tell him how pleasant you are on the phone with customers."

"Thanks. Maybe he'll give me a raise."

"She's lying," Bubba said after Marie ended the call. "There's no such thing as a Dr. Pepper museum."

"Nah, she's not lying," I said, holding up my phone so they could see the results of my Google search. "There actually is a Dr. Pepper museum."

"There is? Where?" Pop asked.

"In Waco, Texas," I said. "And If Nevada's with Kia and Kia's with Bob, then they're in fucking Texas."

"How can you be sure?" Danielle asked skeptically.

"We can't, but there's only one way to find out," I replied. "We're gonna have to go down to Texas."

"Well, at least it's not El Paso," Pop said halfheartedly.

Nevada

39

I'd been lying there, staring at the cracked mirrored ceiling for hours, and to say I was uncomfortable and bored was an understatement. To begin with, the dingy bed I was laying in was hard as a rock, the sheets were scratchy, and the pillows were lumpy. It was a far cry from the bed I'd been sleeping in at the hotel with Mom or my bed at home. But the bed seemed luxurious compared to the nasty stained comforter, which I'd thrown in a corner five minutes after I entered the room. To top it off, the TV was broken, along with the showerhead in the bathroom.

The only silver lining so far was that I wasn't in Texas alone. Kia was there with me. Well, technically, she was in another room at the motel, but still, we were together.

Getting to Texas had been quite an adventure so far. The day my grandmother came by to visit at the hotel and my mother dismissed me, I'd gone into my room and started digging a little deeper into Kia's sister's arrest records. They turned out to be extensive and spread out through Tennessee, South Carolina, Louisiana, and most recently, in Waco, Texas. I couldn't wait to tell Kia, so I slipped out of the suite through the bedroom exit and went to Marie's Hellfire Club.

"So, she's in Texas?" Kia asked when I told her what I'd discovered.

"She was a couple of days ago. I'm gonna go find out."

"What do you mean, you're gonna go find out?" She looked at me like I was crazy. "You can't do that, Nevada."

"Look, my mother is about to ship me off to boarding school. I promised you I'd help you find your sister, but if I'm gonna do it, I gotta go now before my dad and grandpa find out. They've made a living tracking people down," I said.

Kia shook her head. "Well, I'm not letting you go to Texas by yourself. I'm coming with you. She's my sister. I need to be there."

"No. You have to, uh, work," I said. "I don't want you to get in trouble with Marie."

"Marie's my boss, not my pimp. I work when I wanna work, and if I don't, then that's on me," she said, equally defiant. "Now, how the hell are we getting to Texas?"

There was no way I could get on a plane, train, or bus without running the risk of getting caught by my family, who I knew would be out in full force looking for me once they discovered I was gone. I only had one option.

"We can hitchhike."

"Hitchhike? Are you trying to end up in the hands of a serial killer?" She sighed. "No, I have a better idea."

"What is it?"

"You're just going to have to trust me. I'll get us to Texas. You okay with that?" She stared into my eyes. Even if I didn't trust her, I still would've said yes.

I didn't even realize I hadn't answered her question until she said, "Nevada?"

"Yeah." I nodded. "If you think can pull it off, do it."

That was a day and a half ago, and she was right. She'd gotten us to Texas. I just wasn't so sure how happy I was about how we'd gotten there.

I heard a knock on the door, and I jumped up from the bed to open it. I was greeted by Kia's smiling face. Seeing her standing there was like somebody had plugged me in and repowered my battery. I was grinning from ear to ear.

"Good morning," she said.

"Morning." I wanted to hug her but decided against it when friggin' Bob walked up and affectionately placed his arm around Kia. She looked embarrassed.

Bob was a bald, middle-aged, out-of-shape white guy who owned a Copy Hut store in Manhattan. He was one of Kia's regular clients and very much in love with her, which was apparent in his willingness to drop everything and drive us to Texas. This guy had been kissing her rear the entire way down to Texas.

"You ready?" Kia asked.

I looked up at Bob with his arm around her and simply said, "Yeah, I'm ready. I just have to get my backpack."

"Good. I've calculated we'll only need one bathroom stop until our destination," Bob replied, pushing back his Coke-bottle glasses, which kept sliding down his greasy face. Bob's picture could have been in the dictionary next to the term *degenerate nerd*.

"If we hurry, we can catch McDonald's before breakfast hours end."

"You do know McDonald's serves breakfast all day now," I said.

"That's a very limited menu. But I wouldn't expect someone your age to understand. Your mommy probably tries to keep things very simple for you."

I glanced at Kia, but she just turned and began walking toward the car. When this was all over, I was going to hack this guy's accounts and send all his money to Oprah's school for girls in Africa.

We got into the car and headed to our destination, Waco, which was about an hour from where we were. The entire time he was driving, Bob kept telling Kia how beautiful she was, how he had no problem helping her whenever, wherever, and constantly asking if she was okay.

"Is the air too cold, Kia? Do you need me to turn it down some? Are you hungry? Do you need to stop? You are the most beautiful girl in the world, Kia."

He was making me want to throw up, especially when he reached over and grabbed her hand and kissed it. I felt a slight twinge of jealousy, even though technically we were just friends and there was nothing between us.

"I'm fine, Bobby." Kia smiled and rubbed his arm. She turned to the back seat and gave me a look that said *I'm just going along with this to get what we need*. I shrugged, leaned back in my seat, and went to sleep.

After we arrived in the city of Waco, which really seemed more like a town, Bob asked. "So, where exactly do we need to go, sexy?"

"Find the downtown area," Kia told him.

When he found it, she said, "Just drive. I'll tell you when to stop."

We went up and down the streets of downtown Waco for almost thirty minutes.

"You sure you know where you're going, beautiful?" Bob glanced over at Kia, who was staring out her window.

"Wait. Stop. Pull over there." She pointed at a small shop.

"Here?" Bob asked. "At the Asian foot massage place?"

"Yeah."

"You think she's in there?" I asked.

"It's possible. Asian foot massage is a usually code for massage parlor that offers a whole lot more than foot rubs." Kia slid close to Bob. "Bobby, I need you to go inside and ask for something."

I listened as Kia gave him specific instructions and showed him the mug shot of her sister on her phone. She rubbed his head and whispered something in his ear. Whatever she said, he must have liked it, because he couldn't get out of that van fast enough. I watched him fast-walk into the massage place.

"You okay, Nevada?" she asked, turning to me as soon he exited the car. "I know this is kind of awkward for you."

"Yeah, yeah, I'm good. I mean, I really don't have a choice, do I?" I shrugged. "It's just this dude is kinda weird."

"I know, but he's harmless, and he did drive us all the way here."

"I get it. I'll be okay. I just feel like an outsider. He keeps treating me like I'm a kid," I complained.

"I'll talk to him. I promise." She gave me that look that always gave me butterflies.

"Thanks. So, where'd you guys go this morning?"

"To the Dr. Pepper museum. We were both up, and he wanted to go, so I said yes. No big deal. It was actually a lot cooler than you'd think."

I nodded, and we sat in silence while we waited for Bob, who came out a few minutes later.

"Did you see her? Was she there?" Kia asked him.

"No, she wasn't there. There was a girl who looked like her that they offered me, but you know I only have eyes for you. I would never do that." He reached for her hand, but Kia moved before he could touch it. She looked a little annoyed.

She reached into her purse and took out several bills. "Bobby, listen to me. Take this money and go back in there. Tell them you *really* wanna find this girl and spend time with her."

"She wasn't very friendly when I turned the other girl down. I don't think she'll tell me anything," Bob said, looking at the money.

"You offer her this five hundred dollars, and she'll tell you whatever you want to know. The girls who work at the front desk are just locals. They don't make any real money. It's enough to get the information."

"I don't know about this."

"Well, if you don't think you can handle it, I'm sure Nevada can. Right?" She turned around and held the money out to me.

"No problem." I reached for the cash, but Bob pushed her hand away from me.

"Never send a boy to do a man's job." He glared at me as he stepped out of the car. "I'll be back."

"Bob, the money!" Kia yelled.

"Don't worry. I'll pay whatever," he said as he ran back inside the building.

"Never send a boy to do a man's job." I repeated his words, pretending to be gruff. Kia couldn't help but laugh.

"I told you he's harmless, Nevada. And I really do appreciate you doing this for me. There's no one else I'd rather have going through this with me."

Our eyes met, and we stared at each other for a few seconds. Bob had been right about one thing: she really was the one of the most beautiful girls in the world.

"And if anyone is an outsider, it's him," she continued. "He's doing this because he wants sex. He has some fantasy about who I could be to him, but you're doing this because you're my friend. I know the difference."

"I got it!" Bob announced, ruining the moment as he opened the door.

"What did she tell you?" Kia asked.

"The girl we're looking for works somewhere else."

"Did she tell you where?"

"Not exactly, but she's in El Paso, so I guess that's our next stop." He leaned in to kiss her, and she turned her head.

"You know the rules," Kia chastised him. "No kissing."

Roman

40

After a few days of negotiating with Lex on the phone, we finally got him to agree to pay us the two hundred grand a piece. We were supposed to meet him for the exchange at midnight in a parking lot on the Queens side of the Throgs Neck Bridge. When he pulled up in a passenger van, I was the only one waiting with the truck.

"Where's your partner?" Lex began to inspect the truck the moment he stepped out of the van.

"We decided he should stay somewhere safe just in case this was a setup and you tried to kill us. That way, one of us would be around to return the favor." I smirked.

"I get the premise, but I don't operate that way. It's bad for business." I swear he was looking at that truck like he wanted to make love to it. "Everything looks okay."

"Good, then give us our money," I demanded.

He opened the passenger side door of the van and retrieved a large black bag, then walked over to me. "It's all right here, four hundred K. You boys drive a hard bargain."

"I'm sure you'll make out on the deal."

"Oh, I'll do all right." He handed me the bag. As I reached for it, he pulled it back. "Roman, a little advice."

"What?" I said with an attitude, thinking he was about to give me some bullshit about our money being short.

"You guys need to disappear for a while. Just get in your car and drive out of town immediately. And I'm not talking Atlantic City. I'm talking Colorado or California. Just stay the fuck out of Texas." His tone was dead serious.

"Man, I ain't going nowhere. My mama's in ICU about to have a transplant thanks to this money." I snatched the bag from him.

Before I knew it, Lex collared me and pulled me close. "I like you boys, which is why I'm trying to save your fucking lives. This isn't Louie the Jeweler you've stolen from. These people are animals. Unless you want your sick mama to have to bury your dumb ass, disappear for a couple of weeks. Once I unload this shit, I'm taking off for a few months myself."

"A'ight, Lex, I hear you." I pushed him off of me and straightened my shirt. "What the fuck is in that truck anyway?"

Lex stared at me and said, "You don't wanna know. Now, go."

I jumped in the minivan and headed out of the parking lot to the small road that led to the Clearview Expressway, then quickly veered off to a dirt road and parked behind some bushes. I got out of the van, taking the money with me. I ran up a slight hill, where I found Denny laying down in the grass, looking at the parking lot I'd just left with a pair of binoculars.

"Did he open it yet?

"Nah, he's doing something to it now. Must be some type of electronic unlocking device. I don't know." The story about Denny staying behind as an insurance policy was true, but after driving around playing hide and seek with that truck for two days, we wanted to know what was in it. So, we'd decided to stick around and see.

"You get all the loot?" he asked.

I tapped the bag. "I didn't count it, but it damn sure feels heavy enough to be all there."

"It better be. So, was he pissed about us upping the amount?"

"Nah, not as much you would think," I said. "But he did say we need to lay low for a while. I ain't never seen him act that way. Like, he was all shook."

"Well, with that extra two hundred, we can do that." Denny stuck his fist out, and I bumped it. "Oh, shit! He's got it open." He handed me the binoculars.

"What the fuck?" I mumbled as I watched one, two, three women step out of the truck.

"What's going on?"

I handed the binoculars back to him so he could see.

"What the fuck?" Denny said. "Is he on some human trafficking shit? That truck's full of girls."

"I counted three, but there are more getting out?" I asked.

"I got eight so far," he replied, still peering through the binoculars. "A few of them are running away from him." Denny laughed.

"Heads up. There's another car approaching," I said as a black Jeep Cherokee with tinted windows pulled into the lot. "Must be his buyer."

"I don't think so," Denny replied. "The guy in the Jeep's getting out. White guy in black camouflage. He's got a AK—oh, shit!"

Suddenly, we heard rapid gunfire, and even without binoculars, I could see the three runaways falling as they were gunned down. I'd played my share of video games and even shot a couple of brothers in real life, but I'd never seen anything like this before.

"What the fuck! He—he j—just shot three of them," Denny stammered.

I snatched the binoculars to get a better look. The gunman pulled out a handgun, then walked over to each of the fallen women and put a bullet in their heads to make sure he'd finished the job. He pointed at the truck, and the rest of the women scurried back in. He then turned to Lex, who looked like he was going to shit on himself when the man approached him. I zoomed in with the binoculars to get a good look at this sadistic son of a bitch. Whoever the fuck he was, he looked like something out of the movie *Natural Born Killers*.

"What the fuck is he doing?"

"It looks like he's talking to Lex."

Lex was now down on his knees with his hands clasped, pleading for his life. Lex said something, and then the man lowered his gun as Lex reached into his pocket and handed over his phone. The man studied the phone for a minute and gave a satisfied smile. It looked like old Lex might be okay—until the man raised his handgun and shot him in the head.

I watched him fall backward and then lowered the binoculars. "Fuck."

"Rome, let's get the fuck outta here, man." Denny looked scared shitless. Not that I was feeling very courageous.

"We're not going anywhere until that motherfucker is gone," I said with finality. "Now, stay down. The last thing we wanna do is bump into him on our way out."

Denny nodded his agreement.

I lifted the binoculars and couldn't see the gunman. I almost started to panic because losing sight of him could be dangerous. Then I realized he'd closed up the truck and was in the cab. I heard the truck rumble to a start, and within a minute, it disappeared from the parking lot.

KD

41

By the time I'd swallowed the third shot of bourbon, I was feeling quite nice. It was only ten in the morning, but I'd been sitting at the airport bar for an hour and had no plans to leave any time soon. My eyes were glued on the TV screen, where some broad on the news was talking about three women and a man being killed under the Throgs Neck Bridge. What the dumb bitch hadn't mentioned was that those girls were worth a hundred and twenty grand a piece, and they belonged to me.

"Morning, KD."

I turned around to see Slick pulling out the bar stool beside me.

"Well, if it ain't Superman just flown in to save old KD's ass. I gotta tell you, I'm mighty impressed with the work you did last night finding that truck. Mighty impressed. I would have never thought to put GPS on the trailers and the trucks."

"Just doing my job, boss. You did put me in charge of loss prevention." Slick grinned with pride.

"Speaking of losses, what the fuck happened? Why did you kill three of the girls?"

"Sorry, boss, but I had no choice. They were out of the truck, running away. I needed to get the situation under control. Better we lose three than the whole load, right?" Slick replied in no uncertain terms. "There's a million niggers, spicks, and chinks for you to sell on the black market, but you would be screwed if the cops got a hold of that truck."

It didn't take a rocket scientist to realize he'd done the right thing.

"I can't argue with your logic, but more importantly, I appreciate you looking out for my best interests." I motioned for the bartender. "Gimme another. What you drinking, Slick?"

"I'll have whatever you are."

"Bring us a double," I said, then turned back to Slick. "Did you deliver the merchandise to Greer?"

"Yes, sir. The merchandise was hand delivered by me. Then I drove the truck back to New York and delivered the girls."

"Good, good." Hearing that made me feel as if I could relax, at least a little, for now. I picked up my glass and motioned toward the television screen. "You know, bringing you on board may have been the best decision I made since I fucked my son's mother and got her pregnant in the back of my pickup." I laughed then asked seriously, "You do realize we have one loose end that you haven't taken care of?"

Slick lifted the drink the bartender placed in front of him. "What's that?"

I waited until the bartender was out of earshot. "The one person who knows those dead girls came out of my truck. The driver, Johnny Brooks," I told him.

"Well, then I better drink up. I've got work to do." Slick gulped down his bourbon.

As I watched him leave, my phone rang. I took it out of my pocket. "Hello."

"KD." It was Greer, and he sounded emotional.

"Yes, sir, how can I help you?"

"I just wanted to say thank you. That blood you sent us was a perfect match. My daughter's having a transfusion as we speak," Greer said tearfully.

"Well, that's good news, Leo. I'm glad we could help."

"You did more than help. You saved my child's life." Greer continued to weep. "If ever there's any way I can help you, don't hesitate to call."

"Thank you. Give my best to the missus and your fine daughter." I hung up, feeling rather touched and a whole lot more confident about my next move.

42

In Waco, Vegas and I went straight to the Dr. Pepper museum. We showed Nevada's picture to every employee, but none of them recognized him or said they'd seen him. I was starting to wonder if I should have stayed in New York and helped with the search up there, because it was possible Nevada wasn't with this guy Bob. We were back to square one, and it seemed that finding my grandson was going to be like finding a needle in a haystack. But, if our family was able to find a known drug lord in the streets of Kingston, Jamaica, then we'd locate Nevada.

"Any ideas?" Vegas asked as we walked toward the rental car.

"Not off the top of my head. Only thing we can do now is hope Junior finds us a lead," I told him.

As soon as I got into the car, I got a call. "What's up, Junior?"

"Hey, Pop, I got some information for you."

"What did you find?"

"I went by Bob's job, the Copy Hut, and found out he's traveling in his company van. It's wrapped so it shouldn't be hard to spot. I'm gonna text you the make, model, and tag number."

"Ask if he added the credit monitoring," Vegas said.

I held my hand up to signal for him to calm down while I continued talking to his brother. "That's good. Anything else?"

"Actually, there is. I signed him up for credit monitoring and got a pop on a credit card he's been using. It was used at the Dr. Pepper museum, a gas station, and Victoria's Secret yesterday in Waco. And it was used at a Best Buy about fifteen minutes ago," Junior said.

"That Best Buy has Nevada's name written all over it. Your grandmother takes him there all the time. Where exactly in

Waco is it?" I was happy to hear we finally got some useful information.

"That's the thing, Pop. It wasn't used in Waco."

"Damn. Where was it last used?" I asked. If this boy said New York, I was going to lose my mind right there in the car.

Junior hesitated. "In El Paso."

"Shit!" I closed my eyes and exhaled my frustration. Of all the places for Nevada to have run off to, El Paso was probably the most dangerous for a Duncan.

"What's wrong? What did he say?" Vegas pressed for answers again.

"What do you want me to do, Pop?" Junior asked.

"I want you, Sasha, and Paris on a fuckin' plane within the hour. And bring enough fire power to wage a fucking war if we have to!"

"You got it, Pop," Junior said. "I'll see you in a few."

I hung up, looking up in the sky. "Why do you keep doing this to me?"

"Pop, what the hell is going on?" Vegas was beyond frustrated at this point, which I could understand.

"Your son is definitely in Texas." My phone chimed, and the information that Junior sent about the van came through. "This is the car they're in."

Vegas took my phone from me. "Okay, good. But what's this about waging war? And why are Junior, Paris, and Sasha coming?"

"Because your son is in El Paso, which makes this entire situation a little more difficult."

Nevada

43

Although I was only sixteen, I had been to more countries and islands than most people, thanks to my mother. But I had never been anywhere as hot as El Paso, Texas. The walk from the car to the entrance of Best Buy was a short one, but I felt like I was going to suffocate by the time I made it to the door. While Kia and Bob went to look for a laptop that we'd decided we needed, I went over to the cell phone section and picked up two burner phones and a couple of pre-paid phone cards. After waiting near the registers for a few minutes, I decided to go and see what the holdup was.

"Why would you even want this cheap thing?" Bob was asking as I walked up. "Get the MacBook. It's a better laptop. And we can FaceTime each other on it."

Jesus, did this guy ever quit?

"Bob, we don't need anything expensive right now. This right here is fine." She picked up the simple Chromebook she was standing in front of.

"You guys almost ready?" I asked.

"Yeah, let me just grab this right quick." She reached for one of the Chromebook boxes.

Bob sighed. "Sweetheart, just let me—"

"Bob, please. We're getting this laptop, and that's that," Kia snapped at him, then walked off. "You can get me something more expensive when we get home."

He blinked for a few seconds then turned to me, glaring. "Is this everything?"

"Uh, yeah," I said, realizing he was referring to the phones and cards in my hand. "I can get it, though."

"I don't need you to get anything. I promised Kia I would take care of things, and I meant it," he said, pushing his glasses on his nose as he waited for me to give him the items.

After paying for everything, we entered the sweltering heat and went back to the van. Bob, who'd been fairly quiet since losing the laptop argument in the store, asked softly, "Where to next?"

"We can find a motel, I guess." Kia shrugged, then added, "I'm sorry I was short with you. You've been nothing but kind the entire trip. I guess the heat is getting to me."

Bob lit up like a kid at Christmas. "It's okay, Kia. You never have to apologize. Let's find you a nice upscale hotel so you can cool off."

Instead of a cheap motel off the interstate, Bob decided we'd stay at the Marriott in downtown El Paso. Staying in a large chain hotel wasn't something I thought we should be doing. Large hotels had national databases, and they could be hacked. As Bob parked the van, I voiced my concern.

"I don't think this is a good idea," I said, leaning forward.

"You got something against the Marriott?" Bob turned around to look at me.

"No, I just think we should stay somewhere a little more low-key, like the places we've been staying," I suggested. "More off the grid."

"Listen, Kia is a classy woman. We stayed at the other cheap motel because it was late and we were traveling. She needs to be somewhere a little more comfortable, like what she's used to, and I'm gonna give her that." Bob smiled as he grabbed Kia's hand and kissed it.

I looked at both of them and said, "Look, I've been gone long enough to know that my family is looking for me. If we stay here, Bob, I'm telling you, I got a feeling about this, and not a good one."

Kia sighed. "Listen, we'll just stay here for one night. Then we'll go find another ratchet room somewhere else. Tonight, I just want to be someplace where I can take a long, hot bath, eat a good meal, and get a good night's sleep."

"And that's exactly what you're gonna do while we stay here, baby," Bob said, opening the door.

I grabbed the Best Buy bags, along with my backpack, and followed her inside to wait while Bob checked in.

"I'm telling you I don't have a good feeling about this, Kia," I mumbled.

"It's one night, Nevada. Besides, we need wifi to use the laptop to look stuff up." Her fingers ran along my arms as she spoke. She pulled them back when Bob approached.

"Okay, all checked in," Bob announced. He held up two hotel key cards. "Here's the key to your room, Nevada. You're on the fourteenth floor. Kia, we're on the fifteenth floor, in the suite."

"Great," she said. "Nevada, you can come to the suite so we can get to work."

From the disappointed look on Bob's face, I could see that this wasn't what he had in mind. I was sure he'd had some kind of sexual escapade planned for the two of them, but Kia had one goal and one goal only—to find her sister—and that couldn't be done without me. I gave Bob a smile.

"Okay, where do we start?" I asked thirty minutes later after I'd set up the laptop.

"How about we start with Asian foot spas in the area," Kia suggested.

I typed the words into the search engine, but nothing popped up. "Nope, nothing."

"Try massage parlors," she said, looking over my shoulder.

"Just chain places like Massage Envy and Red Door. Nothing that we're looking for." I sighed.

"Hmmmmm, brothels maybe?"

I tried searching for brothels, and still nothing. I leaned back in my chair, trying to come up with more ideas.

Bob, who was sitting in the living room of the suite, indulging in snacks from the mini bar, called over to us. "Y'all are doing this all wrong."

"What do you mean?" I asked, slightly offended. I didn't know who he thought I was, but I had no doubt my ability to hack into highly secured systems far surpassed his.

"You're looking for the wrong things." He walked over to the desk where Kia and I sat. "We're in Texas. You need to be looking for a damn dude ranch."

218 Carl Weber with La Jill Hunt

"A dude ranch?" Kia and I said at the same time. Our eyes met, and we both stifled a laugh. "That doesn't make much sense."

"Sure it does. Every state has its own code word. Type in dude ranch and El Paso," Bob prompted.

Deciding to humor him, I typed the words in, hit search, then read aloud the first name that came up. "The Horseshoe Ranch."

"She's probably there," Bob said with certainty.

"Bob, this makes no sense. This place is advertising a rodeo experience. Horseback riding, cattle drives, and stuff like that. It's not the place we're looking for," Kia tried to explain to him.

"That's what they want you to think they're offering. Trust me. They have way more to offer than that. Click that menu over there." He pointed.

I clicked the menu, and there was a drop down.

He clapped. "See, right there."

"It says members only." I frowned.

"Click it," he insisted.

"It wants a membership number and passcode," Kia said.

Bob reached into his back pocket, taking out his Velcro wallet. It made a loud ripping sound as he opened it and took out a shiny black card that he handed to me. "Here. Type these numbers in."

"You're a member of a dude ranch?"

"Along with other establishments. My black card status allows me around the country."

I paused before taking the card from him. This wasn't gonna work, I thought as I typed the numbers into the laptop and hit enter. My mouth gaped open as wide as my eyes as the screen changed to display a woman, naked except for the cowboy hat, boots, and gun holster that she wore. She had the biggest breasts I'd ever seen, and the caption above her read: *Welcome to the Horsehoe Ranch, where just like Texas, everything is bigger.*

"What the fuck?" Kia whispered the exact words that I was thinking. "Bobby, is this how you found the Hellfire Club?"

"Yeah, it's not like they put a big sign outside that says brothel," he admitted, pushing his glasses on his nose as his eyes remained on the woman on the computer screen.

"Okay, so now what?" I asked.

"Click on her," he told me. I did, and another woman appeared on the screen. "Keep clicking."

I continued clicking through the images of naked women. There were plenty to choose from: all races, all sizes, all beautiful. After a few more clicks, Myesha's naked picture appeared on the screen.

"Oh my God, it's her!" Kia screamed.

"I told you." Bob beamed with pride.

"I can't believe it. We actually found her," Kia said.

I looked at her and saw tears in her eyes. "We did it."

"Now click and ask for a date." Bob nudged my shoulder.

I clicked on the photo, but a message came up saying no dates were available.

"What does that mean?" I asked.

"It can mean one of two things: either she's booked up, or she's not there anymore," Bob answered.

"What do you mean, she's not there?" Kia panicked. "How do we find out?"

"We can always go and see," Bob suggested.

I turned around, and Kia's eyes met mine. "What do you wanna do?"

"Let's go," she said.

LC

44

"You do realize this is his town. The minute we walk in there, someone is gonna call KD or his son, Tyler," Vegas stated, making his thoughts very clear. It wasn't as if my thoughts were any different. It's just I that had a little more information than my son.

"We don't really have a choice." I sighed, staring at the American flag and Texas state flag waving in the wind above the tan brick building. The sign in front proudly proclaimed: *El Paso County Sheriff's Office: We serve with pride*

"Come on. Let's get this over with. We only have an hour before the others arrive," I said, leading the way.

We stepped inside, and as expected, all eyes were on us. I'm sure it wasn't every day two well-dressed black men entered that place with confidence. It took a moment before anyone came over to the counter to assist us.

"What can we do for you boys?" a heavyset officer asked. The toothpick in his mouth moved as he talked.

"I'd like to speak with the sheriff," I said, ignoring the fact that he'd addressed us as "boys."

"And just who are you?" He peered at us. "We don't hold no prisoners here. They're down the highway at the jail if you're looking for someone who's been arrested."

"Look, ain't nobody—"

I put my hand on Vegas's arm to stop him from speaking. "We aren't looking for anyone who's been arrested. We're here to meet with the sheriff." I mentally began counting backward from ten.

"What's your name?" Another uniformed officer, this one tall and skinny, walked up and asked.

"Are you Duncan?" A voice came from behind them. The other two men backed off, indicating that this was their boss and the man I'd come to see, Sheriff Roscoe Porter.

"Yes," I answered. "I take it Sheriff Kline from Arkansas called you?"

"He did." Sheriff Porter nodded. "You boys come on back."

He buzzed us through a door near the counter and escorted us back into his office. Vegas and I sat in two small chairs in front of his desk, which he sat behind.

"Thank you for seeing us, Sheriff," I said.

"Kline said you'd come a long way and I should hear you out." He folded his hands in front of him. "What's this all about?"

"We're looking for this young man and this young lady. We have reason to believe they're here in your city with an older man." Vegas showed him the picture of Nevada and Kia.

"Sounds like you need to file a missing person's report. Billy coulda helped you do that out front," Roscoe said.

"We don't want to file a missing person's report. We need you to use all of your resources and help us find them and the van they're in," I told him. "And neither KD Shrugs or Tyler can know anything about it."

The room went silent for a few seconds, and Roscoe looked at me as if I'd just proposed making a nuclear strike. His face screwed up in confused amusement. "Let me get this straight. You want me to utilize all my manpower and means to help you find two young people and a vehicle, and also make sure KD and Tyler Shrugs don't know what I'm doing? In El Paso, Texas?"

I nodded.

"What else do you need? You looking for Cinderella, or maybe a couple of dwarves and Snow White? What other fairytales you want me to bring to life? 'Cause keeping anything from those two in this part of Texas is damn near impossible. Besides, why would I want to help you do this, other than a colleague from Arkansas asked me to hear you out?" He raised an eyebrow.

I stared at him without saying anything, while Vegas stood and placed a bag on the desk, then sat back down.

"What the hell is this?" Roscoe asked, staring at the black leather bag in front of him.

"Open it and find out. I'm sure you'll be satisfied with what's inside," I said.

Roscoe pulled the bag near him and clicked it open. I watched as his eyes become wide and he gasped ever so slightly, then closed it quickly.

"Mr. Duncan, are you boys trying to bribe an officer of the law?" He glared across the table at us.

I leaned forward slightly and said, "Sheriff, that's exactly what we're trying to do."

Nevada

44

The Horseshoe Ranch definitely lived up to its name on the outside. The huge ranch sat at the end of a long road visible from the highway, and the driveway in front of the massive house was in the shape of a horseshoe. Unfortunately, I never got to see the inside, because there was a big sign in front that said: 21 YEARS OR OLDER, NO EXCEPTIONS. It wasn't worth trying to sneak me in, because if we drew too much attention, we'd never get what we were looking for. So, Bob dropped me and Kia off at the Marriott, and he went back to the Horseshoe Ranch on his own.

"You think this is going to work?" I asked Kia. Bob had just left, and we were sitting in the hotel restaurant.

Kia sighed, stabbing her salad weakly. "All we can do is wait and hope Bob comes through."

I nodded my head in agreement. "Kind of crazy, huh? We're actually in Texas tracking down your sister."

"Yeah," she said warmly. "And I don't know how to thank you enough for everything you've done."

"You don't have to thank me."

"I can, and I will. I don't have much, but if you think of something, it's yours." Kia's voice purred, and something about the way she looked at me made my heart start racing.

"Bob's not going to be back for a while," she said.

I swallowed hard. I was pretty sure I knew what she meant, and a week ago, I would have jumped at the chance. But somehow, that wasn't important—or what I really wanted anymore.

"I appreciate the offer, but I'm good. I didn't do this for that." I sat up straight, picking up my milkshake and making a loud slurping sound with the straw.

"You sure?" Kia looked a little disenchanted by my response.

I nodded. "Yeah, but I do have a question."

"Uh, sure. Ask away," she said distantly.

"On our way here from Waco, Bob tried to kiss you and you pushed him away."

"Yeah, so? What about it?" She seemed to have an attitude all of a sudden. I guess I'd hurt her feelings.

"Why'd you push him away?"

"Because I never kiss clients." She sounded annoyed. Was she mad at me, or at the question?

"But that doesn't make much sense. I mean, you do a lot of other things with him, don't you?"

She cut her eyes at me, but I wanted to get to the bottom of it, so I pressed on.

"What's wrong with kissing?"

"Nothing," she snapped. "Kissing is emotional. It's romantic. It's what I fantasize about, Nevada."

"And having sex isn't?" I was totally confused.

"No, not for me." She was on the verge of tears, but I had no idea why—until she dropped some harsh reality on me. "I've been raped so many times and had so many vile men inside me that there is no emotion left in sex."

I was starting to understand. "Maybe that's because you've only had sex, not love. You've been forced to give your body to people in a transaction. Maybe it just needs to happen naturally and not be traded. You need someone to give you unconditional love."

"You never cease to amaze me, you know that?" she said, finally cracking a smile. "Yes, maybe one day a man will romance me and make me feel special, but for now, this is my situation, and kissing is one small thing I have control over. I'm not giving a kiss to anyone who pays me. If I kiss a man or a woman, it's because I genuinely care for them."

"So, do you think you'll ever find that person?"

"Yes. I already have."

"You have? It's not Bob, is it?" I was going to be pissed if it was that loser.

"No, silly." She laughed, hurting my feelings, but I tried not to let it show. "You're the only person other than my sister I care about," she said. "I'd die for you, because I know you'd die for me."

"So, does that mean . . ."

Our eyes locked. I swallowed hard as she moved a little closer. "Does that mean you'd kiss me?"

"That's not something you ask a girl, Nevada," She slowly leaned toward me, and like a magnet, my body drew closer to hers. I closed my eyes and held my breath.

"You just do it," she told me.

"My, my, there's a whole lotta people lookin' for you two." A loud, obnoxious Southern voice startled us away from each other.

I looked up, and there was a tall, fat man wearing a tuxedo and a black cowboy hat. Standing behind him were three cops also wearing cowboy hats.

"Is there a problem?" Kia asked.

"It would appear so. We're gonna need to see some ID," the fat man said.

Kia pulled out her ID right away, but I just sat there. I knew what this was about. My dad and grandfather had sent them. Grandpa worked with police a lot and was always making donations to their civic groups and unions, even playing golf with the police commissioner of New York City. He always joked that cops were some of the best employees he had.

"Did my family send you?" I asked.

"Come on now, son. You already know the answer to that question." He put his hand on my shoulder. "Now, let's see some ID. I don't want Tyler here to have to cuff you two."

"No." Kia shook her head. "No need for cuffs. Nevada, give him your ID."

Reluctantly, I handed him my driving permit. He showed it to one of the other cops, and they both started laughing.

"Nevada Duncan." The fat man read out loud, smiling from ear to ear. "LC's gonna be mighty surprised when I call and tell him you're with me."

"How about I give you a thousand dollars not to make that call?" I asked.

He laughed even harder. "Boy, you are definitely related to LC Duncan. But you're worth a lot more to me than a thousand dollars. Let's head on outta here and get you two where you need to be."

We stood up and followed him out of the restaurant.

I whispered to Kia, "I told Bob's dumb ass not to use his credit card to pay for the hotel."

"I know. I don't know why I listened to him," she responded.

The fat man nodded at the people in the restaurant who were watching us as we walked out into the hotel lobby. Talk about embarrassing. Every eye in the place was on us.

"Is my dad upset?" I asked as we walked through the lobby.

"He ain't a happy camper right now, that's for sure. But I think he'll be forgiving once I call and let him know I have you in my care," he assured me. "I'll talk to him. Don't worry."

"Okay, good," I said as we walked out the door, though I was more than a little skeptical that this guy would have any influence over my dad.

LC

45

It didn't take very long for Roscoe to accept the generous donation we offered in exchange for helping us find the kids. Within twenty minutes of us sitting down with him, every El Paso deputy, on and off duty, was looking for Bob's van. Of course, now that word was out about my missing grandson, I had to worry that news might get back to KD. Time was of the essence.

"If they're in this city, I guarantee we'll find them by the end of the day," Roscoe promised.

"I hope so," I responded from the back of his vehicle. He'd offered to let me and Vegas ride along with him as he patrolled the area, asking around about the van.

Vegas sat up front with Roscoe. He'd been fairly quiet since our arrival, understandably. Nevada's disappearance had everyone worried, but I was sure it was even harder for him to deal with as his father. I hoped for all of our sakes that Roscoe was right and we found him soon. Back home, Chippy and Consuela were losing their minds, threatening to hop on a plane to come search for Nevada themselves. That was the last thing any of us needed to deal with.

When I looked at my phone and saw Junior calling, I hoped it was good news, and not that his mother was on her way.

"Yeah, Junior. You all made it?"

"We just landed, Pop. I got another credit alert," he said.

"Where?"

"There's a charge at the Marriott Downtown El Paso."

"Roscoe, where is the Marriott?" I yelled so he could hear me over the radio.

"About three miles up the road." Roscoe looked at me in the rearview mirror.

"We need to be heading there. I think that's where they are," I said.

"See you in a few, Pop," Junior said.

Roscoe radioed for backup, then turned on the flashing lights and sirens. Within seconds, another sheriff's vehicle was right behind us as we sped down the road. I could see the tension in Vegas's jaw and squeezed his shoulder to reassure him that everything was going to be okay.

By the time we pulled in front of the Marriott, there were two other cruisers already sitting out front with the official seal of the Texas Highway Patrol displayed on the doors. Roscoe parked directly behind them.

"Pop!" Vegas shouted, bolting out of the car.

I looked at the entrance of the hotel, and my heart was seized with fear. Nevada was being led out of the building by the man I found it hard not to hate—KD Shrugs. Because there was no handle on the rear door, I was unable to get out on my own.

"Open the fucking door!" I commanded. Roscoe quickly moved to open it, and I pushed it so hard that I knocked him backward.

"Nevada!" Vegas ran toward his son. He quickly found himself facing the barrels of multiple guns aimed at him. He stopped, raising his hands.

"That's far enough," Tyler Shrugs shouted.

Roscoe and I rushed to his side. Nevada, Kia, Tyler, and KD now stood between the two patrolmen who had drawn their guns.

"Dad!" Nevada yelled. He tried to run to us, but KD snatched him back. Seeing that man touch my grandson sent a wave of anger through me.

"KD, I'm telling you right now, get your hand off of him," I warned.

"Calm down there, LC. I ain't hurting the boy. Yet."

KD's evil grin turned my anger into pure rage.

"Let my son go right now," Vegas yelled.

"Now, why in the hell would I do that?" KD taunted.

That's when I saw the little .38 he had pointed in Nevada's back. I could see Vegas pick up on this, and it was obvious he was about to make a move, guns or no guns.

"KD, let the kids go," Roscoe pleaded. "We ain't lookin' for no trouble." He really was trying to defuse the situation, but he didn't have long, as a blue SUV pulled into the parking lot with Junior and the rest of my family.

"Roscoe, you was looking for trouble the minute they showed up and you didn't call me," KD chastised him. "I always knew you were slow, but now I'm starting to think you're just plain stupid."

"Let them go," Vegas growled.

"I can't do that," KD replied.

"Why not?" Roscoe asked.

"Because these two young people are under arrest. Ain't that right, Tyler? Now, we're taking them into custody, and they'll call you when—"

"Under arrest? For what?" Kia yelled. "We didn't do anything."

"Dad. Grandpa!" Nevada pleaded.

"Now, KD, you know just as well as everybody else you don't have no jurisdiction to do shit. You ain't the sheriff no more," Roscoe told him. "I am. So let those kids go."

If looks could kill, then Roscoe would have been a dead man after the dark glare that KD gave him. "Fuck you, Roscoe. Highway patrol supersedes your jurisdiction. Tyler, put them in the car."

"That ain't happening," Vegas stepped up and blocked their way. Tyler pulled out his gun.

"Or what?" KD said.

"We should be asking you that." Vegas suddenly smiled, raising his arms in the air. "What are you gonna do, shoot two unarmed black men and the El Paso sheriff in front of two million people?"

"Two million people?" KD questioned.

"Smile, bitches!" Sasha yelled. "You're on Facebook Live." She was holding her phone and aiming it straight at KD and his crew as she approached them. Junior and Paris stepped up near me.

"The state of Texas and the highway patrol will be hit with a lawsuit so big they'll have to sell half the land in it to recover," I added. "And you don't know how many more witnesses might be watching you from the hotel lobby right now. Sounds like a slam dunk lawsuit to me."

Tyler walked over and leaned closer to his father. "Daddy, we can't be taking no chances with this social media stuff. Texas law enforcement got enough problems right now. They'll hang me and the boys out to dry." He turned around and spoke to the patrolmen. "Put down the guns, boys."

"You'd better listen to your son, KD. Sounds like he's giving you some good advice," I said. "Let them go."

KD finally removed his hand from Nevada's chest. "I was just havin' fun with the boy."

Nevada ran to Vegas and threw his arms around his neck.

"All right, LC. You got your kids. Now, I would advise you to get the hell outta Texas. All of you," KD said.

"That's exactly what we plan on doing." I turned to my niece. "Okay, Sasha, you can stop the live feed as soon as we're all in our vehicles safely," I said. I knew she was lying about Facebook Live since our family didn't need that kind of attention, but she was recording a video just in case. With her free hand, she reached for Kia, who was standing to the side, looking unsure about what to do.

I could hear KD murmuring to Tyler, but at that point, the immediate threat was over. All I wanted to do was get home.

Nevada ran over and gave me a hug. "Thanks, Grandpa."

I rubbed the top of his head. "Glad you're safe, Nevada. You had us worried."

"I know, and I'm sorry. Can we just go home now?"

"Yes, that's exactly what we're going to do." We were going straight to the plane and getting the hell out of this godforsaken place. KD saying we should get out of Texas wasn't a suggestion. It was a warning, and one I knew could not be ignored.

"Come on, Kia. We're going home." Nevada waved his friend over.

She walked over and grabbed his arm. "Nevada, I can't go. What about my sister?"

He turned to me. "Grandpa, I never ask for anything, but I promised I'd help her. That's why I'm here. You always told me a man's only as good as his word. I gave her my word."

I glanced over at KD and Tyler, who didn't look like they would remain passive if we hung around too much longer. "Tell me what's going on, and tell me fast," I said.

He gave me the short version of the story, and my first instinct was to tell him there was nothing I could do. But then I remembered what I'd told Vegas a few days ago: sometimes you have to do things for your family even if it makes you uncomfortable.

"What do you think?" I asked Vegas.

"I think we should help her, but not from here. It's not going to take them long to regroup."

Vegas put his hands on his son's shoulders and looked him in the eye so he understood the severity of what he was about to tell him. "Did you hear when that man told Pop we needed to get out of Texas? He was not playing. The moment we pull out of this parking lot, we are moving targets for Texas law enforcement. We gotta go."

"But Dad . . ."

"Hold on a second, Vegas. It's a long shot, but let me try something." I turned to KD, who was about to get in a car. "KD! Can I speak to you for a moment, please?" I hated to say it so politely, but it was possibly the only way we would get out of there without a major confrontation.

KD

46

LC shouted across the parking lot just as I was about to get in the car. I hesitated, wondering what the fuck he could want. Considering the fact that we were just pointing guns at him and his family, it surprised me to hear him say please—and it made me curious.

I looked at Tyler with my eyebrows raised. "What do you think?" I asked.

He nodded. Obviously he was just as curious as I was about what LC wanted. It must have been something important for LC to waste even a minute getting his black ass out of Texas like I'd told him to. I took a few steps toward him in the parking lot.

Maybe there was something left to say between us; something that would salvage a day that had turned to shit after that two-faced asshole Roscoe showed up before I could get the Duncan kid into Tyler's car. It really would have been something to get that kid back at my ranch. The ultimate negotiating chip against LC Duncan.

When Tyler had first told me that LC Duncan was in town looking for two teenagers, I didn't know who the kids were. I just knew that if LC wanted them, then maybe I should be looking for them too. So, I had Tyler make a few calls, and sure enough, we found them. When the kid handed over his driver's permit and I realized he was LC's grandson, I thought I'd hit the fuckin' jack-pot. Unfortunately, LC and some more of his unruly brood had shown up and ruined all the fun. Things could have gotten ugly if I hadn't let the kid go.

"What do you want, LC?" We'd both walked halfway and met in the center of the parking lot. "You got three minutes. I've got a party to attend." I'd been getting ready for Congressman Bell's event across the border when Tyler told me he'd found the kids.

"Nice tux." He gave me a smile that I could tell was fake. He was trying so damn hard not to be his usual arrogant self.

"Stop beating around the bush. What the fuck do you want? It was pretty disrespectful for you to show up in my city to do business without letting me know."

"I didn't come down here on business. It was personal. We're looking for a girl," he said.

That didn't make much sense. I'd been told he was looking for the two kids, and now he'd found them. What was I missing?

"There's a lot of girls in Texas, LC."

"Yeah, I know, but I'm looking for one girl in particular. She's in the sex trade."

"The Horseshoe Ranch is right down the block." I pointed south. "I'm sure you'll find plenty of whores there."

"We've been told this girl no longer works there. I'm hoping she's still in Texas. If anyone could find her, you can."

For the first time in twenty years, this arrogant prick was acting like he needed me. Ten minutes ago, I was ready to blow him and his whole damn family away, yet now he was kissing my ass because he needed a favor.

"Who is she to you?" I asked, pulling on my tuxedos suspenders.

He looked back at his grandson and the girl. "She's the girl's sister. My family promised to help find her—which means I could be down here a few more times if I don't get some help."

"I see." I wondered if I should call his bluff. Would he really be stupid enough to come back to my neck of the woods knowing I'd be gunning for his ass? Then I realized, yeah, he probably would. If nothing else, LC Duncan was one persistent nigger.

"So, she's no kin to you?" I asked.

"No, she's not."

"Then she must not be worth much to you." Putting a dollar amount on the girl would tell me exactly how important she was to him. "Which means she's not worth much to me either. You're familiar with the old phrase, *time is money?*"

"I'll give you fifty grand if you find her," he said.

That surprised me, but I wasn't about to take that deal. If he was willing to give up fifty grand that easy, then he would be willing to pay much more.

I laughed. "I don't get outta bed to take a piss for fifty grand."

I could see the wheels turning in that pea-sized nigger brain of his. He'd beat me today with the brats, but whoever this girl was, she was going to cost him dearly if he really wanted my help.

"A hundred grand," he said, and I shook my head.

What the fuck was I missing? He really wanted this girl.

He looked back at his grandson and the girl again and sighed. "Two hundred and fifty thousand."

"Two hundred and fifty, huh?" Hell, if I could get him up another hundred and ten, I could make up for those girls that Slick shot. "You got a name and a picture?"

"Hold on a second." He walked over to the kids, and the boy smiled at him like he was Jesus Christ reincarnated. He said something to them, and then the girl wrapped her arms around his neck and hugged him. This girl might not be important to him, but she was definitely important to them.

"Her name is Myesha," he said when he came back.

He handed me a phone that had her picture on the screen. I had to bite my tongue to keep from shouting. I knew this girl— oh, too well. Unfortunately, I didn't hide the recognition in my facial expression.

"You know her?" LC asked.

"I might, but I can tell you right now she's gonna cost you a hell of a lot more than a two hundred and fifty thousand dollars." This girl Myesha was the one with the AB negative blood we'd given to Greer. I thought she wasn't worth shit to me now because we'd drained six pints of blood outta her, but LC had just upped her value significantly.

"Let's stop bullshitting each other," he said. "Obviously you know her because she's part of this secret sex ring you've got going on down here."

"You have no idea what I've got going on, LC, otherwise you would have gotten in a long time ago," I said smugly.

"What do you want for the girl?" He was back to his old ways, arrogant and direct.

"I don't know if she's for sale. She's one of our best moneymakers. You'd never believe how much she made for me this week," I bragged without giving any detail.

"Everything has a price. What's your I-don't-wanna-sell price?" He looked like he wanted to hit me. I loved getting a rise outta this nigger.

He was right. Everything did have a price, and I'd already lost a whole lot of money this week when Slick killed three of my girls.

"A million dollars," I said.

"Half a million," he countered.

"Two million." I laughed, and he just stared at me angrily, then looked back at his grandson. "What the fuck, LC? Should I go over there and talk to the kid?"

"You son of a bitch. I'll give you a million, but I want her at the airport in thirty minutes."

"I have a party to go to, but these two nice troopers over there will deliver her. I expect the wire will be sent directly?" I smiled, thinking about the nice profit I'd just made.

"You'll get your money."

"Nice doing business with you, LC," I said, heading back to the car.

"What was that all about, Daddy?" Tyler asked as we got in the car.

"I need you to have the boys bring Celeste's Asian friend to the airport."

Tyler's eyes went wide. "You're giving her to him?"

I chuckled. "A million dollars isn't free, son, and from what Lizbeth tells me, that girl's no good to us now that we drained damn near seven pints of blood from her. She has acute anemia."

Vegas

47

I'd never been so happy to step foot on a plane. We were in Texas for less than twenty-four hours, but it was still too long. All I wanted to do was take my son home, shower, eat one of my mom's home-cooked meals and get into bed.

As soon as I entered the jet cabin, the eyes of my sister, cousin, son, and his friend were on me. I could sense the anxiety and anticipation.

At that moment, Junior entered, carrying Kia's sister, who was so weak that she could barely walk.

"Kia." The girl's voice was weak.

"Oh my God, you found her!" Kia jumped up and ran to her. She tried to hug her sister in Junior's arms, but the girl didn't even have the strength to hug her back.

Kia stepped back, looking scared. "What's wrong with her? Is she sick?"

"It appears so. This is how they gave her to us. Don't worry," Pop said. "We'll make sure she gets some medical attention when we land. But right now, we've gotta get the hell out of here. Sit down, buckle up, and let's go."

He didn't have to tell me twice. I made my way to the back of the plane and sat in one of the leather seats. I looked up and saw Nevada hugging my father.

"Thanks again, Grandpa," he said.

"You're welcome, Nevada. We're still gonna have a little chat when we get home, though."

I should've warned my son that it was probably not going to be a cheerful conversation, but Nevada was smart. He would figure that out soon enough.

Kia and Nevada got settled into their seats, and Junior placed her sister in the seat next to her sister. Then he came to the back of the plane with Pop. Within minutes, we were in the air.

"Pop, I hate to be the bearer of bad news," Junior said about fifteen minutes into the flight, "but I got a call right before we took off. We have another problem." Junior kept his voice low so that the kids wouldn't hear him.

"Of course we do." Pop groaned, pouring himself a drink. "What now?"

"Lex is dead," Junior said.

"Are you fucking kidding me?"

"Lex the fence?" I asked.

"Yes." Pop looked over at me. "I hired him to find out what KD was doing. He was supposed to hijack his truck. What the hell happened to him?"

"He was found dead, shot execution style."

"By who?" I asked.

"Nobody knows who the shooter was, but I have an idea who was behind it," Junior replied.

"KD," Pop and I said at the same time.

"The crazy thing is that his body was found along with the bodies of three women," Junior explained.

"What about the truck?" Dad asked.

Junior looked at my Dad seriously. "There was no truck, Pop."

"They killed four people and then took the truck? What the hell was in the truck?" I asked.

Junior shrugged, and Pop went into deep thought for a second. Then he turned to me and said, "You think Johnny could have been the person driving that truck when it was stolen?"

"I don't know. It's possible."

"As soon as this plane lands, I'm gonna need you to find Johnny Brooks."

"I'm on it. Let's just hope he's still alive when I find him."

"I was just thinking the same thing," Pop said.

I settled back in my seat to take the nap I knew I'd need. Being a Duncan sure didn't make for a restful, easy life.

I slept for the majority of the flight home. When we arrived, my mother was there, waiting along with Consuela.

"Grandma." Nevada hugged my mother first. It made sense since she was the only one with a friendly face. Consuela didn't look too pleased as we descended from the plane. No doubt she was ready to whip Nevada's ass for disappearing like he did.

"We were so worried about you. I'm glad you're safe," Mom told him.

"Me too," he said.

My father walked over to my mother and gave her a big kiss. "I missed you."

"Is there something you want to say to your mother?" I said to Nevada, motioning toward Consuela, who stood nearby, watching the family reunion.

Nevada's head hung low as he walked over to her. "I'm sorry I ran away, Mom."

Consuela pulled him to her and held him tight. "Mi amor. Thank God you're okay. *Estaba tan preocupada por ti, hijo mío.*"

Nevada wiped the tears from her eyes and said, "I love you too, Mama. I'm sorry you were worried."

"Duncan family, let's go home," Pop announced.

Nevada looked around and asked, "Where's Uncle Rio?"

I hadn't even noticed my baby brother's absence until then. It was odd, because he and Nevada were so close. I would've expected him to be waiting with my mother and Consuela.

"I tried calling him when I found out you all were on the way home, but I couldn't reach him. He should be at the house by the time we get there," Mom said.

We all headed toward the various vehicles waiting to take us home. Consuela kept staring at Kia and her sister, who was being carried by Junior.

I walked over to her SUV.

"That's the girl who caused all of this?" she asked me.

"Yes, that's her. But it's not her fault."

"It's not?"

"How about I explain it all to you tomorrow night over dinner?" I asked.

She looked surprised by my invitation. "Dinner?"

"Yes, just the two of us. How about Tavern on the Green? We have a lot to discuss. What do you say?"

"I say yes, I'd like that." Consuela smiled. "And, Vegas, thank you for bringing my son home."

"Our son," I reminded her with a smile. Then I turned and called out, "Nevada!"

He ran over to me. "Yeah, Dad."

"Ride home with your mother."

"But I was gonna go over to the hospital with—"

"No, Uncle Junior and Aunt Paris will make sure she's good. You need to go with your mom," I told him, reading the disappointment on his face. "Listen, I'm proud of you, son. You did the right thing and handled it like a Duncan."

"Thanks, Dad. Are you coming home with us?" he asked.

"Not right now. I got something to handle for your grandfather. But I love you." I hugged him again.

"Love you too, Dad."

"Thank you, Vegas," Consuela said softly.

I looked at both of them and said, "Don't worry. It's all going to work out for all of us."

48

"And so, I'd like to thank you all for coming here tonight, and for your support over the years. I've enjoyed representing this great state up in D.C. and working hard beside our fine president to make America great again. But now it's time to rid the state-house of the corruption, outrageous overspending, and the kiss-ass policies toward immigration—which is why, tonight, I'm announcing that I'm throwing my hat into the ring to become the next governor of New Mexico. I'm gonna make sure nobody gets in here that ain't supposed to be here!"

The room erupted in applause, and the band began playing "Born in the USA." Wesley walked through the crowd, shaking hands and giving hugs. It was very clear why we'd been gathered here. If Wesley was running for governor, he was gonna need money. Based on the reaction to his announcement, he would have no problem getting it.

"Wesley Bell, governor of New Mexico. How 'bout that, Daddy?" Tyler gave me a knowing smile. One thing was for damn sure: if he won, he would definitely be one of the most powerful allies in my corner and good for business.

"Sounds like music to my ears. His ass got my vote, or at least the ones I plan on buying, since technically I'm not from New Mexico," I said with a hearty laugh.

"Well, we got something else to tell you that I think you'll be happy about."

From the way Tyler was grinning, I just knew he was about to tell me that Duncan's plane had crashed and LC and his brats were dead. I prepared myself to hear the great news.

"What's that, son?"

He pulled Elizabeth into his arms and held her close to him. "Lizbeth and I are getting married. She's moving into the house."

"Well, now, that's wonderful news." I was a little stunned; nevertheless, I was happy for my son. He'd been a man-whore long enough, and it was time for him to settle down with the right woman and give me some grandkids to carry on my legacy. Besides, I liked Elizabeth. She was smart, sexy as hell, and knew how to keep her damn mouth shut.

"Congratulations, you two. I'm happy for you. For both of you. Welcome to the family, Lizbeth."

"Thank you, KD." She hugged me, and though it was hard, I tried not to enjoy the feeling of her melon-sized breasts against me. After all, she was about to be my daughter-in-law.

"Tyler, you made a fine choice. I'm proud of you." I grinned. "Go grab us some champagne so we can have a proper toast."

"We'll be right back," Tyler said as they walked away hand in hand.

I sat alone at the table, observing everyone and everything around me, until I was surprisingly joined by Leo Greer. He took the seat beside me.

"Leo, I wasn't expecting you to be here. I thought you'd be with your daughter. How is she anyway?"

"She was doing fine until last night." Greer's voice was as serious as his face.

"I'm sorry to hear that. What exactly is the problem?" If his daughter wasn't well, what the hell was he doing in New Mexico? He sure took this political shit seriously.

He looked around at all the people in the crowd. "Can we step outside for a moment?"

We got up and walked into the lobby of the hotel to find a spot where no one could hear our conversation.

"I came to see you. I need to talk to you about my daughter."

"You're not blaming your daughter being sick on us, are you?" Even though no one was nearby, I lowered my voice. "'Cause we busted our asses to get you that blood. That girl looked like a walking corpse after we drained her. You got what you needed, right?" I asked him.

"I'm not blaming you at all. The blood transfusion saved her life, but I'm finding out now it was just a temporary fix," he said.

"Shit, I'm sorry to hear that."

He was tearing up again. "Yeah, the prognosis isn't good, but there's still some hope."

"I'm sure glad to hear that," I said.

Greer stared at me and said, "I need that girl. The one that's a perfect match?"

"I don't know if that's possible, Leo. She's in pretty bad shape to be honest with you." I hated to hear that this was happening to Greer's daughter, but I needed to be honest and let him know what he was up against.

"But she's alive?"

I shook my head, unwilling to tell him she was with LC Duncan. "I guess, if you wanna call it that. The girl looks like a living corpse. We couldn't drain enough blood outta her to fill a Band-Aid right now."

"You're not hearing what I'm saying. My daughter's in organ failure and will need a liver and possibly a heart. I ain't asking for more blood. I want the girl."

I was so stunned by what he was suggesting that I needed to sit down on the cushioned bench against the wall. "Do you know what happened the last time I helped someone like this? What you're asking me to do landed my ass in jail. I took the fucking fall for everyone. No one went down for that shit but me, and I wasn't the only one involved."

"So I've been told. But this is my daughter we're talking about, and I got way more resources than the person you helped, and you know it. I promise you won't be going anywhere you don't wanna go," Greer insisted. "I'll pay whatever. Do whatever."

"You already owe me a favor," I reminded him.

"True, but I'm a man who likes to get what he wants. You seem to be the same."

"There's a lot of truth to that," I replied.

"So, how'd you like to be sheriff again?" He grinned like he could make it happen. "I heard it's your dream job."

"Yes, sir. Another year or two as sheriff and a couple of grand-kids, and I could die a happy man." I glanced at Tyler and Elizabeth. "But even a man like you couldn't make that happen. I've got too much baggage. Those pussies in the party will take my money, but they'd never let me on the ballet."

"You'd be surprised what I can do with the help of my friends—like POTUS. We could have a rally right in El Paso here. He'd endorse you. What the fuck are they gonna do then?"

"Kiss my lily white ass, that's what they'd do." I laughed then stared at him hard. "You could really do that?"

"I don't say things I can't do," he replied. "Now, what about the girl?"

"Tell you what. Let me think about it, and I'll let you know by tomorrow."

"Sure thing. But what's there to think about . . . Sheriff?" Greer grinned.

Roman

49

My mother's hospital room provided a safe haven for us while we tried to figure out our next move. After witnessing Lex and those women get killed, we'd gone underground, staying as far away from the streets as possible. Li'l Al had already heard rumors that some crazy-looking white guy was spreading money around, looking for the driver of the truck. If he was looking for the driver, then no doubt he was looking for the guys that stole it. I'd done a lot of shit with Denny and Al over the years, most of it illegal, but usually it was pretty low risk. Now we'd gotten into something that truly put our lives in jeopardy. To say we were concerned was an understatement.

"You think Lex told him it was us that stole the truck?" I asked.

"Lex wouldn't sell us out. He was a stand-up dude," Denny said for the fiftieth time, which pissed me off.

"Dammit, Denny, even if Lex was a standup guy—which I don't think he was—he had a gun to his head. Whatever the fuck that dude wanted to know, he told him," I snapped at my friend. "That gangster code of silence you be watching on TV is just Hollywood bullshit. Life on the line, motherfuckers be tellin' it."

"Not me. I'm true to this. I ain't snitching for shit." He tried to sound hard.

"Bro, I love you, but your pretty ass will be the first to talk if the time comes," I said, and Li'l Al laughed his ass off. Denny glared at both of us, but deep down, he knew it was true.

When he finally stopped laughing, Li'l Al said, "I don't know about y'all, but I'm about to steal me a car and go see my people down south. This shit is a little too hot for me."

"I might just take that ride, too," Denny replied. "What about you, Rome?"

"Man, you know I can't leave yet. At least not until . . ." My words drifted off as I looked over at my mother, who was asleep. I could tell that she was getting worse by the day because she was sleeping almost all the time, and when she was awake, she was becoming more and more incoherent.

As if she could sense me talking about her, she moved her arm slightly and opened her eyes. "Roman?"

I slid my chair closer and grabbed her hand. "Yeah, Ma, I'm here."

"Oh, baby, I'm glad you're here. I told your brother you would be here so you could talk."

"Brother?" Denny whispered.

I shook my head at him. "She's out of it, man. It's the medicine, probably."

There was a tapping on the door, and then Dr. Ford walked in the room. He washed his hands at the sink and then came over to check my mother.

"How're you doing, Ms. Johnson?" His voice was calm and soothing.

My mother didn't speak. She just nodded at him, and then closed her eyes to go back to sleep.

I stood up and asked, "Man, Doc, what's going on?"

"Right now, we're doing everything we can to keep her comfortable. She's very sick."

I shook my head angrily. "I need you to do more than make her comfortable. I want her better. Do you know how much fucking money I just paid this hospital? I got the other money for the transplant, too, once we find a donor."

"Why don't we talk over here so your mother can rest?" he said as he stepped into the far corner of the room.

I went to stand with him. "What's going on?"

Dr. Ford took a deep breath and released a sigh. He couldn't even look me in the eye. "Mr. Johnson, I'm sorry, but your mother's name has been removed from the transplant list."

I felt like he'd just punched me in the gut. "What? Why would you do that? You said that's the only way she would survive." I began to panic. "I told you I could pay. I got the money."

"It's not about the money. With your mother's age and her weakened state, the transplant coordination team feels that she wouldn't be able to survive the surgery even if a donor was located," Dr. Ford said.

"What are you telling me? Are you saying my mother is going to die?" My eyes were welling up as I waited for his answer. I didn't even care that my boys could see me crying.

He nodded slowly, confirming my fears. "I'm saying that we've done all we can at this point."

I looked back at my mother. She looked so frail and small in that bed. "How much longer does she have?"

"Based on her numbers right now, I would say two weeks, give or take."

Two weeks. That's all I had left to spend with my mother. Fourteen days. I should have been spending every last second with her, but instead, I'd been out trying to get the money for a surgery that she was too sick to have.

"Shit," I whispered, wiping away tears. "I gotta tell Aunt Coretta."

"Would you like me to talk to her sister for you?" Dr. Ford offered.

"No, I'll do it." My mother wouldn't want her sister to hear about this from a stranger. It would be the hardest conversation I'd ever had, but I owed that much to the woman I loved more than life itself.

"Rome." I felt Denny's hand on my shoulder. "Let's go get some air."

"Nah, man, I can't leave her." I shook my head and went back to sit by the bed. "I'ma be here with her for the next fourteen days. I ain't going nowhere."

"Listen, I've given her a fairly strong sedative. She's going to be asleep for the remainder of the night. Why don't you go home, get some clothes, and come back in the morning?" Dr. Ford suggested. "If anything happens, and I'm saying that's a big if, then we'll call you."

"A'ight," I said reluctantly. "But I'm coming back tonight."

"I understand," Dr. Ford said.

I leaned over and kissed my mother's forehead. "I'll be back in a little while, Mama."

Vegas

50

While the rest of my family headed to the house, I went out to look for Johnny Brooks. He didn't answer the number he'd called me from earlier, so I hit up some of the spots he used to hang at. No one had seen or heard from him. It was like he'd vanished, which worried me. Had KD's people already gotten to him? I was tired and about to call it a night when he finally sent a text, telling me where to meet him.

"Lemme get a rum and Coke," I said as I sat down at the bar at Benny's, a spot we used to frequent back in the day. Even though it was damn near two in the morning, there was still a good number of patrons inside the dark hole-in-the-wall, shooting pool and listening to outdated music coming from an old jukebox.

Benny Jr., the bartender who also happened to be the owner, mixed my drink and placed it in front of me. He leaned over and whispered, "Why don't you take that drink into my back room?"

"Johnny?" I asked.

He nodded, sliding a key across the bar.

I got up and walked behind the bar. The key he'd given me opened the door to the back room, where I walked in and saw Johnny sitting at a small table, nursing a bottle of Jack. I locked the door behind me.

"You drinking? I thought you stopped a couple of years ago."

"Man, I did, but I'm dealing with some shit right now. I gotta cope. Hell, you may wanna get a refill yourself," Johnny said, nervously shaking his head.

"Johnny, what the hell is going on?" I asked.

"I just can't believe this. You ain't . . . I mean, nobody would even believe this. I don't know how to tell you."

"I'm gonna need you to calm down and tell me what the hell is going on." I pulled up a chair and sat at the table with him.

Johnny looked around nervously like there were people listening through the walls or something. "Man, listen. I'm in trouble."

"What kind of trouble?" I folded my arms and got straight to the point. "Trouble with KD Shrugs?"

Johnny winced like even the sound of the guy's name scared him. "Yeah, man, he's after me and . . . and when he finds me, he–he's gonna kill me," Johnny stammered.

"What did you do?"

"I know too much."

"Were you driving that fucking truck?" I grabbed his arm and forced him to look me in the eye.

He held eye contact for half a second then dropped his head, looking down at the table. "It wasn't just that truck."

"Damn it, Johnny. Did you kill those girls? And Lex?"

He snatched his arm away. "Hell no! I ain't kill nobody. You know me better than that," He sounded offended. "And I don't know who did. Some young boys jacked me. But KD don't care about that. He's just gonna kill me."

"No, he's not."

"Vegas, you don't know what he's capable of. KD is a sick man."

Finally, we were getting somewhere. I needed Johnny to open up and give me whatever information he had on KD Shrugs. This wasn't just about Johnny—this was about my family's safety.

"What's KD up to?"

"We been friends a long time, Vegas, and I know I fuck up a lot, but this . . . you . . . your family . . . you're the only one who can help me. LC Duncan is the only motherfucker KD is afraid of, and I'm not even sure he's afraid of him anymore." Johnny's face was full of terror. "I need you to promise you'll protect me.

"You know I got your back, and my dad does too. You're like family. Now, tell me what KD is doing."

Johnny looked around again then leaned in and spoke in a whisper. "That sick bastard is selling girls, Vegas. He's shipping them all over the country and making a fortune."

"Sex trafficking?" That shit didn't surprise me. KD Shrugs was a scumbag, for sure. But then Johnny blew my mind when he explained how much deeper it really was.

"Nah, not that. That's his front, believe it or not. This is something way different. He's taking them and fattening them up like pigs for slaughter. Prostitutes, working girls, runaways, especially illegals. He brings them to his place and cleans them up, feeds them good, gives them medical care and the whole nine. Makes them healthy. It's like a fucking lab. He tests 'em and uses 'em for whatever he can. Blood, plasma, bone marrow. Rich motherfuckers with sick relatives call him, and he'll get them what they need.

"He's saving lives out here, but for a big-ass price and at the expense of other people's lives. There's a sick bastard in New York doing womb transplants. That's one of his biggest clients. This ain't no sex trafficking." Johnny's eyes were wet like he was tearing up just thinking about it. "He's selling these girls to the highest bidder, knowing that they might be killed for their body parts."

My mouth fell open. Johnny was right; I couldn't believe the shit that he was telling me. It was something straight out of a horror movie. Now I understood why Kia's sister had been so sick when we got her. I wondered what they had taken from her. If we hadn't gotten her out of there, who knows how badly they would have carved her up.

I also now realized why Johnny was so afraid. If what he was saying was true and he had proof, he was a walking dead man. Pop was going to have a fit when he heard this. It was worse than anything that he was probably thinking KD was into.

"Shit, Johnny, do you have any kind of proof?" I asked.

"I do, but if I give it to you . . ."

"I give you my word."

He reached into his pocket and slid a jump drive across the table, motioning for me to take it. "Guard that with your life."

"Come on. Let's get out of here. I'm taking you to one of our safe houses," I told him.

When we stepped out of the back room, Johnny insisted on one more drink at the bar. I let him get a shot. The poor guy looked like he needed it after everything he'd just revealed to me. He threw back the shot, and then we headed out the front door.

"That was probably the last drink I'll have. I just wanted—" Before Johnny could say another word, shots rang out, then the sound of screeching tires.

I ducked down to take cover while trying to see where the commotion was coming from. Everything happened so fast that I didn't have time to retaliate.

"Shit! Johnny, you a'ight, man?"

When he didn't answer, I looked over and saw that he'd been shot. I eased over to his body. Blood was seeping through his shirt and onto the pavement where he was lying on his back. I took off my own shirt and placed it on the open wound on his chest.

His eyes met mine, and the last thing he said before closing his eyes one final time was, "You . . . gotta . . . stop . . . KD."

KD

51

"A'ight, tell me that you've got something for me," I said, walking into Dr. Baker's office in Building 5. He was sitting at his desk, looking through some folders, while Elizabeth sat at a small table with her laptop.

"Not yet. We're still working on it." Elizabeth swiveled around in the chair to face me.

"Well, then work faster. I gotta get this guy Greer what he needs. It's the difference between steak and hamburger around here, goddammit!" I didn't usually yell at her, but I'd promised Greer results, and he'd promised me my old life back. "What about the two new girls I got from Peter Lee? They're Chinks. Can't we use them?"

"Not all Asian people have the same blood type. And I'm pretty sure Greer's daughter isn't Asian," she lectured. "It's the same way that all white people or all black people don't have the same type. It's about genetic makeup, not race. You know that."

"Right now, Lizbeth, I don't know shit other than we need to find another match for this man's daughter." I exhaled as I heaved my body into one of the empty chairs. "It looks like I'm just gonna have to figure out a way to get the other one back from LC. And somebody please tell me how the fuck I'm gonna do that."

I was surely regretting having turned her over to LC. His little million was nothing compared to the money Greer would be willing to pay—not to mention the endorsement he could get me from the President of the United States that would put me back on top. I'd sent Slick to try to get her back, but the Duncans had a shitload of security around them at all times in New York, so I was doubtful he would succeed.

"That's not going to work either," Dr. Baker said. "We took so much blood from her in such a short amount of time that her organs aren't viable to use at this point. Maybe in a couple of months she will be okay, but not now."

I remembered the pretty girl that was with LC's grandson. "What about her half-nigger sister? Can we use her?"

"You said she was half black, which means they have different fathers. There's no guarantee they would be a match," Elizabeth pointed out.

"I'm sorry," Dr. Baker said. "The probability of finding another match within the next few days is unlikely. I've had people taking blood samples from migrants at the border checkpoints for two days."

"Goddammit, Baker! I'm getting sick and fucking tired of you shooting me down!" I stepped toward him, totally willing to take all my frustration out on his skinny ass. "Stop fucking being so negative and find me a solution! Double the motherfuckers up. Do whatever it takes!"

"Calm down, KD. He's not being negative. You just don't want to hear the truth," Elizabeth snapped, surprising me with her sass.

"Fuck the truth! I need a goddamn donor, Lizbeth. I got a lot riding on this, and so do you."

She huffed loudly, clearly not happy with me. "The only chance we have is checking the national registry, and there are hardly any people on the living donor database list who match."

"You said *hardly*, which means there's someone up there." I felt a small glimmer of hope.

She swiveled back around and clicked on her computer. "Well, here's one in Brooklyn. Roman Johnson, age twenty-six . . . and look at that! He's black, not Asian."

I walked over to look at the screen. "You don't say? I actually have someone taking care of something for me in that area."

"Well, there's your donor. He was just added to the database a couple of days ago," she said.

I turned to Dr. Baker. "Doc, what's your thoughts?"

"He solves your problem. But if you're sending somebody to get this boy, there's one thing you must remember."

"What's that?"

"When you deliver him, he's going to have to be alive."

Roman

52

"Aaaaaahhhh!" Aunt Coretta screamed when I poked my head through the living room window. She was standing over me with a skillet, about to bash my brains in.

"Aunt Coretta, no!" I lifted my hands to protect my head.

"Roman! Boy, you scared the hell outta me. What the hell is wrong with the you, busting up in this house like that?" She clutched her chest and leaned on the wall, still holding on tight to the skillet.

"Sorry, Auntie," I said, pulling myself in the window the rest of the way. "I forgot my key at the hospital."

"Why didn't you just knock on the door or call me?" she scolded.

"I did. You ain't been answering your phone."

"Oh, I forgot to turn the ringer on after I got up from my nap. I was just fixing me something to eat before I went back over to sit with Sister. You want me to fix you a plate? The food's almost ready. Pork chops, collard greens, and macaroni and cheese. Your favorites," she said.

"Yeah, let's sit down and eat. I gotta talk to you about something."

"Okay, the pork chops will be ready in about ten minutes. You go on up and take you a shower. You been wearing them same damn clothes the past three days." She smiled and pointed at the stairs.

I went up to my bedroom to grab my bathrobe and toiletries. When I opened my closet door, I had to pause for a minute. It seemed like something was off. Things were kind of shifted. I wrapped my fingers around the handle of the gun tucked in my waistband, then snatched back the row of shirts, expecting to find someone hiding there. But the only thing there was a large stack of Nike boxes.

"Yo, you trippin', Rome," I whispered to myself as I sat on the side of my bed. For some reason, I thought about Kandace. It dawned on me that I hadn't heard from her in a couple of days. As fucked up as my head was, it would be nice to talk to her, so I called.

"Hey, baby," I said when she answered.

"Don't *hey baby* me, motherfucker," she snapped, catching me totally off guard.

"What the hell is that all about?" I snapped right back.

"The same thing that was up with you the other night."

"What other night? What are you talking about?"

"Don't play stupid, Roman. I ain't got no time for the shit. You know what I'm talking about," she answered, full of attitude. "And you know the fucked-up part about this is I really like you."

"Kandace, I swear I don't know—"

Crash! A loud sound came from downstairs.

"What the hell? Did you hear that?" I said to Kandace.

"Yes. What was that?" Kandace yelled.

"I'll call you back. I think my aunt fell," I said and hung up.

I came out of my room and yelled my aunt's name. She didn't answer. Step by step, I slowly descended the stairs, afraid of what I would find when I got to the bottom. I heard a noise coming from the kitchen.

I yelled her name louder. "Aunt Coretta!" Still no answer.

I stepped into the living room, and that's when I was confronted by a horrific sight. There in the kitchen doorway was my aunt's body, slumped into a crumpled, bloody mess. I ran over and cradled her head in my arms. Her throat had been sliced open. She was already dead.

"Fuck." I gasped, swallowing the huge lump that had formed in my throat.

"Don't worry. She didn't suffer." The voice came from behind me.

I turned and saw a tall white man standing there, smiling at me. My heart started pounding when I realized it was the same crazy dude who had killed Lex and those girls. The kitchen door was wide open. He must have forced his way through there and ambushed Aunt Coretta.

"You motherfucker!" I reached for my gun, but it wasn't there. I'd left it upstairs on my bed. Here I was, holding my dead aunt, her killer standing in front of me, and I was unarmed.

"Now, are we gonna do this the easy or the hard way?" He lunged at me, and I scurried onto my feet.

I hopped the stairs two at a time and ran into my bedroom, but before I could reach my gun, he grabbed me and tossed me across the room. I landed so hard against the dresser I thought I could have broken my spine. I tried to brace myself to stand, but he gripped my shirt, and his fist connected with my stomach. Dude went crazy on me until I finally got in the right position to kick him. I scrambled away on all fours, reaching onto the bed to feel for my gun.

"Looking for this?" He held up my gun and smiled. I expected him to take aim and shoot, but instead, he pulled out a stun gun and zapped me.

"Damn, that looks like it hurts," he said, mocking me.

You damn right it hurt. I'd never felt anything like it. I was numb and in pain at the same time as I fell flat on the floor.

That's when I heard two ear-shattering shots ring out. He dropped on top of me like a damn tree falling, knocking the wind out of me. Between that and the stun gun, it took me a minute to recover and realize that—*holy shit!*—I was still alive.

I pushed the crazy man off me, patting all over my body to make sure I didn't have any bullet wounds.

"You all right, Roman?" There was a man standing in the entrance of my room, holding a gun. He looked a lot like me but with purple hair. I was pretty sure he was the reason I was alive, but how and why?

Rio

53

"Go get your brother. Bring him back here so I can tell you together. Hurry now. I don't care what these doctors say. I don't have much time."

Miss Margaret was becoming so weak that she could only whisper the words in my ear. I knew time was running out.

Although I hadn't planned on returning to the hospital anytime soon, the whole scenario kept playing over and over in my mind. It was all I thought about. Could it be that Roman was my twin, and not Paris? That would be entirely devastating for me and her. Paris was more than my sister. She was my best friend, and we shared an unbreakable bond. I couldn't imagine sharing that kind of relationship with anyone else, not even an identical twin brother.

Paris was a Duncan in every sense. She had equal parts of our parents: my mother's beauty and strong intuition, and my father's no-nonsense attitude and low tolerance for bullshit. I couldn't imagine her not being the child of Chippy and LC Duncan. But if that were the case, then who was I?

I had no choice. I had to go back and talk to Margaret and get to the bottom of all of this before it drove me crazy. When I arrived at her bedside and saw how sick she was, I knew I had to get the story from her before it was too late. She had a different plan, though. She told me she wouldn't speak on it until Roman was there too. So, I had to go to his house to get him.

I heard a commotion coming from inside the house just as I was about to knock on the door. Standing on my toes, I looked through the small window at the top of the door. Roman was running up the stairs with a white guy right on his heels. *What the fuck?*

I tried to open the door, but it was locked, so I ran around to the back door and found that it had been kicked in. I took out my .22 automatic and stepped inside. There was a woman's body bleeding on the floor. One look at her eyes and there was no doubt in my mind she was dead.

I didn't have much time to think because there was a loud crash above me. I bolted up the stairs two at a time and followed the noise to Roman's room.

The man was standing over Roman with a gun in one hand and a stun gun in the other, zapping the shit out of him. Roman looked like he was having convulsions as the electricity entered his body. It was like an out-of-body experience watching someone who looked just like me on the floor with an attacker hovering over him. So, it was almost like self-defense when I raised my arm and fired two shots into the white guy's back. He landed on Roman with a loud thud.

Blood oozed from his body, forming a deep red pool underneath. There was no doubt he was dead. I grinned, thinking Pop would have been proud of my marksmanship.

"You all right, Roman?" I asked when I saw him start moving. He pushed the body off of him.

"Who the fuck are you?"

"I'm Rio. I'm your brother."

He didn't say anything, but I could see him studying my face.

"Kind of like looking in a mirror, right?" I said as I helped him to his feet.

"Yo, thanks for that," he said, looking down at the dead man. "As far as what you just said, I don't know who the fuck you are, but I know I don't have no brother."

"Actually, you have a few," I said.

He shook his head like he was trying to clear his thoughts, then yelled, "Shit! Aunt Coretta!" He pushed me aside and ran down the stairs.

I followed behind him but stopped in the doorway to the kitchen to give him some space as he knelt down and caressed the dead lady's head. If she was his aunt, then was she mine also?

"Listen, don't worry. It's gonna be okay," I told him.

"How? How the fuck is this gonna be okay? There's a mother-fucker dead in my bedroom, and he fucking murdered my aunt."

I took my phone out of my pocket, and he started spazzing out.

"Don't call the cops! What the fuck is wrong with you?"

I stepped back so he couldn't snatch the phone away from me. "First of all, chill out. Ain't nobody calling no damn police." I put the phone to my ear.

"I need you. It's an emergency," I said when Junior picked up the call.

"What is it?"

"I don't need you to ask a whole bunch of questions, but I need a cleanup crew for two." I pulled my phone away from ear because I knew he was going to yell.

"Two! Rio, what the hell did you do?"

"I promise you I'll explain everything when I get home. Just take care of it for me, please."

"Fine. Text me the address," he said. "But I'm telling Pop."

Any other time, I would've pleaded for him not to do that, but I figured everything was going to come out soon enough. I was also worried about getting back to Margaret's room before it was too late. I didn't want to waste time arguing with Junior.

"Come through the back door. It's open. And Junior, thanks," I said and hung up.

I turned to Roman, who was looking at me like I was from another planet.

"What?"

"Cleanup crew?" he said. "Who the fuck are you, James Bond? What the hell is going on?"

"I'm your brother and the man who just saved your fucking life. Now, let's get to the hospital if you want answers. Your mother's the only one who's going to give either of us the answer we want," I said.

"My mother? She knows about this?"

"Let's put it this way: she's the only one willing to talk about it."

I checked my watch. Junior's people would be there in anoth-er twenty minutes, and I wanted to be gone by then. "Listen, you need to take a shower and change your clothes. We gotta go."

***

Twenty minutes later, we were in my car, headed back to the hospital. He spent the entire car ride in silence, and I wondered if he was in shock—which was understandable considering his aunt was murdered, a big white dude died on top of him, and I'd just told him I was his brother. Not to mention the fact that his mother was dying.

"Mama," Roman said softly as he walked to her bedside after we arrived. He touched her hand, and she opened her eyes.

She looked from him to me, smiling weakly. "You got him."

"I did." I nodded. "We're both here now."

"Mama, I have a brother?" Roman asked.

"Yes, that's him. Your brother Rio," she said, gasping for breath.

"How?" he whispered.

Margaret

54

26 years earlier

"How much longer do you think it'll be?" Mr. Duncan, the nervous father-to-be asked. He'd been pacing nervously for hours, from the moment his pregnant wife was admitted.

"LC, please stop asking her that," his wife groaned. "It'll happen when it happens. And for God's sake, can you please stop walking around this room? You're making me dizzy."

I smiled and gave him a reassuring look. "Well, the last time we checked, she was almost seven centimeters dilated, so it won't be much longer."

"Oh, okay," he said as he went back to walking back and forth in front of the hospital bed.

"You're acting kind of nervous. I thought you said this wasn't your first child," I teased.

They appeared to be very much in love. His pretty wife, Charlotte, was a little more calm than he was, but it was apparent that she was worn out from her pregnancy. It was also clear that the couple had money, not only because of the large diamond ring she wore on her left hand, but also because they were immediately brought to the larger, nicer birthing room that was normally reserved for "special patients," which was code for the ones rich enough to afford it.

"This definitely ain't our first rodeo. As a matter of fact, it's our fifth time going through this," Mrs. Duncan told me.

"Fifth? My goodness. You're a pro at this," I said.

"He should be, but he's like this every time." She shook her head, then grimaced in pain. "But I think you may be right. It's almost time. Oh my God."

"Chippy, baby, are you okay?" Mr. Duncan rushed to his wife's side and grabbed her hand.

I looked at the long piece of paper that the monitor near the bed had just put out, then checked Mrs. Duncan's blood pressure. "Let's go ahead and call Dr. Preston to come in."

Mr. Duncan gave me a panicked look. "Is it time? Is she all right?"

"She's fine, Mr. Duncan. Her blood pressure is a little elevated, and she's in a lot of pain, but that's to be expected with twins. He'll probably give her a little something to make her a little more comfortable," I explained.

Mrs. Duncan moaned. "He needs to give me a lot of something."

"Owwww!" Mr. Duncan yelled out in pain from the grip his wife had on his hand.

I paged Dr. Preston, and a few minutes later, there was a knock on the door.

"Hey, Maggie, you paged?" the tall, gray-haired doctor asked, and I tried not to cringe. It didn't matter how many times I'd told him that my name was Margaret. Most of the doctors and a few of the older nurses still referred to me as Maggie. I hated it.

"Yes, Dr. Preston. Mrs. Duncan is having a lot of pain and discomfort," I told him. "And her blood pressure has increased a little."

Dr. Preston walked over to Mrs. Duncan. "Hello there, Charlotte, LC. Great to see you both."

"Hey, Dr. P. This is the worst pain I've ever felt in my life. I knew it was gonna be harder because this entire pregnancy has been rough, but not like this," Mrs. Duncan told him.

"I understand. Well, let's see what we've got going on." Dr. Preston lifted the sheet that covered Mrs. Duncan's legs. "Oh, my."

"What's wrong?" Mr. Duncan frowned.

"Well, it seems that we won't be able to give her anything for pain," Dr. Preston told him.

"Why not? She's hurting, Doc." The panic in her husband's voice matched the look on his face.

"Because she's crowning, and the baby's head is pretty much out. All right, Charlotte, get ready to push," Dr. Preston told her; then he said to me, "Maggie, can you—"

"Wait!" Mr. Duncan yelled before Dr. Preston could finish his sentence.

"Yes?" I asked.

"So, she's having the baby now? At this moment?" His eyes were wide with fear. "I . . . I need to call Nee Nee. She's supposed to be here."

"LC, go. Get out. It's fine," Mrs. Duncan moaned.

"But . . ." He looked over at her.

"Ahhhhhhhh!" She yelled. "Gooooooo!"

"That's it, Charlotte. Push," Dr. Preston encouraged her.

"Don't you wanna be here for the birth of your baby?" I asked Mr. Duncan.

"He wasn't there for any of the others," Mrs. Duncan said when she stopped pushing. "He's . . . always . . . conveniently outside in the hall."

"Chippy, now, you know that's not—"

"Ahhhhhhh!" His wife screamed, and the next sound we heard was that of a crying newborn.

"It's a girl, and a big one," Dr. Preston announced and held up the sticky, blood-and-mucus-covered baby.

"She's gorgeous," I said as I wrapped a blanket around the baby girl and took her into my arms.

"Well, he wasn't in the hallway for this one." Dr. Preston laughed.

"We have a daughter, Chippy." Mr. Duncan now beamed with pride.

"Yes, LC. Paris has made her arrival." Mrs. Duncan exhaled.

I took the baby's vitals and cleaned her up, then wrote the last name Duncan and time of birth on one of the tiny ankle bracelets and slipped it on her. Once I finished, I swaddled her and took her over to her mother, who looked exhausted.

"She's beautiful," Mr. Duncan said. "You did good, Chippy."

"We did good, LC. She looks just like you," she said, but the smile she wore was brief and replaced with a grimace. "My entire body is hurting."

"One down, one to go. How much longer until the next one, Doc?" Mr. Duncan asked.

"Could be here in five minutes, or as long as five hours," Dr. Preston told them. "But I'm gonna go ahead and give you a light sedative, Charlotte. Okay?"

Mrs. Duncan gasped in pain. "I think it's definitely going to be five minutes."

I quickly took the baby from her arms and called for one of the pediatric nurses to come assist while we got ready for the next birth. Mrs. Duncan was in the middle of pushing when Naomi, another nurse, came into the room.

"Well, what's this cutie's name?" she asked.

"Paris," Mr. Duncan told her.

"Paris. Pretty name for a pretty girl," Naomi said. "I'll go ahead and take her down to the nursery."

"You may want to wait a few seconds, Naomi, or you're gonna have to make two trips. Her sibling is just about to arrive," Dr. Preston said. "Here comes the surprise."

"Surprise?" I asked.

"We knew one baby was a girl, but she would steal all the attention during the ultrasounds and block the other baby, so we couldn't tell the sex," he said. "But we're about to find out. One more push, Charlotte."

Mrs. Duncan groaned and leaned forward. Her husband's eyes grew huge as he stared at the lower part of her body.

"What is it? Is it another girl?" he asked.

"It's a boy!" Dr. Preston said. The second baby was smaller than his sister, and he was quiet. Dr. Preston quickly passed him over to me, and I took him over to the warming bed, where Naomi was waiting with the other twin.

"He's not crying," Mrs. Duncan said. "Is he okay?"

"He's fine, Charlotte. Maggie and Naomi are going to take good care of him. You just lay back and relax for a second," Dr. Preston told her.

I rubbed the back of the baby boy and whispered, "Come on, baby. Breathe."

As if he heard my instruction, he gasped slightly, then finally let out a tiny cry. The tension that had filled the room moments before was now gone. I followed the same process for him as I had earlier for his sister, and then held him up for his parents to see.

"We need to hurry and get him to the nursery because he's gonna need a little more attention than Miss Paris," Naomi said. "What's his name?"

"Rio." Mrs. Duncan sighed. "LC, go with the babies."

"Are you sure?" Mr. Duncan asked her.

"Yes, please. You need to make sure they're okay."

"You can go ahead, LC. We're gonna get Charlotte settled and comfortable," Dr. Preston said.

"I hope that means something for pain, Dr. Preston. My back is still killing me."

Dr. Preston nodded. "We can definitely give you something."

Mr. Duncan kissed his wife, then followed Naomi and the babies out of the room. When they were gone, Dr. Preston gave her a sedative.

Just as he was about to help Mrs. Duncan deliver the afterbirth, another nurse popped her head in the room.

"Dr. Preston, we have an emergency down the hall. The baby's heartbeat is dropping fast," she said frantically.

Dr. Preston looked at me. "Maggie, can you take it from here?"

"Of course," I said.

He leaned over to speak to Mrs. Duncan. "Charlotte, you're in good hands."

She smiled, looking a little more relaxed as the sedative entered her system. "I know that. Go ahead and take care of your other patient."

With that, Dr. Preston followed the nurse out of the room. I covered Mrs. Duncan with a warm blanket and went about gathering the items I would need to start cleaning her up. She was in and out of consciousness by this point as the sedative took full effect.

I was doing another vital check on her when her eyes fluttered open.

"Thank you again, Maggie," she whispered.

"It's Margaret." I smiled. "And you're welcome."

"Oh, I'm sorry, Margaret."

"It's fine. Congratulations again. Two new bundles of joy."

"I'm tired already, and I haven't even started breastfeeding yet. After these two, I definitely don't think I want anymore." She gave a half smile. "Do you have any children?"

"No, unfortunately that's a blessing the good Lord didn't see fit for me to have," I told her.

"You'd make a great mom. I can tell. You're so patient and nurturing. You deserve a baby." She closed her eyes again.

"Thank you, Mrs. Duncan," I said. Then I noticed her grimacing again. "Are you still in pain?"

"Yes. My back is still killing me. And my stomach. It hurts so bad."

"Let me increase your pain meds just a little." I put a little more of the sedative in her IV and waited a few minutes. "Is that better?"

"No, it still hurts, but I'm so sleepy, Margaret. Oh, God. I feel like I gotta push again." She winced.

"You're probably having a bowel movement. It happens sometimes." I rubbed her arm reassuringly.

"I don't think I'm gonna make it to the bathroom." She slurred her words. "I'm sorry."

"It's okay. Just go ahead, and I can clean you up. It's natural."

She let out another loud groan, and suddenly I understood that whatever was going on couldn't have been a bowel movement. I lifted the sheet and looked between her legs, and to my surprise, a tiny head was emerging. I looked around the room and grabbed a nearby blanket.

Mrs. Duncan's eyes were now closed. I gently pulled the baby from her. It was another baby boy, even tinier than his siblings. I held him in my hands. Even though he wasn't crying, he was breathing.

Mrs. Duncan had been carrying triplets and had no idea. As I cradled him in my arms, I thought that it somehow didn't seem fair. Here I wanted a baby but couldn't have one, and this woman had three, one of whom she didn't even realize she had. Hell, no one knew other than me—not even the doctor.

My eyes went from the baby, then back to the mother, then back to the baby.

No, Margaret, you can't, I told myself. *Why can't I? She said she didn't want any more children anyway. Now she doesn't have to have any. She already has twins, and she won't miss what she never had.* As crazy as it sounded, I knew what I was going to do, and there was going to be no stopping me.

"Margaret?" Mrs. Duncan's voice startled me, and I almost dropped the newborn.

"I'll be with you in just a minute, Mrs. Duncan." I kept my back to her as I grabbed another blanket and covered him, then placed his tiny wrapped body in the nearby sink, praying he wouldn't make a sound. I located another bracelet and wrote the name *Carmichael* on it before slipping it over his foot. Carmichael was my mother's maiden name, and also the last name of another patient who'd come in three days earlier and had been released.

I turned around and went back to Mrs. Duncan.

"I didn't make too much of a mess, did I?" she asked with her eyes still closed. She was very groggy from the medication.

"No, Mrs. Duncan. You didn't make a mess at all. I need to grab some more supplies, though, and I'll be right back. Okay?" I told her.

"Okay, and Margaret?"

"Yeah?"

"Thank you again."

I quickly gathered the baby into my arms again and eased out of the room, leaving Mrs. Duncan asleep. A slight wave of relief came over my nervous body when I entered the corridor and saw that it was completely empty. Even slipping past the nurses station to get to the nursery was easier than I anticipated. The charge nurse was so busy on the phone that she didn't even look up at me.

When I got to the door of the nursery, I silently prayed that the plan that I'd come up with would work.

"Well, who is this?" Naomi asked when I walked in holding the baby.

"Baby Carmichael," I said, trying to sound casual.

"Carmichael? I thought she was discharged yesterday."

"Um, she's back for observation. High BP, so we just need for him to stay in here for a couple of hours, that's all."

"Oh, okay." Naomi shrugged as if it was no big deal, then pulled one of the empty bassinets over to me.

I gently laid the tiny boy inside, and he opened his eyes and stared at me. My heart melted, and I placed my pinky finger into his tiny hand. He was absolutely perfect.

Margaret

55

26 years earlier

Sneaking a baby into the nursery at the hospital was one thing. Sneaking a baby out of the hospital was a whole other obstacle I had to face. I knew I would only have a few hours to figure out how to make that happen. I also needed to come up with an explanation for my family about how I suddenly had a newborn. During my one-hour lunch break, I went to the department store closest to the hospital and grabbed a car seat and a few necessities—bottles, diapers, pacifiers, and newborn clothing, among other things.

When I got back to work, the charge nurse told me that the Duncans had been asking about me.

"What's wrong?" I asked as my heart pounded.

"I'm not sure, but I told them I'd send you in as soon as you got back."

A million scenarios ran through my mind as I slowly returned to Mrs. Duncan's hospital room. I tapped lightly on the door and prayed she was asleep or didn't want to be disturbed.

"Come in," she called out.

"Hey, Mrs. Duncan," I said with fake cheerfulness. "I heard you've been asking for me. I was at lunch. Is everything okay?" The room was full of family members. Balloons, stuffed animals, and flowers were everywhere. Three boys and a girl surrounded the bed where Mrs. Duncan sat up, looking radiant. Mr. Duncan sat in a chair near the bed, and another man and woman were there also.

"Everything is fine, Margaret. We just wanted to thank you for everything you've done. I told my sister-in-law Nee Nee here that you were by far the best labor and delivery nurse I've had, and as you see, I've had quite a few," Mrs. Duncan told me.

"That's so sweet, and your family is beautiful. How are you feeling?" I asked as I checked her vitals and IV.

"I feel so much better. That extra sedative dose had me pretty much out of it, but I'm fine now."

"I'm glad to hear that." A slight wave of relief came over me, and I relaxed a little. "Well, everything looks good right now. How are the little ones?"

"As you can see, they're doing great too." Mr. Duncan nodded toward the babies, who were in the arms of happy family members.

"Daddy, I wanna hold my sister," a little girl sitting in Mr. Duncan's lap announced.

"You will, London. I promise," he told her, then said, "London has been the only girl for so long. She's excited to finally have a sister."

"Me too," one of the boys said.

"Yes, you too, Orlando." Mrs. Duncan hugged the little boy, who was sitting by her side.

"Well, I'll go ahead and leave you all to enjoy your family time," I said. "My shift is almost over, and I'm off this weekend. But I wish you all the best."

"Aw, well, thank you again, Margaret. I don't know what I would've done without you," Mrs. Duncan said.

"You don't have to thank me. I was just doing my job, really."

"At least let me give you a little token to show our appreciation." Mr. Duncan went to reach into his pocket.

"Oh, no. I couldn't take that. It's against hospital regulations. And like I said, I was just doing my job." As I looked around at the family, I wondered if I had done the right thing. Clearly, they not only had plenty of money, but they had plenty of love, too. They were decent people. But I was decent too. And although I probably didn't have as much money as they did, I had plenty of love to give the tiny baby boy that was waiting for me in the hospital nursery. The Duncans had enough. It was my turn.

The last hour of my twelve-hour shift seemed to creep by. I went over the plan in my head like an escape plan in case of fire. When it was time, I gathered my nerves and went to the nursery to get my baby.

"I thought you were gone." Naomi greeted me when I walked in.

"I'm leaving as soon as I take baby Carmichael to his mom. She's being discharged," I told her.

"Really? I thought she was gonna be here at least overnight. Let me get him together." She went to get up.

"No, keep doing your paperwork. I can get him," I volunteered.

Naomi remained in her seat, and I hurriedly located the designated bassinet. There he was, sleeping peacefully, as if he were waiting for me. I began rolling it out of the nursery.

"Bye, baby Carmichael!" Naomi waved.

I had barely made it into the hallway when I heard her calling out.

"Margaret, wait!"

I froze.

"You forgot this." She held out one of the hospital-issued diaper bags that we gave to all of our new moms. "I know his mom probably got one already, but hey, he's a return customer, so he gets another one."

My hand was shaking as I took the bag from her, and I prayed she didn't notice. "Oh, thanks. I'm sure she'll appreciate it."

"You're welcome, Maggie," she teased.

"I'll see you later," I responded nervously and went back to pushing the bassinet. Luckily, Naomi didn't even notice that I was headed in the opposite direction of the maternity side of the floor. Instead, I made my way to the supply closet, where I'd placed the oversized coat and infant carrier I purchased earlier. I slipped the carrier over my shoulders, then placed the baby inside.

He began to whine and wiggle a little, and I rubbed his back as I reached into the diaper bag Naomi had given me. I closed my eyes and prayed as my hands found a pacifier, which I gently placed into his mouth. He quieted down and closed his eyes.

"That's it. You're such a good baby. Now, I just need you to stay quiet a little while longer for me while we get up outta here."

I don't know whether it was my constant prayer or the fact that the baby listened to my pleas, but I was able to walk out of the supply closet, down the hallway, into the stairwell, and out of the hospital undetected. No one stopped me, and when I reached my car in the employee parking garage, I was so overjoyed that I almost cried. I was sweating, but I didn't take off the coat.

There were still cameras in the garage, and I didn't want to risk being seen as I put the baby in my car. Instead, I pushed the driver's seat of my car all the way back so I could comfortably drive with the baby still in the carrier until I was several blocks away. When I thought it was safe, I pulled over into a parking lot and placed him into the car seat. Then, I headed home, hoping the rest of my plan would work.

"Maggie, did you bring the potatoes like I asked?" my sister Coretta asked as soon as I walked into the house.

"No, I forgot."

She rushed out of the kitchen and into the living room with a look on her face that told me I was about to get cursed out, until she saw the car seat I had just placed on the sofa.

She stopped in the doorway. "Margaret, whose baby?"

"Mine."

"Heffa, stop playing with me and tell me whose baby you got." Coretta walked a little closer and looked into the car seat. "That's a little baby. That baby shouldn't even be out the house yet. Is he a newborn?"

"He is." I picked him up out of the seat, cradling him in my arms so she could get a better look at him.

"He's precious. But I don't understand. Where's his mother?" Coretta asked.

"I'm his mother."

"Margaret, you play too much." She became serious. "Your ass wasn't pregnant when you left the house this morning, so how the hell are you his mother? Where the hell did you get this baby from?"

"I was leaving work, and I saw a young girl by the back door. She was about to leave him. She saw me staring, and she was scared and crying. She said she couldn't take care of him, and I promised her I would make sure he was safe." I told her the story I'd been creating in my head the entire time I was driving home.

"Okay, so she left him at the hospital, but why is he here?" Coretta waited for me to continue.

"Well, I kinda didn't take him inside. I brought him home. For us."

"What? You just brought him here? This isn't a damn puppy, Margaret. It's a baby! Have you lost your mind?"

"No, I haven't. Listen, I know this sounds crazy, but if I had taken him inside, they would've put him in the system. And you and I, of all people, know what would've happened to this beautiful bundle of joy if that happened."

I stepped closer to her and held the baby out to her. She hesitated, then took him into her arms.

My sister and I had both spent time in the foster care system while our mother was incarcerated, and our father was the same place he'd always been our entire life: God knows where. It was not a pleasant experience for either one of us. Luckily, a distant aunt and uncle finally rescued us from the hell that we'd lived in and raised us. I knew my sister would see this as a chance to pay it forward. At least I hoped she would.

"I don't know, Mar." She called me by the only nickname I answered to. "We don't know anything about this baby or his mother. Hell, he may be a crack baby or have some kind of illness."

"He's not a crack baby, Retta," I assured her. "He's a perfectly healthy baby boy. He's just a little small. But I'm sure you ain't gonna waste no time fattening him up."

Coretta leaned her head and inhaled the tiny body she was holding. "This is crazy."

The baby began wiggling and whining. I grabbed one of the small, pre-made bottles of formula from the diaper bag and handed it to her. She placed it into his mouth, and he began sucking.

I smiled. "See, you're a natural at this. He needs us, Retta. This is the baby both of us have been praying for."

"Lord, Margaret. I don't know. We don't even know his name," she whispered.

I had been thinking of the perfect name ever since I'd decided that he would be my son. I wanted his name to reflect someone who would be strong and powerful, yet kind and nurturing, like his father seemed to be.

"His name is Roman," I told her. "Roman Carmichael Johnson."

"Roman Carmichael Johnson," Coretta repeated. "It's perfect."

Together, my sister and I raised Roman. We told people that we'd taken custody of the newborn from a cousin down south. No one ever questioned it. It also helped that Roman's complexion was on the lighter side, much like me and my sister.

Things were fairly easy for our little family. Roman was a decent student and a good athlete who loved basketball and baseball. We doted on him and made sure he was well taken care of. When he was younger, he'd occasionally ask about his father, and I told him he'd passed away before he was born. That satisfied his curiosity, I guess, because he stopped questioning.

After high school graduation, he didn't have a job, but somehow he always had money to help pay the bills. I knew he was running the streets, but I was older and too tired to keep fussing at a grown man. So, I just prayed for him. Prayed that he wouldn't get shot or locked up, and prayed that I'd made the right decision all those years ago. But I knew that one day, the truth would come out, and now, the time had come.

Roman

56

All I wanted to do was jump up and run out of the room. Instead, I remained by my mother's bedside while she held my hand and, with each word she spoke, shattered my world as I knew it. I stared in disbelief, shocked by her confession. Rio, the twin brother that I'd just learned about, stood beside me, holding her other hand.

"Wait, so you're really not my mother?" I tried to comprehend what this all meant.

"Roman, I'll always be your mother. You'll always be my son. But, no, I didn't give birth to you. Charlotte Duncan did." Her eyes fluttered open and closed.

"I don't believe none of this, Mama." I shook my head. I had some other mother, and I actually had a father? That couldn't be true. "I know you're high off these meds they giving you, but this shit is ridiculous."

"She's not lying," Rio said. "Our mother—"

"Man, fuck you. You don't even know us," I hissed at him.

"Roman, no." Her eyes opened, and she squeezed my hand tighter. "It's the truth."

"No, Mama."

Her eyes went to Rio. "Take care of your brother, Rio. Tell your parents I . . . I'm sorry."

A loud, sharp tone screamed from one of the machines. My mother's hand released mine as her head fell to the side.

Rio gasped and stepped back.

"Mama!" I yelled. "Mama!"

I called her name over and over, but she didn't respond. I could hear the footsteps of the nurses as they ran into the room.

"Sir, we're gonna need you to move." One of them tried to maneuver past me, but I remained still, afraid to release my mother's hand.

"She's coding. Call a Code Blue!" another nurse yelled.

The doctor on call entered, and he was a little more direct in instructing me. "Move out of the way."

"Mama!" I yelled again. My heart was racing, and I could feel the sweat pouring down the sides of my face. I was more afraid at this moment than I'd been earlier when I was attacked. I couldn't lose my mother. She was all I had left.

"Get him out of the room, now!" the doctor ordered.

Someone grabbed me, and I was finally pulled away, but I remained in the corner of the room, watching them work on my mother.

"Push one of epi and get a crash cart in here!"

"It's en route, doctor," the first nurse told him just as a large cart was wheeled into the room and over to the bed.

The doctor grabbed the two paddles and ordered, "Clear!"

My mother's body bounced up, then fell back to the bed. Her eyes remained closed, and the long beep continued. I began praying, begging God to spare her just a little while longer. I needed her.

"How long has she been down?" Dr. Ford rushed in, and I felt like it was a sign. God had heard my prayer and sent him to save her.

"Six minutes and counting," someone answered.

He grabbed a pair of purple plastic gloves and slipped them on as he rushed to her side. "Push another one of epi. Start manual CPR."

"Please, God, don't let her die," I prayed as he pressed on her chest. I went to move again, wanting to be by her side, but someone was holding me back.

After a while, he stopped, and they all looked at the screen above her bed. It was a flat red line.

He stepped away and said, "Someone call it."

"Time of death, 10:45 p.m."

"What? No!" I tried to lunge for the bed, but the same strong arms that had pulled me away held me back.

"Roman." Rio spoke my name, and I realized he was the one who'd been holding me this entire time.

"Mr. Johnson, we did all we could for your mother. I'm sorry," Dr. Ford said to me.

I couldn't get any words past the huge lump in my throat.

"Thank you," Rio said, his arms still wrapped around my chest. "Can we have some time alone with her, please?"

"Certainly," Dr. Ford said. "Let's clear the room."

The medical staff filed out, and Rio finally released me. I rushed back to my mother. While I felt so lost and alone, she looked so peaceful, like she was sleeping and didn't have a care in the world. I finally swallowed the lump in my throat, and the tears began to flow.

"Mama, damn." I touched her face. "What am I gonna do now?"

"It's okay, Roman. I got you," Rio whispered, putting his hand on my shoulder.

I shook my head. "I don't have nobody else. Aunt Coretta is dead. My mama is dead. I'm alone."

"Roman, listen to me." Rio turned my body to him. "You're not alone. You got me, and you got a family. I promised Miss Margaret I'd take care of you, and I will."

I stared into the face that looked exactly like mine—even more so now that we both had tears streaming. I still hadn't processed everything my mother told us, and I didn't know what was going to happen from here or how I was going to handle it. But I was glad that I wasn't alone.

Chippy

57

"Is it almost ready, Grandma?" Paris's son, Jordan, asked as he hopped in the kitchen.

I stirred the pot of homemade sauce. "Almost, baby. Just a few more minutes. Aunt London is making the salad."

"Ewwwww, salad." London's youngest daughter, Ria, as we called her, was right on Jordan's heels. She turned her nose up. "Grandpa says salad is rabbit food."

"Girl, don't even try it. You love salad." London laughed as she cut up vegetables. "Your grandpa loves it too."

"Yes, he does." I smiled.

"Can I have a carrot?" Jordan asked. "I like rabbits."

"Here." London handed both children a carrot. "Now, go wash up and get ready."

"What do you say?" I asked.

"Thank you," they said simultaneously.

As I turned to take the pot of noodles off the stove, I heard the front door opening, and a few seconds later, Rio's voice.

"Hey, Ma."

"Uncle Rio!" Jordan yelled.

"Jordan, what did I tell you about being so loud?" I warned, my attention still on the hot stove.

"Whoa! It's two Uncle Rios," Ria said.

"Cool," Jordan said.

"Rio, who is—?" London stopped mid-sentence. "Oh my God. Talk about creepy."

I finally looked up to see what she was talking about. Sure enough, standing near the doorway was Rio and another man who looked exactly like him with a mustache and goatee. The resemblance between the two was so strong that it was scary, and if I hadn't given birth to Paris myself, I would've thought that it was his twin brother.

"Ma," Rio said. "Uh, this is Roman. He's my, uh, brother."

"What do you mean, your brother?" I asked, the pot of noodles now in my hand.

I knew damn well LC didn't have a baby with some other woman and now his indiscretion came home to roost. Surely, that couldn't be what was happening. But there was no doubt this boy was related to the Duncan family somehow. Anyone with eyes could see that.

Rio swallowed so hard that I could see the movement of his Adam's apple. "He . . . he's your son."

I frowned. "Rio, I don't know what kind of mind game you're trying to pull here, but I don't have time for your foolishness. You two do look alike, though."

"It's not a game, Ma." Rio stepped closer.

Something inside me understood that this moment was huge, but I was still resisting it. "Stop, Rio."

"He really is your son. You didn't give birth to twins when you had me and Paris. You had triplets."

"Rio, that's not funny, and this is a horrible joke," I said, fighting against the awakening that was happening inside of me.

He shook his head. "It's no joke, Ma. He was born the same day as me and Paris in the same hospital."

My knees began to wobble, and the pot slipped from my hands, crashing to the floor with a loud clang. The hot water splashed all over, and I felt a few drops scalding my bare ankles, but I couldn't move.

"Ma!" London grabbed me.

"Grandma!" Ria gasped.

"Ria, Jordan, go upstairs. I'll call you when dinner is ready," London ordered the children.

"But—"

"Now!" she growled, and they scurried out the door, both of them still staring at their uncle and his duplicate as they passed.

"Mom, come and sit." London touched my arm.

"I don't want to sit." I snatched away. "I want to know what your brother is talking about."

My eyes went from Rio to Roman, who was still silent. Other than the hair color, they looked identical. But there was no way I could've had three babies. Granted, it was a difficult birth, but that's something I damn sure would've remembered. How could I have given birth to a son and not have known?

"His mother—well, the woman who raised him, was the nurse in the delivery room," Rio explained. "Her name is Margaret Johnson."

"Margaret Johnson," I repeated. I remembered her very well, because she was so nice. She took excellent care of me the entire time. I vaguely remembered LC even offering her a tip after the delivery.

"After you had me and Paris, you were sedated and didn't even realize you had another baby. She took Roman right after you pushed him out," Rio said.

I closed my eyes and tried to recall everything that happened that day—the birth, the exhaustion afterward, and then Margaret helping me while no one else was in the room. I'd had a bowel movement, and she cleaned me up. Or had I? It was such a long time ago, but could it have been possible that it was another baby I'd pushed out?

"Who told you all of this?" I asked.

"My mother." Roman finally spoke. "A little while ago, before she died."

"Margaret is dead?" I whispered. "And she said all of this?"

"She did, Ma," Rio confirmed.

"Oh my God," London said. "This is crazy."

"So, you're my son?" I stepped closer to Roman, and my eyes met his. I searched deep within them, hoping to see something that would somehow confirm this revelation. But I only saw hurt and confusion.

"I guess." He shrugged.

My hand trembled as I reached out and touched his handsome face. It was a face that LC and I had created, a child I'd birthed without knowing and who had been stolen from me. I had another son. We had another son. Another Duncan. A missing link of our family that we didn't even know existed. My heart leapt, and tears began to fall from my eyes.

"Ma, is this for real?" London's hand was on my shoulder.

"It's real," Rio told her.

"Roman." I said his name, then wrapped my arms around him. "My son."

"What's going on here?" Paris walked in the kitchem. "Why is Jordan upstairs talking about he has two Uncle Rios? And Ma, why are you crying? Whoa . . . who the fuck is that?"

"Paris, this is our twin brother, Roman," Rio said.

"Get the fuck outta here." She laughed.

I let go of Roman, and we turned to face her. As she stared at Roman, I could see the same look of shock and confusion on her face that had been on mine and London's a few minutes earlier.

"It's true, Paris. It appears this is your brother," I told her.

"Looks like you're gonna have to share that Wonder Twin title with someone else now, huh?" London smiled. "Wait until Daddy hears about this."

I thought about LC, who'd gotten on a flight hours earlier. I needed to tell him, but this wasn't a conversation that could be had over the phone. Our son was home, and he needed to see this for himself.

LC

58

I felt like I was part of a scene in an action film as I rode in Roscoe's squad car. There had to be at least twenty other law enforcement vehicles from different jurisdictions around the South, in addition to the one Vegas and I were riding in, all traveling with lights flashing. We had no time to spare because there was a strong possibility that the suspects had been given a heads up, and if that happened, then they were sure to be long gone by the time we arrived. I glanced at the infamous PRIVATE PROPERTY sign that was pointed out the last time I visited. The procession of vehicles surrounded the front of the house and most of the outlying buildings. Within seconds, we were out of the car, waiting.

"What in the entire fuck is going on here?" KD yelled as he came rushing out of his front door and onto the porch.

I was relieved to see that he was home. No one had warned him in advance.

"KD, we're here to bring you in." Roscoe walked toward the house.

"Have you lost your goddamn mind, Roscoe? You take another step and I'll put a bullet in your skinny ass." He reached for his gun, aiming it at Roscoe, who continued toward him.

"You don't wanna do that." Roscoe jerked his thumb over his shoulder. "These boys are itching to take you out."

"And just what do you call yourself arresting me for?" KD asked.

"For the murders of Sheriff Derrick Hughes and Sheriff Andy Wilkins," Roscoe countered.

KD began laughing uncontrollably, as if Roscoe had told him the funniest joke he'd heard in decades. His fat belly jiggled, and his face turned fire engine red. After a few moments, he regained his composure and dabbed at the tears in his eyes.

"Is that right? Well, Roscoe, first of all, what makes you think I had anything to do with that? If they're even dead. Because last I checked, them boys was missing. You find their bodies?"

I couldn't listen to that smug bastard another moment. I stepped out of Roscoe's car and held up a manila envelope. "We've got proof, motherfucker, and you're going to jail."

"I swear, LC, you must have some sort of crush on me or something. I have women I've fucked that don't come around as much as you."

I opened the envelope and took the pictures out, one by one, throwing them onto the porch. "You can't talk your way outta this."

His eyes went to the photos at his feet, and I saw his amusement fade fast as he realized what he was looking at. The pictures had come from the jump drive Johnny gave Vegas before he was killed. Somehow, he'd captured images of KD, Tyler, and two other state troopers standing outside Derrick's vehicle. There were additional pictures of Derrick and Sheriff Andy Wilkins' dead bodies in the back seat, and a full photo account of the car, from being loaded onto the back of a flatbed to it being dropped off at a recycling yard.

"What's going on out here?" Tyler stepped out onto the porch.

"These pictures don't prove shit. Anybody can use Photoshop these days and make it look incriminating." KD kicked the pictures.

"We also have an eyewitness," I told him.

One of the officers opened the back door of his cruiser, and out stepped Herman Cooke, who owned Morningstar Recycling and Scrap.

"It's over, KD," Herman told him. "They know everything."

"You stupid—" KD went to step off the porch and nearly fell, but Tyler caught him.

"Tyler Shrugs, KD Shrugs, you're both under arrest for the murder of Sheriff Derrick Hughes and Sheriff Andy Wilkins." Roscoe instructed a couple of his deputies, "Cuff them and read them their rights."

"You'd better not touch me, boy!" KD screamed as the deputies hopped onto the porch and handcuffed him and his son.

As they were led past me, KD turned beet red. "You uppity nigger. This is all your doing, but you're gonna pay for this."

"No, you are. Derrick was a nice young man who didn't deserve to die." I stared at him. "You didn't even have the decency to allow his family to bury him, you bastard. I hope this time, you rot in jail."

"Don't worry, Daddy. We'll be home before dinner. And trust me, there's gonna be hell to pay for every last one of these pricks," Tyler yelled as they were putting him into the back of the car.

Once they were taken into custody, we got back into Roscoe's car and continued farther onto the property until we arrived at a set of buildings. Roscoe had already secured a warrant, and he and his men hurried inside.

"What do you think they're gonna find in there, Pop?" Vegas asked me.

"I'm afraid to even think about it." I sighed. "I'm hoping it's not like a damn morgue in there with body parts all over the place."

Roscoe and his guys came out, looking a little perplexed.

"What did you find?" I asked when he walked over to us.

"Nothing really. Just a whole bunch of storage spaces and enough canned food to feed an army. We're gonna check out the other building. I'm wondering if what that guy told you was true, because right now, it looks like nothing major."

"There's no way Johnny was lying. He was scared shitless, and he couldn't have made this up," Vegas said.

"Sheriff, you need to get over here!" a deputy yelled at the top of his lungs.

Roscoe took off toward the second building. A few minutes later, a nurse was brought out. Then came a guy in a chef's uniform, and another one in a white lab coat. All of them were in handcuffs.

"Guess they found the morgue," Vegas whispered.

Then, the door opened again, and a line of women were escorted out.

"Oh my God," I breathed.

"Pop, how many are there?" Vegas asked.

"Looks like at least a hundred."

A short while later, a few ambulances pulled up, and Roscoe finally emerged and directed the EMTs inside. "There's a few in the back. They're hooked up to some kind of IVs."

"So, Johnny was right?" I asked Roscoe.

"He was. Looks like KD has been providing care for these women and then harvesting whatever folks need. It's like a hospital and a spa in there at the same time. If I hadn't seen it for myself, I wouldn't have believed it," Roscoe said. "I've made a call to the FBI. We've gotta get them involved, because this shit is way above my damn pay grade."

"I feel you," I told him.

My cell phone began ringing, and I took it out of my pocket. "Excuse me. I have to take this."

"LC, I need you to come home." It was Chippy.

"Okay, love. We'll be heading to the plane in the morning."

"No, LC. Leave now and come straight home." There was urgency in her voice.

"What's wrong, Chippy?"

"I can't answer that question right now, but we've been married well over thirty years, and you know me well enough to know that if I tell you to come home immediately, then it must be important," she said. "Lavernius Duncan, I need you to come home now."

I didn't have to give it a second thought. "I'm on my way."

"Pop, what's wrong?" Vegas asked.

I turned to Roscoe and said, "I need someone to get me to my jet right now. I've gotta get home to my wife."

Roscoe looked at me for a second, then tossed me his keys. "Leave the door unlocked, and don't forget to let me know where you park it."

It was full speed ahead as I drove to the hangar. I had no idea what had my wife so vexed, but I knew I had to find out in a hurry.

Epilogue

"We good?" Vegas asked his son, Nevada.

It was a crisp, sunny fall day, and they were both looking dapper in their Italian leather shoes, expensive slacks, and cashmere overcoats. Standing on a hill in Central Park, they took in the spectacular foliage after lunch, and then a leisurely walk in the park with their better halves. It was amazing to Vegas how much his son had matured in a few short months.

"I think so," Nevada replied. "What other choice do we have?"

"None, but that doesn't mean you have to accept it."

"I love you, Dad, just as much as I love being here," Nevada replied. "I want you both to be happy, and this is the only way."

"For now," Vegas replied.

"Happy birthday to you . . ."

They turned to see Marie and Kia walking up the hill, singing. Kia was holding a single cupcake with a candle. She'd been waiting to surprise Nevada for the entire day. And surprise him, she did. He could not help but blush.

"Blow out the candle," Kia urged.

His happiness was evident from the wide smile that covered his face after he extinguished the candle.

Vegas and Marie walked down the hill to give the couple a few minutes of privacy.

"It's so beautiful here," Kia said, removing the candle from the cupcake. "Here. It's strawberry shortcake, your favorite."

"I'm glad you came." Nevada placed a hand on her hip. She began feeding him pieces of cake. "Having you here has made this the best birthday ever. I'm sorry it's coming to an end."

"Me too. I've missed you."

"I missed you too. I wish this date would never end." He closed the gap between them, but then tensed up when he heard her phone chime an alert.

She frowned at the text message. "Unfortunately, I've got a client in an hour."

"How is old Bob?" Nevada teased.

"He's good. He put my sister on his company insurance. Otherwise, I'd blow him off."

"It's okay. We've gotta go soon too."

"You know, he's very jealous of you." She laughed, leaning against Nevada.

"He should be, because I'm getting something he's not." He chuckled happily, pulling her into his arms and kissing her.

Kia put her arms around his neck, and her mouth opened slightly to welcome his tongue. They enjoyed the warmth and passion until he finally released her.

"I could kiss you all day," she sighed with a dreamy look in her eye.

"Tell me about it."

She kissed him again, sweetly this time, just her lips against his.

"Kia," Marie called. She had gotten the same text message.

She gave him another quick kiss. "I'll FaceTime you tonight."

"You better."

She walked toward Marie, who kissed Vegas goodbye before the two women exited the park.

Vegas returned to Nevada's side. "Everything good?"

"Everything's great. They're probably waiting on us. You ready to go?"

Vegas gave him a thumbs up, and they walked in the opposite direction toward the Thompson Television building.

"Where have you been? What took you so long?" Consuela asked when they walked into the lobby. Nevada silently kissed his mother's cheek, allowing his father to speak.

"It is my son's birthday. We were spending a little father and son time together." Vegas kissed her on the other cheek. "Come on. They can't start without us."

Consuela linked an arm into each of theirs, and they entered the main studio of the television station. They spotted Sasha and Junior, who were already seated. Nevada sat beside his uncle and looked onstage at his grandparents, Aunt Paris, Uncle Rio, and his new uncle, Roman. They all looked nervous. Video cameras were strategically placed throughout the room, and the production staff made last-minute adjustments.

One of the producers yelled, "Quiet on the set!" A hush fell, and the lights dimmed. It was showtime. "Close on Savannah. Three, two, one." She pointed at the host.

"Today on the *Savannah Kirby Show,* we have the intriguing, exclusive story of love, tragedy, and abduction," the show's host, singing sensation Savannah Kirby, announced as the camera panned from her to Chippy and LC, pausing momentarily on a close-up of their faces before moving to Paris, Rio, and finally, Roman.

"Twenty-six years ago, Charlotte and LC Duncan gave birth to twins Paris and Rio, or so they thought. Turns out, she didn't have twins, but actually triplets. They weren't aware of the third baby until a string of unfortunate coincidences. Right after his birth, the third baby was abducted by Margaret Johnson, the nurse who delivered him. She took him home and named him Roman Johnson. Now he's here with his birth family, and they are all here to share their amazing story."

Savannah looked into the camera and exclaimed, "Y'all, this story is crazy! Wait until you hear all the details. Please help me welcome the Duncans."

The camera once again panned across the stage, capturing the reactions of each family member as the audience erupted into applause.

"You've gotta be fuckin' kidding me."

Fifteen hundred miles away, at the Allen B. Polunski Prison in Livingston, Texas, KD Shrugs threw a deck of cards at the television in the recreation room. He'd been watching the show with his fellow inmates, and now he was pissed. His angry face almost matched the color of his orange jumpsuit.

"What's wrong, Daddy?" Tyler was dressed in the same type of jumpsuit.

KD pointed at the TV. "Look at that son of a bitch. Can you believe this shit? He's there, and I'm fucking here!"

"Is that LC Duncan?" Tyler squinted at the small screen. "Why is he on TV?"

"Somethin' about a long-lost son." KD wished they could turn up the volume, but that wasn't allowed, so he strained to hear what they were saying. He read the names on the bottom of the screen and nearly shit his pants. *Roman Johnson.*

"Well, I'll be damned. This world is just too damn small."

"What's going on, KD?" one of the guards asked.

"Nothing, Richards. Go back to sleep." KD rushed over to the phones on the other side of the room. He put in his access code, dialed the number, and waited for the operator to connect the call.

A woman answered. "Save Smart Corporate. How may I help you?"

"You have a call from an inmate . . ." the recording began.

The Save Smart operator didn't hesitate to accept the call. She'd been given explicit instructions by her boss to do so should KD ever call.

"Put me through to Leo Greer. I need to speak to him right now," KD demanded.

"I'll see if he's available."

"Tell him it's about his daughter," KD told her. "He'll be available."

"I thought you said you didn't want me to get you out until the heat died down," Greer said as soon as he picked up the phone.

"I don't," he replied. "No reason to bring attention to ourselves now. How've you been?"

"I'm about to go into a meeting. What's this about my daughter? I don't have time to chitchat." Greer sounded a little frustrated.

"Actually, Leo, I'm calling to help you."

"Help me with what?"

"Saving your daughter. What else?" KD replied. "You still looking for a kidney and a heart?"

"Of course I am. They've got my daughter on a damn respirator. I've got all the money in the world, but I can't save her without those organs. My wife's talking about pulling the plug."

"Well, don't pull the plug just yet, because I know where two, possibly three perfect matches are not too far from you."

"You do? Where?" Greer's voice was animated now. He sounded like he was ready to jump through the phone.

"Now, I can't get them for you considering my predicament, but a man with your resources should be able to find the right people to do the job."

"KD, stop fucking with me and tell me where I can find these people!"

"Turn on your TV to the *Savannah Kirby Show* and you'll see all three of them. Roman, Rio, and Paris." KD smirked as he hung up the phone.